SONG OF THE LION

SONG OF THE LION

A Leaphorn, Chee & Manuelito Novel

ANNE HILLERMAN

HARPER

NEW YORK . LONDON . TORONTO . SYDNEY

HARPER

FIRST HARPER PAPERBACK EDITION PUBLISHED 2018.

Library of Congress Cataloging-in-Publication Data has been applied for.

ISBN 978-0-06-282174-4 (pbk.)

21 22 LSC 10 9 8 7

Song of the Lion is dedicated to the men and
women who work in law enforcement on the
Navajo Nation and to the memory of Shiprock
District Officer and U.S. Marine Corps veteran
Alex Yazzie, who gave his life on March 19, 2015,
while responding to a domestic violence incident.

SONG OF THE LION

Navajo Police Officer Bernadette Manuelito stood in the lobby of the Shiprock High School gym, fondly known as the Chieftain Pit of Pain, trying to decide if she should buy a hot dog or a Frito pie from the booster's stand. Despite the decibel level produced by more than a thousand fans screaming and stomping on the bleachers, she recognized the new sound even as she felt the building shake.

She waited for the lights to go out, but they didn't. The crowd in the bleachers grew quieter momentarily, enough that she could hear the shrill whistle of the official as he called a time-out. The older guys, a team assembled for homecoming from veteran players who had captured past state championships, had handed the upstarts more challenge than the kids expected. Spectators cheered every basket and blocked shot.

In Bernie's mind, the noise from the parking lot changed everything. She nudged back her panic and hurried toward the exit, pushing through a few folks also hoping to leave the building. They sensed danger and wanted to escape; she headed toward it.

Her brain raced with scenarios. The explosion could be a bomb, and there might be more bombs out in the parking lot, hidden in the gym, even on the roof. The bomber could be lurking in the dark with a gun, waiting to pick off victims as they came into his sights. And there might be more than one perpetrator.

Because Shiprock, NM, was a small town, Bernie knew the gentlemen hired to provide security for the game. They knew she was a cop, even though tonight, off duty, she looked like a short young Navajo woman in jeans with a red Chieftains sweatshirt under her jacket. She approached the first guard she encountered, a portly man leaning against the wall, sipping on a drink from a blue plastic cup. "Henry, stand by the door. Keep everyone inside. I'm checking to see what happened out there."

"OK. Why?"

"We don't want anybody hurt. Have Larry help you."

"What's goin' on?"

"Just do it."

She ran outside.

The scene took her breath away. Orange flames blazed through a thick smoky haze, illuminating a mound of destroyed metal in the parking row closest to the gym and reflecting off other vehicles with broken windshields. A few car horns blared into the night, but alarms weren't common here. The blast had ruined the security lights closest to the main doors of the Pit, but those farther from the scene illuminated the broken glass, bits of metal, and other debris that had flown everywhere.

She scanned the area for the bomber but saw no one. The wind blew the toxic stench toward her, searing her lungs and burning her eyes.

She jogged closer to the flattened pile of chrome, steel, and melted plastic, near enough to feel the intensity of the fire. She dreaded what she had to do next. If anyone had been inside what was left of the car, he or she wasn't a person anymore. Bracing herself, Bernie peered through what would have been the windshield. Nothing in the wreckage looked even partly human. She exhaled and stepped back.

Had it been a bomb? Probably, she thought. Why else would a car explode in the middle of the night? Was the bomber out here waiting for a crowd to gather before detonating the next blast? Watching for the flash of emergency lights and uniforms to shoot first responders?

She pulled her phone from her jacket pocket.

Sandra, on duty at the Shiprock Police substation in dispatch, recognized her cell number. "Bernie?"

"I need all available backup ASAP to the parking lot at Shiprock High School gym. A car exploded. Lots of damage. I'm starting to look for victims. It's bad."

"Are you alone?"

"Except for the rent-a-cops and the thousand people inside for the game. I need help here faster than fast."

"Got it."

Bernie made a check of the proximity, stepping over or around the debris, using her phone as a flashlight to look inside the ruined cars closest to the one on fire. If the bomber, an accomplice, or a bystander had been injured by the blast, she had to find him.

She heard the gym doors open and close, saw the inside light beam into the dark night. She turned toward the sound and yelled, "I'm a cop. It's dangerous out here. Go back inside."

The door closed. She continued, checked inside and between the nearby cars, and saw no one dead, injured, or hiding. Several of the vehicles closest to the blast site had broken windshields and shattered side glass. Embedded bits of metal from the explosion had damaged others. She felt glass crunch beneath her boots.

Because the veteran players from the school's past state championship teams had family, friends, and old fans in the area, the parking lot overflowed with cars, SUVs, vans, and pickup trucks. Basketball ruled the rez. Shiprock High School fans were famous for their loyalty to the Chieftains, both boys' and girls' teams, current contenders for the AAAA division title. Every Chieftains home game filled the three-thousand-plus-seat arena. Moms and dads, cousins and grannies lined up with folding chairs and coolers before the doors opened for the junior varsity game, followed by the B team, followed by the big event.

Tonight, they had packed the gym to the fire marshal's advised capacity and probably beyond. The numbers meant confusion in the parking lot turned crime scene when the final buzzer sounded. It was the ideal setting for chaos.

Bernie wasn't an expert on explosives—the Navajo Police relied on the federal agents for that. But if, as she expected, a bomb had caused the blast, she knew she and whoever arrived to help needed to preserve as much evidence as possible before the game ended. Among the people in the gym might be witnesses and even the bomber.

Having found no injured people, she used her phone for crime scene photos, beginning with the car that looked like the target vehicle. She stood in front of the flames, working quickly, listening both for help on the way and for the gymnasium door opening to release curious and probably scared basketball fans.

She put her hands in her pockets for warmth and felt the flyer a young man had handed her earlier calling for an environmental protest in Tuba City. Was the explosion a precursor to a weekend of trouble?

Finally, she saw flashing lights on the highway and heard the wail of a siren. It would be great if it were Chee, but it wouldn't be. Her husband, a sergeant, was on duty tonight at the other end of the district, following a bootlegging case. Otherwise, he would have come to the game with her.

The arriving officer was probably Officer Bigman, she figured, at the station ready to call it a day when her call came. She and Bigman, a clan brother, worked well together. He was a steady hand, a good guy in a tough situation who'd had her back more than once.

But the patrol unit cruised directly toward the entrance to the gym and the burning car. She trotted toward it, waving the driver away from the crime scene. It must be the new guy, Wilson Sam. Bigman would know better.

She'd worked with the rookie a few times before and decided he was impressed with himself for no good reason. He didn't seem to like her either.

In the glare of his headlights she noticed more cars and trucks with dents and shattered windows farther away from the site of the explosion. Wilson Sam stopped, turned off the siren, and lowered the window when she reached him. She felt the car's interior warmth escaping as he spoke. "I was getting ready to go home. What's going on?"

"A car blew up. Park by the fence and get right back. Block the entrance until we figure out what's up. Leave the light bar flashing."

"Cripes. What a mess. It stinks out here." She felt his eyes on her casual jacket and jeans. "Are you in charge? I didn't know you were even working tonight."

"I am until the feds get here or someone tells me otherwise." She didn't like his tone. "Park fast and come back to help with crowd control."

"Can't the security guys . . . ?"

"Don't argue. Go."

Sam drove backward to the rear of the lot, left the lights pulsing against the dark Four Corners night. She watched his silhouette against the blue-and-red strobe as he strolled to her, taking his sweet time.

She snapped more pictures of the car at the epicenter and the debris around it, trying to include everything since she didn't know what might be important to give the investigators an idea of the uncontaminated scene.

Sam arrived and watched her take photographs. The way he stood, resting his hands on his hips, reminded her of a disagreeable clan brother. "What if this was just some kind of engine malfunction that made a big mess?"

"Until we know otherwise, we treat it as a bomb. Go to the gym. Tell the folks who want to go home to chill. Keep things calm in there. We have to hold people inside in case there's another bomb out here or a sniper. There are kids in there, and the ground is full of sharp metal, broken glass, who knows what else. We have to minimize the damage and the disruption to the crime scene until we get some backup."

Sam took a step toward her. "You're wrong. If this was a bomb we should start evacuating. There could be another bomb in the locker room, wired to the game clock, anywhere. The whole gym could blow. Do you want people to die because you screwed up?"

She glared at him. "It's my call. I'm in charge. Listen up and don't argue."

Sam stared back. "You go inside that death trap. Not me. I'll take pictures and take my chance out here."

Bernie swallowed her anger to focus on the job. "Don't let anyone near that car or any of the cars around it." She ran toward the gym.

The stifling heat and game-day smell of sweat and food slapped her as she opened the door. The security guards—Henry, the paunchy man she'd spoken with earlier, and Larry in an Atlanta Braves baseball cap—looked relieved to see her. She heard the shrill whistle of an official calling a penalty.

Bernie studied the crowd in the lobby, looking for someone she knew. She saw a man with his hair in gray braids talking to a pair of girls with glow rings around their necks. She noticed a middle-aged woman with a baby, both of whom looked tired. She spotted a Hispanic man who resembled her teacher from the sixth grade, a receptionist she recognized from the medical center, a *bilagaana* in a button-down shirt who seemed out of place, a library aide she'd met in Farmington, and a boy she'd arrested for drunken driving. A few team mothers who had been selling popcorn, fry bread, and Frito pies stood by their food. People looked curious and anxious, but no one had panicked. At least not yet.

She noticed a table littered with promotional material soliciting students to enroll in the military, advertising for a revival meeting, holiday bake sales, and the protest in Tuba City. She swept the papers to the floor and climbed up so she towered over the crowd.

She yelled, "Attention, please. I'm Officer Bernadette Manuelito." She shouted several times, and then one of the food vendors banged on a metal tray with a spoon. People looked up. "There's been an explosion in the parking lot. Until we figure out what happened, no one can leave for a while. Go back and enjoy the game. We don't want anyone getting hurt. Sorry, but I can't answer any questions. Just relax, folks."

She surveyed the lobby crowd again and spotted Mr. Franklin, a man she knew from the Shiprock Chapter House and the area's delegate to the Navajo Tribal Council. She called his name and, when he looked up at her, motioned him to the front of the table. "You've got a strong voice. You're a leader. Take charge here, sir. Please. Try to keep people calm and in the building."

He was an elder, and that gave him extra clout. "What happened?"

"A car blew up. I don't know why. I've got to get back outside."

Franklin turned to the crowd. His deep voice resonated with calm authority. "Do what the lady policeman says. I know her. Go watch the game."

Bernie climbed down from the table and bumped into the man with the braids she'd seen earlier. He smiled at her and said, "Excuse me," first in English and then in Navajo. His voice, rough and musical, reminded her for a split second that the world held beauty as well as the current chaos.

She went back to the parking lot. After the oppressive heat of the gym, the combination of frigid air and acrid smoke called her senses to attention.

She looked for the rookie but didn't see him. "Sam? Where are you?"

"Over here. Somebody's hurt bad."

She followed his voice. A new smell added itself to the stench, the unforgettable odor of burned human flesh. Then she saw the body, a crumpled form in the shadows. How could she have missed it?

"Is he still alive?"

"I don't know."

"Did you call—?"

Sam interrupted. "Sandra said the ambulance is on the way."

Bernie squatted next to the victim, keeping her boots out of the blood. The one eye she could identify was closed. Glass fragments sparkling in the skin of the eyelid, on his cheeks, neck, and his brown jacket. She leaned closer, pushing down her own nausea, and heard a gurgling breath. "Take it easy, sir. We're here to help you."

The person didn't respond. She listened to Sam step away and then heard him vomiting. Probably his first experience with a person nearly dead.

The rookie came back, keeping his distance from her and the victim. "A few people have come out that side door already. They ran to their cars and drove off while I was here with the dude. Is he still alive?"

"He's breathing." She made a judgment call. "Stand by that door. Keep it secure. Don't let anyone come out of the gym. I'll watch this guy until the ambulance gets here."

Sam hurried off, this time without argument.

Bernie straightened up and stared north toward NM 491, the direction from which the medics and fire trucks would come. Waiting. That could be the motto of her experience in law enforcement in the Four Corners. Waiting for an ambulance. Waiting for the FBI. Rarely did the Navajo Police have the luxury of waiting for backup—most of the time, officers were on their own. So few police for so much geography, and a growing population.

Because Shiprock Hospital was closer than the fire station, she figured the ambulance would arrive first, then the fire trucks. Then the San Juan County deputies unlucky enough to be working to-night. Then the New Mexico State Police, the FBI, and whatever other conglomeration of agencies got involved with cars that blew up. Maybe some of them would get there before the game ended and the crush of people wanting to leave the gym intensified.

She heard the injured man groan and squatted next to him. She softened her voice. "I'm a police officer. I'm here with you, sir. An ambulance is on the way. We'll do everything we can for you. Hang in there." It had been long minutes since the explosion. So far, no second blast and no snipers shooting at Sam, at her, or at anyone else. Then she noticed a tall, slim figure in a white cowboy hat walking toward the disaster site. She stood, drew her gun, and yelled, "Hey, you. I'm a police officer. Get over here now."

The man look toward her, surprised, and yelled back as he continued her way. "Didn't mean to startle you. I'm here to help." He stopped a few feet away, and she followed his glance to the injured person. "Holy cow. He looks bad."

"Who are you?"

"Byrum Lee. I'm a medic." Unlike the rookie, Lee kept his cool despite the horror of the body's disfigurement.

"What are you doing here?"

"I had to work late, but I came to see the end of the game." As he spoke, he reached toward his pocket. She automatically raised her gun. "Don't worry, Officer. I'm not armed. I'm getting out my ID. I heard the explosion from my truck just after I turned off the engine. I saw the car come apart and start burning. I didn't know what to do, but when that police car drove up, I thought maybe he could use some help. I didn't realize you were already on the scene."

He gave her his wallet, open to his driver's license. While she examined it, Lee squatted down and gently pressed his fingers against the charred skin of the man's neck. He moved near the man's face and turned so his ear was close to the victim's open mouth.

Lee stood. "I was in Afghanistan. That was a long time ago,

but some things stick with you, like the sound of lungs filling with blood. He's in bad shape."

"The ambulance is on the way."

Behind her, Bernie heard the gym doors open and the heated tones of the tail end of an argument. She turned in time to see a small group of people—they looked like teenage boys—running into the cold. For a split second she considered the wisdom of leaving the victim with an unknown Good Samaritan.

"Mr. Lee, stay right here until the ambulance comes. Tell me if the guy says anything. And don't let anyone mess with the burning car."

"Sure thing. Whatever I can do. Nobody should die alone."

She sprinted toward the boys, almost reaching them before they got to a red van.

"Hey, you guys! Stop. I'm a police officer."

The boys broke into a gallop, increasing the distance they already had on her, splitting off in different directions. She berated herself as she turned back to the burning car. First she couldn't find a dying man, and now she let possible suspects get away.

Then, in the distance, she saw the welcome red flash of ambulance lights against the night sky. Moments later, she heard the wail of the sirens. An ambulance and, behind it, a fire truck. Something wound tight inside her relaxed a fraction of an inch. The situation was bad and could still become disastrous, but in a few minutes she and Sam wouldn't be facing it alone.

She stopped to catch her breath, thinking of what to tell the emergency folks. Then she saw two sets of headlights on the road right behind the ambulance, with turn signals indicating they were headed for the gym. The vanguard of the expected stream of parents, aunties, and neighbors coming to pick up the kids who attended the game. More would follow.

The fire truck and ambulance headed toward the smoldering car, and Bernie ran to meet them. The truck stopped outside the entrance to the gym and two firefighters got out. She knew the taller one, Mike Hannigan, but he looked right through her and headed toward the uniformed rookie standing by the side door.

She yelled. "Hannigan. Bernie Manuelito, Navajo Police."

He stopped. "Hey, Officer. What's cooking?"

"I heard the explosion about half an hour ago. No more since then. Officer Sam and I are the only law enforcement here. We found one victim." She moved toward the ambulance. The driver lowered the window. "Follow me."

She jogged to where Lee waited with the injured man. The ambulance rolled along behind, lights flashing.

The driver called to her out the open window. "Only one person hurt?"

"That's all we've got for now."

She heard another siren and noticed more responder lights approaching from the distance. Much quicker than she'd expected. Thank goodness.

The ambulance crew went to work and Lee stepped aside.

"He's hanging on." Lee kept his gaze on the injured man. "We said some prayers. He didn't speak, but I know he heard me. Poor guy."

"Thanks for your help. I need your ID. I'm sure the feds will want to talk to you."

Lee showed Bernie his Arizona license again and she jotted down the information. The game would officially be over in a few minutes if it didn't go into overtime. For many fans the combination of fear, curiosity, and fatigue would overpower their respect for an elder like Mr. Franklin. She envisioned the chaos and kept moving to coordinate the response.

The firefighters had begun to assemble what they needed to spread flame-retardant foam on the smoldering car when a San Juan sheriff's car pulled into the parking lot.

Sam left his post by the door and ran to the car. Bernie felt her anger rise, but evidently he told the deputy she was in charge because the cruiser drove toward her. She recognized the man at the wheel, an officer she'd talked to that summer when her sister had been arrested. She didn't recall his name at the moment, and didn't recognize his partner. He lowered his window.

"You guys got here quickly."

The deputy stroked his mustache. "Amazing, I know. What's up?"

"A car exploded and seriously injured one man. So far, nothing else has blown up but we have another problem." The fumes had irritated her throat and it hurt to talk. "People already want out of the gym and there's a lineup of cars waiting to pick up kids. The game will end soon, and that's when the real fun begins."

The deputy nodded. "If there's a sniper, another bomb . . ." He turned to his partner, a husky woman with gray in her hair. "You try to keep people in the gym. I'll drive back to the gate and block the entrance. Stop the confusion from getting worse."

Bernie looked at the female deputy. "Mr. Franklin, a tribal official, is helping inside." She described him, and told the officer the names of the security guards.

Already, about a dozen more vehicles had come in. The sheriff's deputy managed to stop them from getting close to the crime scene, and so far, no looky-loos had climbed out of their cars. But that was just a matter of time.

More people began leaving the gym, using the side doors. She heard the deputy yelling, "Go back," and watched as more people ignored her.

Bernie stayed by the bombed car, on the lookout for anyone who took a close interest in it, tried to pick up a souvenir or interfere with the firefighters. She'd warned people away from the flames and smoke and made sure no one drove off in the cars closest to the one that had been bombed. The chaos accelerated as more fans left the gym. When they saw the ambulance and fire truck, some people froze. Some began running. A little girl tripped, fell, and started to cry. A man scooped up the child and hurried away with her bundled in his arms. Bernie saw a woman

whose foot was bleeding from where the sharp shrapnel had pene-
trated the thin sole of her shoe. A growing press of cars and trucks
pulling out of their parking spots created a jam of vehicles and
added engine fumes to the stench of the burning car. The deputy
managed to hold most fans at the exit, at least for the moment. She
heard the ambulance doors close. Then Lee came over to her. She
noticed the blood on his jacket.

"That poor soul didn't say a word. I hope he couldn't feel anything either." He pointed toward the gym. "Want me to stand at
the side door and try to keep some order?"

"Good idea."

"Whatever you want, ma'am."

It wouldn't be long, she hoped, before the FBI team arrived
from Farmington, half an hour to the east. They'd secure the scene
and do a thorough investigation in the morning. If he was available, the FBI contact would be Jerry Cordova, she figured, the
agent based in Albuquerque who spent a lot of time in Farmington
and Gallup these days. A smart guy. Maybe a little too fond of
himself, but a solid, professional cop.

More flashing lights in the distance now caught her eye.
Another Navajo officer, maybe, or the New Mexico State
Police. She heard horns honking, an uncommon sound on the
reservation.

Then she saw a man bend down to pick up something in the
parking lot.

"Hey, don't touch that. Leave whatever that is alone."

He stood straight, startled.

"I'm a cop."

He laughed, "Yeah, sure. And I'm the reincarnation of Mu-
hammad Ali."

Bernie walked closer. "What do you have there?"

He opened his fist and showed her a bent piece of rusted metal.
She showed him her ID.

"Put it down and get back in the gym."

He tossed the metal down and took off, running away from her farther into the parking lot.

She should have made Sam guard the bombed car, she thought. With his uniform and height he would have gotten more respect out here than she could. Now, one of the rent-a-cops, Larry, was running toward the ambulance team. After a brief conversation, attendants went with him back into the building. Meanwhile, a dozen more fans left.

Officer Sam walked up to her.

"It's hopeless keeping people in—you try it."

She looked at him, speechless.

Sam stood a little straighter. "Just so you know, I called a tow company. Some of these vehicles down here aren't drivable."

"What are you thinking? The ones closest to the target can't be moved until they get checked for bomb fragments."

"Who made you God?" He glared at her for a moment, then walked back to the gym.

The New Mexico State Police arrived, and a few minutes later a black sedan with flashing lights glided through the crowd. She recognized the car. Cordova in his usual style. She sighed with relief. There had been tension among the FBI and the Indian cops in the past, in her mentor Lieutenant Leaphorn's heyday. Some ill feelings undoubtedly remained, but she respected Cordova. And she knew he'd take charge.

She watched him park far from the bombed car, climb out, and put on his protective vest with FBI panels front and back. It made her aware, again, that she was out of uniform. He trotted up to her, his badge on a cord around his neck, all business.

"Fill me in."

Bernie told him everything she knew about the explosion and the aftermath. It didn't take long. "When I came out of the gym, I didn't see anyone running away or any vehicles driving off. I called it in. The rookie showed up, and I went back into the building to get the rent-a-cops and a volunteer to keep the spectators calm. Or try to."

Cordova said, "Did you ask security if they noticed anything?"

"No." She should have, she realized, but that could come later. "There's more."

She told him about the pack of teenagers who had ignored her and run off in different directions. She told him about the victim. "The ambulance left about five minutes ago. He was alive then."

"What can you tell me about him?"

"Male. Maybe five eight, one-seventy pounds. It looked like he had on some sort of brown jacket."

"Did he say anything?"

"Not to me. A volunteer stayed with the victim until the ambulance got here."

"Who was that?"

"An army medic who came late to the game." She thought a moment and conjured up his name. "Byrum Lee. I have his info."

"Did you find a cell phone on the injured guy?"

"I didn't search him." Another mistake, she realized.

She noticed Cordova looking at her, realizing she was out of uniform."Why are you here, Manuelito? Just lucky?"

"I came for the basketball. This is a big game."

"So who won?"

"I don't know."

"Who's here besides us?"

"Two San Juan County deputies." She gave him the names. "I saw the state police pull up out there just before you arrived. And Officer Sam has been helping with crowd control at the gym."

"Sam who?"

"Wilson Sam. He's our new guy."

"I haven't met him."

"I'll introduce you when we get a chance."

Cordova bent down and picked up a piece of metal, stood up and showed it to her. It seemed similar to the debris the man had tried to leave with, but it was smaller. "See how this looks rusted? That's from the bomb." He replaced the metal. "ATF has a bomb squad on the way from Albuquerque with a sniffer dog. Our bomb techs should be here tonight, too.

"You keep an eye on the scene here while I discover what's happening in the gym and get some interviews organized. I'll radio the state police team out there, tell them to hold everyone in the lot in and keep everyone outside the fence out. Some bombers like to hang around, enjoy the chaos." He picked up his radio. "Don't let anybody near these cars, even if they own them." Cordova headed for the gym. She shoved her frozen hands into her pockets. Cordova was in charge now, telling her to do what she'd been doing as though the idea wouldn't have occurred to her.

A man with a buzz cut, wearing warm-up pants and a Shiprock Chieftain sweatshirt, walked directly toward the burning car. She took a breath and prepared to repeat what she'd said dozens of times that night: she didn't know what happened, and he should wait in the gym. He turned toward her and spoke first.

His voice trembled. "I can't believe this. It's a nightmare." He kicked at the ground with his Nike. "Did you see what happened?"

"I heard the explosion and saw the fire. I'm a Navajo police officer. I got here right after the explosion. You need to go back into the gym."

"I loved this car. Look at it now." He started to walk to the smoldering metal, avoiding the fire hoses and stepping around the puddles of liquid from the hoses and the car.

Bernie moved in front of him. "Stop. So this is your car?"

"Was my car. My Beemer. My sweet baby." He looked at her. "I know you. You played with the Lady Chieftains, right?"

"Right." She realized the man was the leader of tonight's alumni squad, the star center on the Chieftain team that had won the state championship two years in a row when she was in high school. "And I remember watching you guys win state. Bernadette Manuelito."

The man gave her a worried smile. "I'm Aza Palmer. You guessed that. What happened out here?"

The fumes made her cough. "You know anyone who'd blow up your car?"

"No. People liked that car. You don't see many of them, even in Phoenix."

She rephrased the obvious. "Do you know someone who wants to harm you?"

He glanced at the wreckage again and then turned back to her. "Judging from this, I guess so. In my line of work, you make enemies and I've had some threats." Palmer laughed nervously, then stopped, embarrassed. "Was anybody hurt in the explosion?"

"Yes. Was someone waiting for you out here at the car?"

"No. Not that I know of." Palmer began to move toward the vehicle again. Bernie put her hand on his arm.

He pushed against her grip. "I just want to check out what happened."

"Sorry. It's a crime scene." She gave him a stern look. "There's an FBI agent here who will need to talk to you. He's in the gym." She described Cordova. "Go inside where it's warmer. You can't do anything helpful here."

"But it's my car. And I have to know . . ." His voice trailed off.

She swallowed, and her throat felt scratchy. "Don't argue. Go on in."

The November night was clear. *Níłch'its'ósí*, the month of small winds. She looked up at the stars, icy pinpoints in the dark velvet sky. Her eyes teared from the smoke. The calendar said it was autumn for another few weeks, but thirty degrees qualified as winter in her book. She realized her ears ached with cold and wished she had a hat.

The flow of people from the gym stopped. Evidently Cordova had taken charge. She wondered if he'd given the rookie a lecture.

Who among the people of Shiprock would want to harm Aza Palmer? Half the girls she knew in the high school had a crush on him, not just because he was one of the starters on the boys' team but because he was a nice guy. She'd read the article the *Navajo*

Times had put together about the game, mentioning that ticket sale proceeds would benefit a program to end domestic violence. The article had a picture of the championship team from the old days and a "where are they now" paragraph. Palmer seemed to still be the star, a partner with a law firm in Phoenix, one of those with eight names on the letterhead.

Bernie remembered something else about him. In his senior year, back when she was a sophomore, someone Palmer dated, a quiet girl named Lona, got pregnant and everyone knew about it. After Palmer graduated, they got married and moved away.

Cordova came out of the gym a few minutes later. "I'd like you in there with me so we can speed things up and let these folks get home. You're good with people. I told your rookie to guard the car."

"Sure. Did Palmer find you?"

"Palmer?"

"The guy who owned the car."

Cordova blinked. "Where was he?"

"Out here, assessing the damage. I sent him to look for you."

Cordova looked at the smoking ruin again. "I haven't seen him yet, but he's not going anywhere."

Cordova and the San Juan deputy, with Councilor Franklin's help, had done a good job of organizing the crowd. Teachers in the audience had come forward to stay with anxious children and teenagers waiting for parents who had been detained outside the fence. Bernie got their names and then arranged for the kids to meet their grown-ups near the administration building. Next, she took the names of parents waiting with children, then the elderly and their companions and asked them each a few questions. Lastly, she focused on able-bodied adults—some impatient and grumpy, some philosophical, most wondering what all the fuss was about. She assessed who might be helpful for follow-up interviews if needed. Although no one she spoke to said they'd seen anything unusual, some hesitated. They might recall something later.

Not a single man or woman she interviewed mentioned someone missing, or asked about the person who had been taken away
by ambulance. Did he have no friends? Was he the bomber? Was
he associated with the teens who ran, or with some of the fans who
left the scene before Bernie could talk to them?

She noticed Cordova and Palmer deep in conversation and then
Palmer sitting alone on the bleachers, head in his hands. Then
Cordova was standing beside her in his FBI vest, waiting until
she'd finished getting information from a distraught woman in a
fringed jacket.

"Take a break, Manuelito. You don't want to make a mistake."

"I'm OK."

"You are. Take a break anyway. Come outside with me. I'll tell
your rookie to come in, warm up, and do some of this."

The stench of the burned car still hung in the night air. Cordova
had cajoled or persuaded the San Juan deputies to guard the crime
scene. The fire truck remained, the crew waiting to see if their services would be needed again. Behind the yellow-and-black Keep
Out tape, the slick puddles of goo that had quelled the car fire glis-
tened in the dim light. When she thought of hazardous duty as an
officer, she'd pictured getting shot at, spit on by drunks, or chased
by guard dogs. She hadn't imagined working with flood victims
when the hard male rain fell too fast for the parched ground to
absorb. She had not anticipated that she'd be working long hours
in a blizzard to help stranded families, hunting for suspects in a
sandstorm, or walking for miles in the merciless sun searching for
a lost child. Now, she could add to the list breathing toxic smoke
and fumes that made her nauseated.

They talked as they walked toward her car. "Did you ever
smoke, Manuelito?"

"No. After all the junk I've breathed in tonight, I'm glad I
didn't."

"I used to. Actually made some interesting contacts that way.
I quit when my wife and I started dating and she said kissing me

was like licking an ashtray." He laughed at the old joke. "So, tell me how come you're here again?"

"Basketball." No one who grew up within thirty miles of Shiprock, or any town on the reservation, would have asked the question.

"You have a nephew on the Shiprock team or something?"

"No. It was a special game, the veterans versus the young hot-shots."

He nodded once. "So, I guess that means there are more people here tonight than usual. I heard it was SRO."

"SRO?"

"Standing room only."

Bernie laughed. "The games always draw a big crowd. Bas-ketball rules the rez. People line up early with folding chairs and coolers, waiting to get into the Pit. If you want a seat, especially at any of the big rivalries, you have to be here for sure when the doors open for the B-team at four."

"No kidding?"

"No kidding."

The lot had partly emptied. Clusters of cars damaged by the explosion, and a few vehicles with flats from running over debris as they headed for the exit remained along with those cars and trucks that had picked tonight to die of natural causes. She saw the rookie looking at the damaged cars and officially introduced him to Cordova.

"The wrecker I called just pulled up." Sam stood straighter and sucked in his gut as he talked. "Where would you like him first?" She noticed that the rookie didn't direct the question to her, but tossed it to Cordova.

Cordova said, "I'll brief him. Go back inside and talk to the potential witnesses. Take names of everyone and contact informa-tion. Make a note of anything that needs follow-up. The gal at the table by the door can help you."

She expected the rookie to balk, but he smiled. "Yes, sir. Glad to. Whatever you want. This is the first time I've been involved with a federal agent."

And then he was gone.

Cordova said, "I'm going to talk to Palmer once more, see if he's remembered anything else. What do you know about him?"

"He's a lawyer and lives in Arizona. He told me he's had some threats and that no one has tried to kill him. Number twenty-three on his jersey. Good from the free throw line."

"Why don't people like him?"

"He didn't say exactly, but he's a lawyer."

The crime scene van was there now, she noticed, complete with a big brown dog straining on its leash. Cordova said, "There's plenty of help around. Go on home. You did a good job."

"Thanks."

"I'll need a statement from you. Make some notes and we can do that tomorrow."

Because she had arrived late, the only empty parking spots had been at the very back of the lot. At the time, she'd pictured herself enjoying the stroll back to her ride after the hours in the hot, stuffy gym. Now, she was glad she'd parked where she had because her car hadn't been damaged. The poor Toyota had been too close to a fire that summer, and getting hit by shrapnel wouldn't have improved things.

A new car, or at least a different car with lower mileage and a working air conditioner, topped her wish list. But something always happened to divert whatever savings she managed to put away. When it came to a choice between replacing her car or helping relatives, there was no choice. And if she or Mama or Darleen needed a hand, her extended family came through for them. That was the Navajo Way.

Bernie drove to the station. It wasn't until she finished her report on the incident that she realized she could barely keep her eyes open. She wanted a shower to wash the smoke out of her hair, warm steam to lift away the sight of the injured person's burned flesh. And then a cup of tea for her scratchy throat and a good book to help her forget. Chee must be long done with his shift and probably asleep. But maybe he'd waited up for her. Maybe he'd even fixed her a bite to eat.

She arrived back at the trailer to find the lights on.

Jim Chee looked up from the movie he'd been watching on TV and smiled at her.

"Sounds like you had quite a night. Smells like it, too."

Bernie put her backpack on the floor and stood next to the couch. She coughed. Chee muted the television.

"You OK?"

"Yeah, just tired and stinky."

"I heard about the explosion on the scanner. Did you have back-up?"

"Eventually. The rookie got there first. Then the fire truck and ambulance, sheriff's deputies, a state police car, and then Cordova. By the time he arrived, it was chaos."

"Did the rookie do OK?"

"I guess. He found the one who was hurt. That guy . . ." She stopped, pushed away the memory.

Chee turned off the TV. "I heard the ambulance took some-body to the hospital, so I guess the victim was still alive at least. I'm glad he didn't die out there. I'm relieved to see you, honey."

And that, she knew, was why he was up, listening to the scanner with one ear while he watched TV, and not in bed as she'd expected. If the situation had been reversed, she would have done the same.

He went to the kitchen. She heard the water running.

"You want something? Tea? Hot chocolate?"

"Whatever you're having." She coughed again.

"Are you getting a cold?"

"I think it's smoke from the explosion. I'm jumping in the shower."

He handed her a garbage bag. "Put your clothes in here until we can wash them."

When she came out, she felt better. She listened to the rustle of dry leaves that still clung to the cottonwood trees along the San Juan River behind their little house, and the quiet song of the water, music that had swayed her heart and convinced her Chee's trailer could be her home. She heard the whistle of the teakettle.

Chee sat at the kitchen table. He had made fried bologna sandwiches to go with the hot chocolate.

She smiled at him. "Thanks. How did you know I was starving?"

"Because I'm a genius, in case you hadn't noticed. But mostly because you're always starving."

She could have argued the point, but instead she sipped the hot chocolate. "I would have loved some of this earlier tonight. I half froze out there in the parking lot."

"I bet."

She watched him take a bite. Chee could eat voraciously, any time of the day or night, and never gain an ounce.

She savored her sandwich, happy to be safe with the man she loved.

Chee took the plates to the sink.

"You want more hot chocolate? I can make some with my magic recipe. No trouble."

"Does your magic recipe involve a packet and hot water?"

"The secret's in the wrist." He demonstrated a stirring motion. "Kind of like basketball."

"Right."

"So, who won the game?"

"I don't know. I got kind of busy after the bomb went off."

"Did many of the championship guys show up?"

"Yes, enough for a bunch of substitutes. I'd love more hot chocolate. I'm still cold from the parking lot."

Chee took her cup and turned back to the counter. "I can feel you watching me. Are you trying to steal my recipe?"

"Never. Then I'd have to make my own hot chocolate."

He poured the water, stirred, came back to the table, and put the cup in front of her. She noticed tiny white specks on the light brown froth.

"What are these?"

"Miniature marshmallows, of course."

"Of course. Did you make them, too?"

"I'm not telling." He slid into the chair next to her. "Do you know whose car blew up? Or was it a truck?"

"It belonged to one of the all-stars. Aza Palmer. He said it was a BMW, his baby."

Chee said, "And there were no more bombs, no sniper attacks, nothing like that?"

"No, thank goodness." She stirred the hot chocolate, watching the marshmallows dissolve. "There are other reasons for cars to explode, but I'm betting, with a new car like that, it was a bomb."

"I think so, too. If you want to kill someone, there are simpler ways. But if you want to make a statement . . ." He left the thought hanging. "Car bombs are a terrorist weapon, designed to spread panic. Usually the organization behind the bombing brags about it. Maybe they've called in something to the FBI, you know, taking the credit?"

"Whoever did this didn't make a very clear statement tonight. An incinerated BMW, a couple rows of damaged vehicles, a whole bunch of annoyed basketball fans and scared kids and parents. I thought it was interesting that Palmer seemed so cool about the incident. He felt bad about his car, but he didn't seem worried that someone probably wanted to kill him. He said it went with the business."

"The business?"

"He's a lawyer. I guess he deals with criminal cases. He must have good insurance." She sipped her chocolate. "How was your shift?"

"Nothing like yours. The bootlegger vanished before I got there. I arrested a drunk for speeding. Lots of time to think about the meaning of life." Chee put his cup in the sink. "Let's get to bed, honey. We're leaving early for your mama's place tomorrow, remember? I promised to move the loom so she can use it. You wanted to get that done before your shift."

"I'll be there in a minute." She tapped her cup. "As soon as I'm done with this."

"There was a message from your mother on the phone when I got home. She said she'd have Kneel Down Bread for us tomorrow."

Bernie laughed. "Great. I love that *ntsidigo'i'*, especially in November."

"Yeah, it's good that your mother froze some of what you two made last summer. I think it will taste even better now."

Bernie finished her chocolate. She took the phone out of her backpack, plugged it into the charger, and noticed a missed call from Mama's house. It was too late to call now. Darleen would still be up, but she didn't want to deal with her little sister—she'd had enough drama for one night.

She switched on the ringer, as they both did each night, in case there was an emergency with Mama or at the station. By the time she got to bed, Chee was snoring lightly.

She thought about the loom. He had made it for her with his own hands in the traditional way as a wedding gift. She had planned to use it but never seemed to find the time. She'd call herself an advanced beginner when it came to weaving. She'd enjoyed it, but other things crowded her calendar. Mama had a student now, Officer Bigman's wife, and a loom at the house would make it easier for them to work together. Mama enjoyed teaching Mrs. Bigman and talked about her all the time. She enjoyed seeing Mama happy, but felt like a bystander in this new relationship.

Bernie had just turned off her reading light and snuggled next to Chee when the phone rang. Had something happened to Mama? Then she breathed a sigh of relief. It was Chee's phone.

IN JIM CHEE'S WORLD, a phone call after ten p.m. never brought good news unless a friend or relative was expecting a baby. None of his relatives were pregnant.

He rose and made his way to the bathroom, where his phone lay charging. The screen read "Largo." Chee seldom cursed but he thought about it.

The captain got to the point. "I need you to come in to the station now. You know about the explosion at the high school? Bernie fill you in?"

"Yes, sir."

Largo said, "Do you know who Aza Palmer is?"

"The guy whose car blew up."

Largo said, "He's also the man running the mediation in Tuba City, Tó Naneesdizí. You know about that?"

"No, sir."

He heard Largo exhale. "Where have you been, man? There's a big meeting about a new proposal for a resort on Navajo land near the Grand Canyon. Our tribal officials, bigwigs from the Hopi, the Havasupai, Hualapai, environmentalists, developers, federal government agency types, Arizona state officials, academics, bureaucrats, you name it. Maybe even some Paiutes. They'll all be there, and Palmer is the ringmaster."

"Ringmaster?"

"The person in charge of keeping things moving."

Chee took the phone into the bedroom and found his clothes. He wished Largo would get to the point.

"This guy Palmer is the mediator, the one who runs the meeting. The attack at the school may have had something to do with that. The issue is a big controversy."

He felt the questions pile up, but he knew Largo had more to tell him.

"Sergeant, this comes from the chief. Pack an overnight bag, get yourself down here, and plan to be gone for a few days. I'll tell you the rest when you get to the station."

"Now? You're in the office, sir?"

"Yep. Me and Mr. Palmer are here and I wanna go home."

Chee silently grumbled into his clean uniform. He looked at Bernie, the blankets pulled up to her chin and still irresistible, her beautiful dark hair flowing loose, catching the light from the bathroom. She opened her eyes.

It was impossible to keep a secret from someone when you spoke on the phone in a trailer. Not that he wanted to. He told her all the details he knew. "I know you'd like this assignment. I hope you aren't jealous."

She chuckled. "Jealous? No way. I already worked tonight, and I wasn't even on duty. Why can't it wait until morning?"

"I'll find out when I get to the station, but I bet you a doughnut I'm driving to Tuba City." He took his duffel from beneath the bed and folded in T-shirts, socks, underwear.

Bernie sat up. "Stay in touch, OK? And take some long johns. It's freezing out there."

"I'll text you when I know what's up." That way, if she was asleep, he wouldn't wake her.

His breath looked like white steam inside his truck, and Chee knew it wouldn't get warm in the time it took to drive to the station. His police unit would be cold, too. But the call made him curious, distracted him from the discomfort. An assignment from the chief. That was a first.

He found Largo at his desk and a tall Navajo in a Chieftains jacket and matching red warm-up pants pacing and fiddling with his cell phone. He'd never met Aza Palmer, but Chee had seen his photo in the article about the reunion game. From the story, he knew Palmer was about his age, but the man's face was lined and his hair gray at the temples. Hard living, Chee thought, or maybe some underlying medical issue.

The captain made introductions and told them to sit. He got to the point quickly. "Cordova noticed one of the flyers in the gym, the one from Save Wild America calling for demonstrations at the meeting at Tuba City. He knew the group had been involved in violence in California, including a bomb that did major damage and sent some folks to prison. Mr. Palmer has received threatening e-mails from them questioning his motives and his character."

Palmer folded his hands in his lap and looked at Chee. "That kind of suspicion is totally misinformed. The mediation brings together the major parties with an interest in and disagreement over the plans for the resort. My job is to keep the conversation civil, on point, and help the parties involved reach some sort of resolution. I'm the referee, not the star player." He straightened in his chair and glanced at Chee. "I tried to keep him from calling you. You guys are overreacting. If someone had wanted to do serious damage, they would have used a bigger bomb and timed it to explode when the game ended. Or just shot me."

Largo drummed his fingers on the desk. "Tell Chee what happened after you left the Pit tonight."

"I couldn't drive my car, of course, so I called Katie, my clan sister, to pick me up after the FBI guy had asked me the same questions several times. I'd planned to spend the night at her place anyway. Well, this car she hadn't seen before blocked the entrance to her road. Somebody got out and started waving at us, motioning for her to stop. I wanted to talk to him, find out what he was up to. But Katie couldn't tell who it was and what happened at the gym spooked her."

Chee noticed the calmness in the man's voice, the tone of a person who had looked danger in the face more than once.

Palmer took a breath and continued. "Then the person started to follow us, right on her bumper. She came here. When she turned into the lot, the other car drove on. Katie called her boyfriend, and he came down, drove home with her, checked things out. Everything was cool at her place, so I assume the incident was about me."

Largo leaned in toward Chee. "The chief called me at home after he heard about the bomb at the gym. He takes this seriously. We don't want the Navajo Nation to be embarrassed by an incident in Tuba. The mediation session is on our home turf. We have to make sure the star of the show stays safe."

Palmer started to protest, but Largo waved him quiet. "Chee, drive Palmer to Tuba in your unit, check into the hotel with him, and stay there until the feds get a handle on this."

Chee grimaced. "You mean, like a bodyguard?"

"More than that. The chief wants you to be on the lookout for any kind of trouble that might disrupt the talks, not just threats to Palmer." Largo held his hands out. "The chief remembered that you'd spent some time in Tuba City. The other officers there have their hands full keeping up with the protesters, the other bigwigs, you name it. I'll tell the captain in Tuba what's up."

Chee frowned. He'd worked with the chief when the man was a captain, before he rose to head the 250-officer Navajo Police Department The man was a decent officer, a good yarn spinner, and a superb politician. Chee wished that he'd made less of an impression. He didn't sign on as a cop to be a bodyguard and chauffeur.

Palmer said, "This is ridiculous. Chee can take me back to Katie's place tonight. I'd like to check on her. I'll rent a car tomorrow in Farmington."

Chee liked the idea, but he knew the captain well enough to understand the situation offered no room for debate.

"Here's what's happening." Largo used the same voice he reserved for scolding those who came to complain about something based on rumors and anti-cop prejudice. "Contact your clan sister and get her to bring the stuff you need to the motel. You're safer without a car for the next few days. Chee will make sure nothing disturbs the mediation and embarrasses the Navajo Nation. We don't want to see you dead, you don't want that either. Do us all a favor. Cooperate."

Palmer shook his head. "You're overreacting."

Largo leaned toward him. "I don't care what you think. This isn't subject to argument. You came to us for protection, remember? That's what I'm offering. Katie stopped here because she was worried about you after those incidents tonight. If you don't want our help, get out. We're not running a taxi service."

Chee registered the look Palmer gave the captain, an expression of someone who issued orders and wasn't used to getting them. Palmer stood. "It's late. Let's go to Tuba City."

Chee had spent more nights than he cared to remember driving the back roads of the reservation, responding to calls about family fights, meth kitchens, runaway children, or stolen cattle. That went with the "serve and protect" oath he'd sworn as a member of the Navajo Nation police force. But this assignment grew from politics as much as Palmer's safety. It bugged him.

Chee liked to drive in silence, using the time on the road to think. Tonight, as he moved his duffel bag from the passenger seat of his truck to the trunk of his Navajo Police unit, he realized he'd probably have to make conversation with a stranger. Perhaps Palmer would fall asleep. But the guy was a lawyer, and Chee assumed he'd want to talk. The drive would take about three hours. The anticipation made him grumpier still.

Palmer climbed in, put his fancy leather bag on the floor, and fastened the seat belt. They rode in silence for a while through the night, the rhythm of the tires on asphalt, the darkness that surrounded them taking hold. Normally, Chee's evening shift involved late-night driving in search of miscreants, witnesses, or people with complaints who wanted him to sympathize. They might mention a stack of discarded tires as a landmark to help him find the turnoff for their place. Navigating to Tuba City was easier. Boring, but easier.

The quiet minutes became a half hour. The heater kicked in. Chee kept the unit a few degrees colder than comfortable to make sure he stayed alert. Even so, his eyelids began to feel heavy. He considered pulling over, getting out into the cold to revive his brain. He glanced at his passenger.

Palmer stared out the window. Now that the car had warmed, Chee noticed the smell of the man's sweat. Palmer glanced away from the darkness outside and patted his jacket pocket. "Mind if I smoke?"

"Yeah, I do. Not in the unit. That's not good for you anyway, man."

Palmer said, "Let's get this straight. Your job is to try to make sure no one does anything to me that interferes with the mediation. It's not to meddle in my personal life. Clear?"

"Clear. I don't like this any more than you do."

Palmer said, "Can I ask you a question?"

"OK." Conversation might wake up my brain, Chee thought. Maybe Palmer would say something interesting.

"Do you know the Navajo officer who was there at the school tonight? The woman? She wore jeans, so I guess she works undercover."

Chee smiled. "Bernadette Manuelito?"

"That's the one. I remember her from high school. A sweet girl, smart as they come, kind of shy. I never pictured her growing up to be a cop. She did a good job." Palmer chuckled. "I could tell she was frustrated when the FBI agent came in, pushed her aside, and took charge."

Chee thought about telling Palmer Bernie was his wife. Decided to save that information and changed the subject. "Do you come back here, I mean to Navajoland, very often?"

"No."

"So, it took the game to bring you home?"

"A coincidence actually. The schedule to start the mediation co-incided with the game, so I figured, why not? It gave me a reason to get in shape."

Chee watched headlights ahead coming toward them considerably faster than the speed limit but not swerving. He turned on his light bar. The truck slowed. Then the empty highway rolled on, the darkness outside the patrol unit's windows unbroken.

"You're lucky you weren't in that car when it blew."

"I loved that car. I dreamed about owning a car like that when I was in high school and most of the boys wanted pickups. When I got my first job out of college and finally could afford to buy an old clunker, I kept visualizing a sleek BMW, the car of my fantasies. I finally bought it last year. Why would somebody blow it up?"

"You tell me."

"I have no idea." And Palmer fell silent.

Traffic was light, the night clear and still. In homes all across Navajoland, it had been a fine evening for stories, Chee thought. These long, cold November nights when the snakes slept made him miss the man mainstream society called his uncle but whom he knew as *shidá'í*, his Little Father. He longed for the wonderful way the old man had of bringing stories alive, retelling tradition with enriching details as he helped Chee grow from a boy to a man. His uncle built a world with words the same way other men could create beauty from the raw materials of silver, stone, or wood. He missed his *shidá'í* always, but especially this time of year.

Chee remembered Bernie's kindness toward Hosteen Nakai and his wife, now gone, too. Before he realized that Bernie would become his partner for life, she helped him kidnap his uncle out of the hospital against doctor's orders so the old healer could die as he wished beneath the open sky and his *chindi* could float free.

Chee said, "So what's it been like for you to go away and then come home?"

"It's sad. Strange and sad."

Most lawyers he'd been around were talkers, Chee thought, but a conversation with Palmer was closer to an interview. The effort made him more alert.

"Sad how?"

"Well, the landscape speaks to me, brings back memories. My mother and my grandmothers are gone, and most of their generation, too. I visited with my aunt, but she didn't recognize me. A lot of friends I went to school with moved away like I did." He laughed. "I met my wife when we were still in high school and that cut back on the time I spent with the guys."

The comment made Chee curious. "Did your wife come with you back to Shiprock?"

"Oh, we split a long time ago."

Chee steered into the darkness. One hundred seventy-two miles, more or less from Shiprock to Tuba City, a trip that usually required about three hours. With the light traffic he hoped to arrive a little sooner, tuck his passenger in for the night, text Bernie, and go to bed.

"So what does a mediator do? I've heard about mediation, but I've never been involved with a session."

Palmer exhaled. "We help people with disagreements resolve them. Usually, the meetings are private, confidential, limited to people directly involved in the conflict. But because the Grand Canyon belongs to America, as they say, the resort development issue is complicated. I will devote the first session or two in Tuba City, in advance of the delegates getting down to work, to public comment."

"How did you get picked for this job?" Fully awake now, Chee turned up the heat.

"I worked with the Forest Service on another Grand Canyon case and also with the Navajo Nation on a couple other major issues and with the state of Arizona. That might have helped. The Tribal Council recommended me along with some others. When I

applied, I didn't know if being Navajo might work in my favor or
go the other way."

Palmer had not bragged, and Chee gave the man credit.

"Have you been following the issue?" Palmer asked.

"Not lately. It seems like the conflict has been going on forever."
It was, Chee noticed, one of the few questions Palmer had asked
him in their many minutes together.

"It has been simmering a long, long time." Palmer adjusted the
heater vent. "Business interests, economic development on one side;
Native groups, environmentalists on the other, but not necessar-
ily in agreement about what they'd like to see done or left alone.
Lots of people in between. Nobody would dare say they advocate desecrating a sacred place. But what's sacred and what's just
nice to look at? What does 'appropriate development' mean, and is
there any room for such a thing at the canyon? Should the Navajo
Nation have the right to do what it wants with its land? It is a
huge, divisive issue, a grand canyon of disagreements."

They drove awhile without conversation, the hum of the tires
on the asphalt puncturing the dark silence. Chee watched the
markings on the highway sail by in the bright ribbon created by
the headlights. He understood the road and drove at a speed that
exceeded the numbers noted on the black-and-white signs.

Palmer said, "What happens next with the investigation into
who destroyed my car?"

"Federal agencies handle the big crimes: murder, car bombs,
kidnapping, bank robbery, stuff like that. They'll work on it. Our
tribal police jurisdiction is mostly Navajo-on-Navajo crime. Missing elders, traffic laws, meth labs in the outback, domestic violence."

"That sounds major to me. Especially domestic violence. That
shapes a kid's life forever."

Chee felt warm embarrassment rise to his face and appreciated
the car's darkness. "I didn't mean it that way. No one likes to respond to those calls. Usually at least one of the people is drunk or

high, maybe both. The children are crying, hiding, traumatized. It's a dangerous situation for everyone, including the officer who gets the call." He knew several officers who had been attacked and hurt on those assignments "Domestic violence, child abuse, is that the kind of law you do?"

"I used to when I started my practice. I worked pro bono child custody and restraining orders and some criminal defense. Environmental law and mediation hold my interest now."

Chee dimmed his headlights for an approaching car, then flashed them back to high. "What do you think about the idea of a resort near the confluence of the two rivers?"

"It's a complex subject. As the mediator, I have to keep my opinions to myself or, better yet, not have any." Palmer looked out the side window, then turned back to face the empty highway unfolding in the unit's headlights. "How much longer before we get to the hotel?"

"Another hour or so."

Chee heard a shuffle and glanced over. Palmer had pulled something out of the leather bag at his feet. In the glow of the light from the big dial on Palmer's watch, he could see that it was a bag of hard candy. The translucent ones that came in fruit flavors. Jolly Somethings. Palmer extended the bag toward him.

"No thanks. I'm not big on sweets."

"I'm not either, but I've got some blood sugar issues. Diabetes."

"That a nice briefcase, or whatever you call it."

"I like it. My ex-wife gave it to me when I graduated from law school."

Then Chee heard Palmer zipping his jacket and watched the passenger lean his head against the headrest. They drove past the intersection for Kayenta, historic hometown of the Wetherill family of traders and explorers, through the little settlement of Tsegi, and over the rest of the route in silence. If Palmer fell asleep, Chee didn't hear him snoring.

They got to the Rest Well *Diné* Lodge in Tuba City about one a.m. Palmer stood at the entrance with a cigarette while Chee went in to start the registration process.

The round-faced girl at the hotel desk wore her smooth hair cut to fall at her jawline. She had the puffy eyes of the sleep-deprived. Chee told her his name and she checked the computer.

"Are you here for the Grand Canyon meeting, Sergeant?"

"That's right." He didn't feel like making small talk. "You should also have a room for Aza Palmer starting tomorrow night."

"I don't see anything for Palmer. We're nearly full—very unusual for this time of year. A lot of people are interested in what's going to happen at the canyon."

A chime sounded as Palmer came in. He walked up to Chee. The girl said, "I have two rooms for you for tonight and one for an additional four nights under your name, Sergeant."

"I hope I won't be here that long."

Palmer said, "Could you put one of those rooms for tonight under a different name?"

The girl looked up at Chee from the screen. "I guess so, if it's OK with the sergeant."

"Book it under Zoom Harris."

She went to the computer.

"Mr. Harris, you have a reservation starting tomorrow. Do you want me to add tonight to that bill?"

"Please."

Chee looked at the man. "Zoom Harris?"

"It's a long story." Palmer smiled. "Sad, and not very interesting."

Chee turned to the girl. "Are these adjoining rooms?"

"No, sorry. When the person called for the reservation, I told him those were all booked. These two are across the hall from each other. That's the best we could do." The girl took plastic cards from a desk drawer. "How many keys do you want?"

Before Palmer could interject Chee said, "Two for his room. One mine."

The girl slipped the white key cards into small sleeves and wrote the room numbers on the outside of each one before she handed them out. She smiled at Chee. "Since you're a cop, could I ask you a favor?"

"What can I help you with?"

"There's a vehicle in the back lot with a dog that's been barking all night. Some customers complained. I went out there and the dog is in an old camper van or bus, whatever they call it, parked along the fence. One of those funny old Volkswagens. I checked the books, and whoever owns it isn't registered here. I'm not sure what to do next."

Palmer said, "This must be the night for trouble in parking lots. At least the dog isn't blowing up anything."

Chee thought about suggesting that the complaining customers put pillows over their heads. The hotel could give them earplugs. Or she could call a tow company to remove the vehicle and its critter while he slept. He said, "I'll check on it for you. Does the hotel take dogs?"

"Yes, and I've got one dog room open."

He walked with Palmer to their rooms, down the long, car-peted corridor. The hotel was quiet, not even the blare of late-night television penetrating beyond the guest room doors. A few room service trays sat neglected in the hallway.

When they found the right rooms, Palmer ran his card through the reader and the green light blinked on. Chee stopped him as he reached for the door. "Let me." He pushed, and the door opened into stuffy darkness. He felt along the smooth wall for the light switch and flicked it on. He checked the bedroom, bathroom, and closet, found nothing suspicious, and motioned Palmer in.

"What are your plans for tomorrow?"

"I'll call Katie in the morning to bring my stuff. Otherwise, I'm going to phone room service and stay here and work until about an hour before the meeting."

Chee handed him a business card with his cell phone number

and jotted down his room number. "Call me if anything seems odd, threatening, out of the ordinary. Or just come to my room. I'd like the other key to your room, just in case. I'll see you tomorrow."

Palmer handed him the key card. Chee walked out the side door to his unit to get his overnight bag. He heard the barking and saw the camper. If the girl at the desk hadn't been so polite, he could have said no, he thought. But now he was committed, so he'd deal with the canine troublemaker next.

4

The barking originated in a vintage orange Volkswagen camper van parked sideways at the edge of the fenced hotel lot. The vehicle had California plates, a rusty dent behind the driver's door, and a Save Wild America bumper sticker. Another read "Earth Day—Love Your Mother" and looked as though it might have come from the first Earth Day. Perhaps tourists, he thought, or protesters in Tuba for the meeting. He hadn't expected out-of-staters.

He noticed light escaping through the drawn curtains. The high-pitched barking grew more ferocious as he walked toward the camper door. He knocked. "Officer Jim Chee, Navajo Police."

A man's voice called out. "Go away. Do you know what time it is?"

"There are some complaints about the dog barking."

"What barking?" The dog continued to bark. "Stop with the harassment already. Find some real crime." And then the man swore at him.

Chee had dealt with rude people for most of his career but never got used to it. He felt a flare of anger. One of the basic principles of the Navajo Way was to treat your fellow creatures with respect,

and he knew the world would certainly move more smoothly if
everyone followed that.

"Sir, do you have a room at the hotel?"

"What do you think?"

"I think you don't." Chee kept his voice level. "The hotel has
a vacancy and you can bring the dog in. Otherwise, you need to
keep your dog quiet and move the van. This lot is only for hotel
guests."

"He'll stop barking once you leave. If you're really a cop and
not just a security goon, go find some bad guys. Like those developers who want to rape the Grand Canyon."

Chee was tired. The November cold moved up from the asphalt
parking lot through the soles of his boots, through his socks and
into his skin.

"The motel will have your vehicle towed. You'd be smart to
move it yourself."

The man swore at him again through the closed door.

The dog kept barking. Chee trotted back into the lobby. "I
talked to the dog's owner, told him he could be towed. He's difficult."

"Thanks anyway." The girl reached below the counter, opened
a drawer, and took out some foil bags. "Here, have some extra
coffee. You look like you might need it in the morning."

Chee's room, a copy of Palmer's, sat on the other side of the
hall with a window toward the parking lot. He put the room key
cards and the coffee packs on the desk along with his wallet and
car keys. He missed Bernie already. He sent her a text: *Tuba 2 a.m.
Wish you were here.*

He adjusted the thermostat to warm the room, hung his shirts in
the little closet, quickly brushed his teeth, and, finally, climbed between the smooth, fresh sheets of the king-sized bed. It seemed like
he had just dozed off when a sound awakened him. He reached to
the bedside table for his ringing phone. It was seven a.m.

"Hey, Jimmie Chee. What's cookin'?"

"Not much. I'm in Tuba." He'd met Albert Dashee, better known as Cowboy, on one of his first assignments. Dashee worked for the Hopi Tribal Police and had become a friend. "What's up, brother?"

"I'm driving to Moenkopi today, just got a little bored and that made me think of you."

"I got a call from the captain to come here late last night to help with the big mediation session after that excitement in Shiprock."

"I heard about that. That's why I have to work, too. The boss figured with you Navajos providing security, we ought to come and supervise. So we'll be running into each other a lot this week."

"Yeah. There's a downside to everything." He hid his surprise that Dashee knew about his assignment; some news travels fast in Indian Country.

Dashee chuckled. "Wanna meet for lunch?"

"Sounds good. You treating?"

"Sure." Dashee didn't hesitate or make a joke; Chee assumed his friend needed a favor.

"When and where?"

"Tuuvi Cafe as soon as the orientation ends. I figured I'd see you there, but I thought I'd call you, anyhow. Start your day off right."

"What orientation?"

Dashee told him when and where. "Captain West set this up, but after what happened at the high school, the feds want in on it, too. I guess they think they can keep it at a two-ring circus instead of a full rodeo."

No one had told him about the orientation, but that didn't surprise Chee and he didn't take it personally. He knew how things worked or didn't work. And if he'd missed the session, someone would have filled him in. But now that Dashee had let him know, he figured he ought to show up.

"So what time does it start?"

Dashee told him.

"Is that Navajo time or Arizona time?"

"We call it Hopi time, but it's all good now, dude, until March. Then we stay sane and you all get complicated with daylight savings. Where do you put all that extra daylight anyway?" Dashee laughed.

As he showered, Chee thought about humans and time. Spanning three states, the Navajo Nation, of which Tuba City was a major metropolis, joined most of the rest of the United States in the switch on and off daylight saving time. People living away from Navajoland in the rest of Arizona, including Dashee's Hopi village, didn't move their clocks forward in the spring and back in the fall. Because Navajo Tuba City and Hopi Moenkopi were neighbors, the hour time change from one side of the street to the other caused tourists considerable confusion.

He dressed and went outside to greet the day with sacred cornmeal and his morning prayer. He noticed the untowed camper van parked by the fence. The dog was quiet. Back in his room, Chee put some water in the little coffeepot, added grounds to the basket. While the coffee brewed he turned on the television, something he never did at home in the morning because there he had Bernie to talk to.

The Shiprock explosion made the morning news. The cameras showed the ruin of the bombed car and the flashing lights of cop cars. The FBI guy looked good on camera and sounded calm, professional, and serious.

He called Bernie.

"Sweetheart, turn on the TV. They've got Cordova on the news talking about what happened. He gave a shout-out to Navajo Police. That would be you and the rookie."

"Did he use my name?"

"If he did, that part didn't make it on broadcast."

"Thank goodness."

"You didn't mention that TV people were out there."

"It was a zoo. We were lucky they didn't get there until after

Cordova took charge. I can't talk long. I'm leaving for work. The captain and Cordova want me to help follow up with the interviews."

"Interviews?"

"You know, all those people in the gym who might have seen something on their way in, but probably didn't. What's Palmer up to this morning?"

"I haven't heard from him. Nothing else has blown up, so I guess he's cool."

He remembered their plan to take the loom to her mother's house. "Do you want me to call and tell her what happened?"

"I'll do it. I need to talk to her anyway."

Chee said, "I miss you. I wish you were here. I'm making enough coffee for two."

5

Bernie had just arrived at the station and slipped off her jacket when Sandra forwarded the call.

The woman on the line didn't identify herself. "I was looking for some information about the bombing last night. Can you help me?"

"The FBI is handling that. I can give you a phone number for Agent Cordova."

"You're a Navajo police officer, right?"

"Yes, ma'am. Officer Manuelito. Who are you?"

"I understand that you guys were the first on the scene, is that right?"

"Correct. Who am I speaking with?"

"This is Lona Zahne."

"Lona? It's Bernie. Bernadette Manuelito. It's been forever. How are you?"

"Bernie? Oh my gosh! You're a cop—I heard you say Officer Manuelito when you answered the phone. A cop?"

"Right."

The phone went quiet for a moment.

"I just learned about the explosion out there on TV," Lona said. "Aza Palmer, you remember him? He was supposed to be at the game. The reporter said someone was killed and, well . . ."

Bernie heard the catch in her voice.

"I talked to Palmer after the bombing. He's OK."

"You were there?" Lona didn't wait for a response. "Gosh, that must have been terrifying."

"Oh, it's part of the job." *Terrifying* was not the word Bernie would have used. Maybe *exciting*, *challenging*, *exhausting*, and *nerve-wracking* while she waited to see if there would be more bombs or a sniper.

"I could never be a cop. So Aza wasn't hurt or anything?"

"He's fine."

"What happened?"

"A car exploded during the game. I don't know much more. The FBI is investigating. Your husband wasn't hurt."

"Great. But Aza hasn't been my husband for a long time. I thought everyone back there knew that."

Bernie pulled out a notebook and jotted down "Lona Zahne" and the number on her phone screen. When something bad happened, like a car blown to smithereens, the victim's discarded spouse ranked high on the potential-suspect list along with former lovers, debtors, fellow gang members, and associates tied to the drug scene.

"You back on the rez these days, Lona?"

"Oh no. I'm in Phoenix. My boy finished high school, got a job out of town, so I'm done with the mothering business. And you, girlfriend, still there in Shiprock where we grew up. Did you ever get married?"

The question surprised Bernie. She was thinking about Lona being "done with the mothering business" and was glad her mother didn't feel that way.

"Me, married? Yes."

Lona's laugh surprised her again. "He must be a special guy. You were always so independent. Do I know him?"

"I don't think you've met him. He's a cop like me. Sergeant Jim Chee." Bernie noticed Sandra standing in the doorway, motioning with her right hand . . . call waiting. "I've got to go, but I'd like to talk to you some more."

"Sure thing." Lona rattled off a second phone number. "Let me know when you're in Phoenix. And I'd love to meet your husband." Bernie ended the call and focused on Sandra.

"FBI on the line for you. And then Largo wants to see you with Wilson Sam in his office."

Bernie picked up the call. "Hey, Cordova, Chee caught you on TV this morning. He said you handled it well."

"I've had some practice. Thanks for last night. Good work. What's the name of the new guy?"

"Wilson Sam."

"Cocky, isn't he?"

She didn't respond.

"We have some preliminary information on the victim in the bombing. I talked to Largo, but I wanted to tell you directly myself." She heard the fatigue in Cordova's voice, waited for him to continue. "No ID on him. He had a phone, but it didn't set off the blast. He's Native American or maybe Hispanic, late teens or early twenties. Critical condition."

"That's it?"

"I know. You figured out he was young and Navajo just by looking at him."

Bernie smiled. "What else about the bomb? Homemade? Professional?"

"We're working on that. Before you ask, no prints yet from what's left of the car. No clue on motive, but Palmer mentioned some threats, including nasty e-mails from an environmental group, the one that had the posters there, Save Wild America. The mediation has had lots of press and he's a controversial character.

"You know, Manuelito, we both said 'bomb.' It could have been something besides a bomb, I guess. We won't know for sure until we get the crime scene report. Largo told me he'd free you up to help with the interviews. Great. We want this solved yesterday."

Bernie switched the phone to her other ear. "I'm going to talk to Largo as soon as we hang up. I'll check to see if any families around here have called about a missing person. This man's relatives could be wondering why he didn't come home last night."

"That's probably not as important as—Hold on."

Then he was back. "I just learned that the man died at the hospital this morning from injuries received in the blast. Tell Largo. We'll cross interviewing him off our to-do list."

The news of the death—and the nonchalance of Cordova's comment—left her speechless.

PERCHED IN THE CHAIR in front of Largo's desk, Wilson Sam looked neat, smug, and a lot more rested than she felt. She settled into the folding seat next to the rookie, wondering what to expect.

Largo looked exhausted. "You hanging in there, Manuelito?"

"Yes, sir. I guess. Cordova just told me the victim died."

Largo sighed. "The FBI and a special bomb team are still at the high school. When Cordova called earlier he said you both did great out there."

Sam adjusted himself to sit a bit higher.

Bernie said, "We were just being cops."

"You weren't even on duty, Manuelito. It was some kind of luck that you went to the game. Good luck for the feds, maybe not so good for you."

She shifted in the hard chair. "No luck involved, sir. Half of Shiprock was there. And Sam, well, he helped."

Largo leaned back in his chair and rested his hands on his belly. "The feds like us today. That's the good news, I guess. They like us so much they want us to work on tracking down possible witnesses. That's the bad news. Let's get this squared away."

"Tell Cordova I'll do whatever I can." Sam's voice dripped with enthusiasm. "Whatever he wants."

Bernie said, "Last night, besides the folks I talked to in the gym, I got the plate numbers of everyone who parked close enough to have their vehicles damaged. I have contact information on the players for both teams and the officials and security guards. Since they all had to suit up early, I thought they might have seen something."

Largo looked at Sam.

"Manuelito assigned me to crowd control. I was breathing in fumes and freezing my toes off instead of doing something useful."

The animosity in his tone tightened Bernie's chest.

Largo turned to Bernie. "Give him half your follow-up list." He looked at the rookie again. "Pay attention when you talk to people. Think about what they might be leaving out." He took a breath. "Questions?"

Bernie and Officer Sam stayed quiet.

"I've got one for you both. Why would anyone do something like that here? I mean, this is Shiprock, not Phoenix or even Albuquerque. People know each other. A lot of innocent folks could have died. Think about that when you do those interviews."

Sam followed Bernie back to her desk. She found her notebook from last night and gave him a page with a list.

"Is this all?"

She said, "These are the basketball players and the officials. They all had to be at the Pit early. Start there. Do you know how to proceed?"

He stood straighter. She could feel his stare on the top of her head. "Well, let's see. What if I ask if they saw anything suspicious?"

Bernie bristled. "Give some examples of what suspicious looks like when you ask the question. You'll get a better response."

"You mean, *Sir, did you see someone walking around with a bomb? Ma'am, did you see a creep plant a little package under the car that blew up?*" He glanced at the paper she'd given him. "Cut me some slack. I didn't sleep through training."

"You slept through the part where they said leave the attitude at home."

He glared at her, started to say something, and then stormed out.

After he left, Bernie stretched and walked to the front of the building, heading outside for some air.

Sandra looked up from her computer. "I gave the car registrations Largo asked me to compile to the rookie. He was whining about needing more to do. Was that OK with you?"

"Fine. If he makes a mess of it, Largo can deal with him."

"What's up with you two?"

"Nothing."

"It didn't feel like nothing. He couldn't wait to get outta here, and you look fried."

Bernie thought about what to say. "We're both on edge today. What happened last night could have been horrific."

"I can't get over it and I wasn't even there. What if there had been a second bomb? What if you hadn't been at the game? What if the bomber had been one of those anti-police nuts?"

"You're right. It could've been worse. We're lucky, I guess."

Sandra reached in her desk drawer and pulled something out. She handed it to Bernie. "I found this last week when I was hiking up by Tsoodzil."

Bernie looked at the rock. Mount Taylor, where it came from, was Turquoise Mountain, the Sacred Mountain of the South, one of four that formed the traditional boundaries of Dinetah, the Navajo homeland. The rock had a slightly yellow tint. Quartz, perhaps. The shape reminded her of some sort of animal. Bernie felt its cool smoothness in her hand. She moved her fingers over it lightly and started to hand it back.

"It's yours."

Bernie looked at the rock again. This time, she saw the shape of the *náshdóítsoh*, the mountain lion, a strong and important animal in the *Diné Bahane'*, the story of how The People came to be, the Navajo Old Testament. *Náshdóítsoh* symbolized protection and healing. She slid the rock into her pocket.

Bernie stood in the parking lot for a few minutes, watching the traffic and remembering an old song about the wisdom of the mountain lion. Then she took her mug to the break room, discovered the empty pot, started some coffee, and went back to work while it brewed.

She didn't mind making phone calls, the task ahead, but she always learned more when she spoke to someone face-to-face. She reviewed the list of fans she'd briefly interviewed last night and marked for follow-up. Then she started an e-mail to Lieutenant Leaphorn, the department's legendary detective. He was recovering from a head injury and still unable to speak clearly on the phone. But technology had enabled him to get back to work part-time as a consultant for the department. Now, when she wanted his advice, she wasn't asking for a favor.

Lieutenant,

Because you have convinced me there is no such thing as coincidence, I need your help in connecting the dots. You probably heard about last night's bombing. The car belongs to Aza Palmer

Then she realized she had too many questions to put in an e-mail. It was time for a visit. Even though he couldn't speak easily, he could listen and maybe give her some answers on the spot. Or do some research and e-mail a response.

When she went back for coffee, Officer Bigman was putting the lid on his traveling mug.

"I heard you were in the wrong place at the right time last night."

"You could say that. And I missed the end of the game, too."

"The old guys won." He chuckled. "You know what they say: age and experience beat youth and exuberance in the long run."

"I thought it was age and trickery."

"Any news about the explosion?"

"The man who was injured died. A young Navajo guy without any ID. Largo has us making a bunch of follow-up calls."

Bigman clicked the lid of his coffee cup into place. "I get to drive out to Sheep Springs and look for the Tsosie girl—you know, the one who likes to run away."

"At least it's not snowing yet."

"I wish it had snowed earlier. That would make her easier to track."

Bernie settled in to start the calls. Sandra buzzed her. "A person here wants to talk to someone about the bombing. He says he knows something."

"Is the rookie around?"

"Sorry."

"I'll be right out."

A middle-aged man in a denim work shirt stood nervously at the counter. Bernie introduced herself with her clan affiliation. Bruce Chino did the same.

"My sister was at the game last night where the trouble happened. She told me she saw a young man, a high school kid or something, and it looked like he was trying to break into cars or something. Acting weird, you know? She told a security guard about it when she went into the gym." Chino paused, rubbed his palms against his pants, continued. "I figured I should mention it to someone like you, you know, after what happened. In case, you know, that boy was up to no good or something."

"Did your sister have any idea who the man was?" Bernie was tempted to add, *You know, or something.*

Chino shrugged.

"Can you give me your sister's name and phone number so I can talk to her?"

"Gloria Chino. She had a phone, you know, but she lost it somewhere. You can call me when I'm over there." Chino gave Bernie his phone number.

"When will you be there?"

"Oh, in about three days or something. I'm driving a truck to Los Angeles. Just on my way out now."

"I'd like to talk to her before that. Can you give me directions to her house?"

"They live out there, you know, just past the place where that house burned down." He elaborated. "She works, so go by later."

Back at her desk, Bernie looked at her interview list. She began with people she knew, or at least had met before the trouble last night. The first two calls went to voice mail, but on the third a woman answered. Bernie heard a dog or maybe a baby crying in the background.

They'd met last year when the woman, Julie Pahe, reported that her truck had been stolen. Bernie reintroduced herself and asked Pahe if she'd remembered anything unusual at the game since they'd spoken last night.

"Well, my big boy plays on the JV, so we have to be there early. Usually I drop him off by the door, because I have to work, but last night I planned on staying because of the homecoming game. That's how I found a parking place close to the entrance. I decided to call my sister before I went in because, you know, she's having a baby any day now. Did I already say that?"

"Go ahead and tell me what you saw." Bernie feared the story would segue into her sister's pregnancy or the births of other children, but Julie stayed on target.

"I noticed a man standing outside the gym. Not smoking a cigarette or talking on the phone or anything. I wondered why he didn't go inside. Maybe he was waiting for a friend, but it was cold out there. Maybe he wasn't doing anything, but when my sister and I finished and I got out of the car, he had disappeared."

"That's interesting. What did he look like?"

"Oh, typical, I guess. Pants, a jacket. On the short side. Not too fat." Julie stopped. "I guess I didn't get a good look."

Bernie remembered the jacket on the man who died. His supine body had seemed reasonably tall, but then most people seemed tall from her perspective. "Could you tell what color the jacket was?"

"It was getting dark," Julie said. "But I think it was blue. It had a hood and he pulled that over his head."

Blue. Not the brown she'd seen on the dead man.

Julie took a deep breath. "Is the gym still closed?"

"As far as I know. Until the experts finish investigating the explosion."

"I hope they figure out what happened. My boy is afraid they will have to cancel practice."

"How did the JV team do last night?"

"They played together really well."

Bernie knew that meant they'd lost. "Thanks for your help."

"I hope the police have more luck finding who did it than you all did finding my truck."

"Yes. Me, too." The truck had never been recovered.

Bernie spent the rest of the workday following up on her list of potential witnesses, learning nothing much, feeling useless and discouraged.

She thought of Bruce Chino's sister, Gloria, and decided to stop by her house before she headed home. Then, rather than eat by herself, she could head off to Mama's for dinner and a visit.

She called Mama's house and her sister answered.

"Hey there." Darleen sounded preoccupied.

"Hi. I'm thinking of stopping by for dinner."

"Sure. I've been too busy to think about food. Could you bring a pizza?"

"I guess. You guys need anything else?"

"Beer. No, just kidding. Three months and fourteen days without a drink."

"That's great. How's Mama?"

"She's OK. She was tired last night after teaching Mrs. Bigman. What's happening with the mad Shiprock bomber?"

"Have you been watching TV?"

"I read about it on Facebook first, and then Mama and I saw the damage on the news this morning." Darleen didn't wait for an answer. "That FBI guy on TV was kinda cute, but he didn't have much to say."

"What kind of pizza do you want?"

"Mushroom. Extra cheese."

Bernie walked past Sandra's desk on her way out.

"Are you calling it a day?" Sandra asked.

"One more interview. Maybe it will lead somewhere."

"You look kinda down, sad or something."

"I'm frustrated. After all those calls, only one lead and it's marginal."

"There's something else, too, right?"

Bernie bristled at Sandra's probing but had learned to tell her friend the truth and get it over with.

"I don't like Chee being gone, and I keep thinking about that explosion and the dead one."

"And the rookie?" Sandra didn't wait for an answer. "You still have that little rock?"

Bernie took it out of her pocket. Sandra looked at it. "See, from this angle it looks like *shush*." Sandra was right. It could be a bear, the spirit of courage. But Bernie saw *náshdóítsoh*, the protector, more clearly.

GLORIA CHINO, THE POTENTIAL WITNESS, lived only ten miles from the Shiprock substation, but her road consisted of deep ruts and gaping potholes. Bernie's unit, an SUV, had good clearance, but she drove slowly, negotiating the challenges, glad there was still a bit of daylight.

She pulled up in front of a manufactured home with a hogan next to it. A committee of three large dogs, each one brown with black on the ears, legs, tail, or muzzle, came up to the vehicle, growling. Bernie waited, and then a squat woman in a sweater the color of crisp bacon, her black hair in a ponytail, came to the door and called the animals. The dogs grew quiet, but Bernie could feel their eyes on her as she walked toward the front door.

"I'm Officer Bernadette Manuelito. I'm investigating the bombing last night." She summarized her conversation with Bruce Chino at the substation.

The woman nodded and introduced herself with her clans. Bernie did the same. On this part of the reservation she frequently encountered clan sisters, but Gloria wasn't related. Bernie followed the woman inside. The dogs stayed out but on the alert.

The house was neat. A well-worn Two Grey Hills blanket covered the couch. A glass case in the corner held shiny brown Navajo pots and painted Pueblo bowls. Bernie saw a well-made wedding basket, sports trophies, and family photos.

"Bruce told me he was going to stop at the police station in case someone was interested in what I saw. Thanks for coming all the way out here." Gloria gave her the hint of a smile. "I remember you from the game, giving orders. I thought you were taller."

Bernie said, "I would have called, but Mr. Chino said you don't have a phone."

Gloria shook her head. "I keep thinking I'll find it. Probably will as soon as I get another one. I can't call it 'cause the battery is dead." Gloria pushed a strand of stray hair out of her face. "Can I get you a glass of water or something?"

"That would be great."

Gloria took a red plastic cup from the shelf and filled it with water from the kitchen faucet. She cleared a pile of mail from the dining table to reveal orange placemats. "Have a seat."

Bernie complied and pulled a notebook from her backpack. Gloria settled across from her. "Shall I start talking now?"

"Yes. Please go ahead."

"Well, we went to the game because my husband, Wilbert, used to play basketball at Crownpoint, and so he remembered playing against some of those guys who won the championship. He knew them a little. Anyway, we had to stop for gas, so we got to the gym kind of late, and Wilbert had to park in the back.

"At halftime I went outside for a cigarette. I'm trying to stop, so I left them in the truck. So I sat there, cracked the window, and listened to the radio while I smoked. It was cold, but warmer than standing outside, you know? On my way back to the gym I saw the inside lights on in a car in the front row. I thought, that person's battery will be dead before the game is over. I used to have a car and the glove box didn't stay closed, so the light came on and then the battery went dead. I went over to check it out, and a guy was sitting in the car. I can't swear that it was the car that went boom, but I know it was in the same row."

Gloria pushed her hair out of her eyes again.

Bernie leaned forward. "May I ask you some questions?"

"OK."

"Could you tell what the man was doing?"

"Not doing much that I could see except sitting there. Like he was thinking or something."

"What did he look like?"

Gloria laughed. "Short black hair, a brown jacket zipped up. No glasses, though, I remember that."

"A brown jacket. Are you sure?"

She nodded. "The seats in that car were brown, too. Looked like leather."

"Was he tall? Short?"

"He was sitting down, so short."

"About how old?"

Gloria pushed her hands together and pressed the upturned fingers against her chin. "Maybe eighteen, twenty, twenty-two. Something like that. He looked too young for such fancy wheels."

Bernie made a note. "Had you seen him before?"

"I don't think so."

Bernie heard the hesitation. "But you might have?"

Gloria waited to answer, studying her fingernails. "Well, just between us, I go to AA meetings. I'm not supposed to talk about who else is there, but I might have seen him. But maybe not. Like I said, it was dark."

The dogs started barking, and Gloria stopped talking until they fell silent. Then she said, "Do you think that man put the bomb in the car?"

"I don't know. Can you give me his name?"

"It's against the AA rules."

Bernie said, "I think the man you saw died in the explosion. His name will help me find his family, let them know what happened to him."

Gloria pressed her lips together. "I only know the first name. Rick. I hope it wasn't him."

"*Ahéhee.* Thank you for telling me that, and what you saw. Anything else?"

Gloria said, "When I was walking toward the car, it looked like he was bending down. Like he dropped something on the floor maybe, and was getting it."

Bernie finished her water. "If you think of anything else, anything at all, let me know."

Gloria nodded. "I'll walk out with you because of the dogs."

The pack, clustered outside the door, followed them to the Navajo Police SUV. None barked or growled. Bernie figured they didn't object when visitors left.

It was dark now, and colder. The heater in Bernie's unit sounded like a motorcycle revving up, but it worked quickly. The SUV had almost warmed to comfortable when she reached the station.

She added notes from the interview to the rest of the day's results and sent a message about the man Gloria identified as Rick to the captain with a cc to Cordova. She mentioned the AA connection, and the fact that this meeting lead, if it was verifiable, tied him to the Shiprock area. She told Largo she'd check in at the AA meeting, out of uniform, tomorrow.

She ordered the pizza and left the station, happier than she'd been all day. A lead. A small one, but it could mean that the man who died—she'd call him Rick—would be more than another lost soul. Someone would have to tell his relatives. She snuggled into her warm Navajo Police jacket and climbed into the frigid Toyota. Despite the miles she'd put on it, the car kept going and she appreciated it. It had been in her life longer than Chee. She turned off the heater to spare herself the blast of cold air until the engine had a chance to warm. The Tercel started right up.

She encountered the normal handful of vehicles on US 491. Everyone seemed to be behaving. She searched the folds of her brain for a glimpse of a man in a blue jacket, or maybe a blue sweatshirt with a hood, among those she'd encountered in the gym, the person Julie Pahe thought could be suspicious. Were two men involved in the explosion, or was blue hoodie just a guy who enjoyed standing outside in the cold?

She thought about Leaphorn, and how skillfully he called attention to the details she overlooked. She needed to brainstorm with him.

Curious to see the site of the explosion again, she turned onto US 64. The parking lot stood empty, cleaner than it had been before the incident, the crime scene investigators done with their jobs. It was rare to find it vacant in November; the school events on the schedule must have been canceled. All that marked the death of a man in a brown jacket was the scar on the pavement made by the blast.

She wondered what the dead man's family thought about his absence. Did he have a girlfriend, a brother who worried about him the same way she had worried about her sister last summer when Darleen hadn't come home or answered her phone?

Her Toyota seemed colder, the night darker. She gave her head a quick shake to dispel the bad memory, feeling the weight of her hair as it moved. She turned on the heat. The whirr of the fan and the cold air turning to warm on her feet and legs helped to push the image of the burned man aside.

At home, she took a shower, put on her soft old jeans, a sweater, and her favorite silver-and-coral earrings. She thought about the warm pizza and a sweet, bubbly Coke to go with it and about the pleasure of being with Mama and Darleen. She thought of how lucky she was to have them close enough that they could share dinner.

The pizza sat boxed and ready when she got to the restaurant. She placed it in the front seat next to her and wrapped it in a blanket. As she drove the dirt roads she knew so well to Mama's house, the aroma of yeasty crust, cheese, and tomato sauce deliciously filled the car.

Darleen had set the table with plates, forks, and little packages of cheese and red pepper left over from previous pizzas. Mama pushed her walker from the living room and sat in her usual place. Bernie opened the box, and the smell of warm crust, melted cheese, and pepperoni made her mouth water.

"Hold on," Darleen said. "I'll get the salad." She put a bowl of lettuce, chopped cucumbers, bell peppers, and what looked like little beige balls on the table, went back to the fridge, and brought out two bottles of salad dressing. "It won't hurt us to eat some vegetables. I asked for mushrooms, but I know you always get pepperoni pizza."

Mama said, "I like it."

"Me, too." Bernie put her napkin in her lap. "The sauce has tomato—that's a vegetable. Add the pepper flakes and we're practically vegetarians. Except for the meat."

Darleen said, "In my class, we had these people come in and they talked about eating the old ways like our ancestors, and how people are getting sick—diabetes, heart disease, other bad stuff—because of so much fake food."

Her sister had given her a glass of water, not the bubbly sweet Coke she'd dreamed of. Bernie served some salad to Mama, then put a slice of pizza on her plate. She gave herself a slice with plenty of pepperoni and added some packaged cheese and red pepper flakes. She offered Mama a packet of cheese and passed the salad to Darleen.

Mama said, "We saw that car that blew up on TV. The one at the high school. Do you know about that?"

"Yes."

Darleen filled her plate with salad. "That whole deal weirded me out. Why would someone do that? This isn't New York freakin' City."

"Motive is a big question right now. A bunch of federal agencies are working to figure it out."

"It's crazy." Darleen put her fork down. "I was almost there. Stoop Man and I were going to go to the game, but then his car wouldn't start."

"I'm glad you weren't there. I've never seen so much confusion. The parking lot was a mess. Some people spent hours there and had to have their cars towed. It was lucky that only one person was hurt." She meant killed, but *hurt* was good enough.

Mama said, "Were you there?"

"I wanted to watch the game—you know some of those old guys went to school with me." Bernie took another bite of the pizza, thinking of how to avoid this conversation. "The FBI handles major crimes like that and they offer all kinds of special training for those officers. They know what to do if something blows up."

"I'd think one of those FBI schools is near Washington, right?" Darleen laughed. "I'd like to go to Washington, see the White House and stuff like that. I'd like to go anywhere. Road trip!"

Bernie enjoyed the chewy, salty pepperoni. Chee always wanted different toppings, things like eggplant, pineapple, and Canadian bacon. Not her. She liked predictability. Why mess with perfection by adding mushrooms?

Darleen passed her the salad again. "Here, have some. It's good for you."

Bernie put the bowl on the table. The little balls the color of coffee with milk did not belong in a salad. "What are those round-ish things?"

Darleen stabbed two with her fork and held them up for inspection. "They're garbanzos, a kind of bean that's really nutritious."

"How do they taste?"

"Great. They're kind of nutty, sweet, and starchy. Right, Mama?"

Bernie noticed that their mother had separated the garbanzos from the greens and was eating them, one by one.

"I like them." Mama put two in her mouth. "Try it."

"I want to enjoy the pizza while it's hot."

But Mama passed the bowl to her anyway with a look that said, *Take some.* So Bernie spooned some greens and chopped tomato and cucumber onto her plate. Even though she tried to avoid the garbanzos, she accidentally scooped up a few. She poured on the Thousand Island.

"What's the Cheeseburger doing tonight?" Darleen asked. She used the nickname she and Mama had invented for Jim Chee.

"He's in Tuba City at that big meeting on the Grand Canyon development."

"I heard about that. Why did he have to go?"

"A bunch of VIPs will be there, and after the car blew up, Chee got asked to help as a sort of bodyguard for the mediator. At least he doesn't have to drive back and forth. The department pays for a room at a motel there."

"How long will he be gone?"

"I don't know. Neither does he."

"As long as it takes," Mama said. "He can bring the loom over later. We've been using the one at the senior center and that works. Over there, we get coffee and cookies, too. I'm glad you sent that lady to me. She's real nice."

Bernie pictured Mama and Mrs. Bigman sitting at the table, drinking coffee from white Styrofoam cups. Laughing together. The image made her heart ache.

After dinner, Bernie cleared the table, secretly disposing of the garbanzos she'd hidden under a lettuce leaf and hoping Darleen's experiment was a one-time adventure. She washed the plates and silverware and then joined Mama and Darleen in the living room. She noticed some books on the coffee table. Darleen and Mama must have been to the library, she thought. Then she realized they were textbooks, probably part of Darleen's work for her GED, her long-delayed high school diploma.

After they had watched TV for a while, Mama patted her hand. "Come with me to the bedroom." She used Bernie's arm to rise from the couch. Her grip was strong. She eased herself to her walker, straightened up, and then moved smoothly down the hall. Her balance seemed better, too. She and Darleen had learned that there was no point in asking Mama how she felt; she always said she was fine. Mama never complained about her health, saving that energy to give advice to her daughters.

Mama sat on the bed.

"Can I help you, Mama? What can I do?"

"You can tell me what is bothering you."

"What do you mean?"

"You know what I mean."

"I worked all day. I'm tired."

"What else?"

"Nothing."

"No, something. Something troubles you."

The house was still except for the murmur of muffled conversation from the television in the living room. Bernie was comfortable with silence, but Mama, the person from whom she had learned to respect silence, was better.

"Well, I interviewed people to find out if anyone knew what happened or why." She might as well get the interrogation over with. "Some of the children were upset. That's always hard to take."

Mama patted the space beside her. "Sit down. Something else troubles you."

The powerful quiet that filled the room made her think of the mountain lion, *náshdóítsoh*, the one the Holy People sent to guard Turquoise Girl on Mount Taylor. She stroked the fetish rock in her pocket. This was at least the fourth time Mama had asked. Bernie had to be honest in her answer.

"I did see something that upset me, a person who was badly hurt, burned. Then I learned that he died. I don't want to talk about it."

"Daughter, stay here tonight."

"I can't, Mama." Her body felt heavy, her brain unfocused, weary. "I have to get up early tomorrow for work." She wanted to call Chee, go to bed.

Mama nodded. "Then drive safely. Rest. Say your prayers."

Bernie pushed down the surprise of tears building in the back of her eyes. Mama's concern made a Navajo policewoman feel like a treasured child.

She went to the living room to gather her backpack and say good-bye to her sister. Darleen had put the TV on mute and was fiddling with her cell phone.

"So, what did Mama lecture you about?"

Bernie hesitated. "Oh, she figured something was bothering me and wanted me to tell her."

"Did you?"

"You know how she is. She could pry a secret out of a stone." Bernie shrugged, waited a few beats. "How are your classes?"

"Fine. Mama wanted to know about the bombing, right?"

"Yes."

"Was the Cheeseburger there, too?"

"No. Only me at first. Then backup arrived."

Darleen twisted a lock of her straight black hair around her index finger. "It's a good thing you were there. I'm proud of you."

"I was off duty actually. It's no big deal."

"Yeah, it is. So who won?"

"I think the old guys squeaked it out, but I missed the end."

Bernie motioned toward the books on the coffee table. "How are your classes?"

"You already asked me that. They're fine. Sometimes interesting." Darleen slipped off her shoes and pulled her feet beneath her. "There's a guy in my math class. He makes videos. He's cute. I call him CS because he's a veggie, you know, vegetarian."

"Sea Yes?"

"The letters *CS*, short for Carrot Soup. I'm enjoying classes this time, more than high school. I guess I'm not as dumb as I thought I was."

"You're not dumb. You just got distracted."

Bernie walked into the kitchen and filled her water bottle. She waited for her sister to say more about CS. Darleen picked up her books and headed into the kitchen, too. When they were children, Mama had told them to do their homework at that table after they had cleared the dishes. The lesson stuck.

Darleen got a pen and opened a notebook. "Sister, did you ever think about not eating meat?"

"You mean give up hamburgers? No pepperoni pizza?" Bernie shook her head. "That guy I married cooks the best steaks on the grill. No way I could live on lettuce and those ugly ball things."

"Garbanzos. CS told me not eating meat is healthier and helps Mother Earth. You know about all those cows chowing down on the rain forest?"

"That's not exactly what's happening, but I've read about it. What's Carrot Soup's real name?"

"Why?"

"Because I'm a cop and you're my baby sister." Bernie put the water bottle in her backpack. "I want to make sure he's not a serial killer."

"CS is OK. A little offbeat, but hey, so am I. The only cereal he kills goes in the bowl with soy milk."

"Soy milk sounds questionable. What's his real name?"

"Don't stress out about him. He's a good guy, and he's even got Code Talker in his heritage. Don't be so suspicious."

"I'm just curious."

"You can ask him when you meet him."

On the dark, empty road, Bernie thought about Darleen. She still worried about her little sister, but she worried less these days. She'd been around enough drinkers to know that sobriety didn't always last. Maybe Darleen's would. Ever since she'd been arrested, her little sister had seemed happier, less angry.

Bernie focused on the swath of pavement her headlights illuminated, and thought about what awaited her at home. Or what didn't await her. Chee. She'd never believed in love at first sight, but she'd been attracted to him from her first day as a neophyte with him as her boss. She hid her feelings so well that he treated her as one of the boys until she left for an assignment with the Border Patrol. Then, finally, he realized she was a woman in addition to a police officer. He was the man she'd always hoped to find.

And now, she headed home to an empty house. She rolled down the window to let in a blast of winter air scented with sage and dust and to allow her melancholy to escape. Instead her thoughts circled around the man who had died. Long before Bernie became a cop, Mama made her and Darleen promise they would never make her ride in an ambulance because of the *chindis*, the spirits of the dead.

After the cold stiffened her neck and shoulders, she rolled up the window and switched the heater to high. She replayed the conversation with Lona. Why would an ex-wife call to check on her ex-husband after a bomb exploded? Because they were connected through money—alimony, child support, a shared business interest? Because she still had feelings for him? Because she'd tried to kill him?

Bernie smiled. She was getting ahead of herself. She hadn't spoken to Lona for years, and now she was accusing her of murder. But she'd mention the call when she talked to Leaphorn and to Cordova.

The Lona she remembered was smart, smart and quiet. When she dropped out, people were surprised. And then, when she came back to school, everyone knew about the baby. Lona returned with a new attitude, more serious and more grown-up. She never mentioned the baby or Aza Palmer at school, and they avoided each other on campus. Then, shortly after Palmer graduated, he married Lona and they moved away.

Bernie drove up to her empty house and turned on the lights. She put on the kettle and, while she waited for the water to heat, jotted down a to-do list, which included a follow-up call to Lona. She was working the early shift the next day, which gave her time to check on Darleen's new friend.

The buzz of her phone startled her. Bernie glanced at the screen: the captain trying to reach her.

She picked up the incoming call.

Largo got right to the point. "Cordova says they ID'd the body. A guy from right here in Shiprock, Richard Horseman, with no record of prior involvement in bombings. You know him?"

"No, sir. Richard could be Rick, the man Gloria Chino knew." She filled him in.

"Horseman was in the system because he got arrested for car theft, but the charges were dropped. Cordova wants you to go with him tomorrow morning to interview Horesman's grandmother. You can put the AA stuff on hold."

"Yes, sir. I felt funny about that anyway."

"How did you do with your contact list?"

"I gave some to the rookie. The rest is done. Nothing much new. Someone might have seen the dead man sitting in the car that blew. Someone saw another suspicious character out there. It's in my report."

Largo said, "After you do the interview with Cordova, take the next couple days off. The FBI is on this like ants on jelly and the rookie will come in." She could practically hear him thinking over the phone. "How did he do out there?"

"He made some mistakes, but he didn't panic. There was a lot going on. He tried to show some initiative."

"Anything else you'd like to say?"

"No, sir." Wilson Sam's attitude toward her was something that she'd deal with privately.

"One more thing. Leaphorn wants you to give him a call."

"Did he say about what?" She remembered that she needed to stop by and see the Lieutenant. Her days off would be perfect for that.

She heard Largo's rumbling chuckle. "No, but if I had to guess, I'd say he needs to give you some advice or wants a favor. Or maybe some of each."

6

Jim Chee walked from the motel to the Tuba City police station. He could have driven, but it was only a few miles and the early morning was crisp, cool, and bright with sun. The newscaster noted that a major winter storm could be on the way, but that was always the case in November. No use worrying. Enjoy today's beauty.

The receptionist at the police station looked up when he entered.

"The meeting is down the hall."

Chee knew the way. A pair of officers—a tall, thin sergeant and a shorter, younger, more muscled fellow with the posture of a Marine—stood in the hall.

"Hey, Chee, I heard you'd be up here," the tall man said.

Chee nodded. "*Yá'át'ééh.*" He remembered Sergeant Art Redbone as a quick wit and a good cop. Redbone introduced the other man, Officer Billy Silversmith.

"I just found out from the sergeant that you worked with Lieutenant Leaphorn." Silversmith looked serious. "He's been consulting on a case up here. He was telling us about when he worked as a PI, helping a woman from Santa Fe find her granddaughter, and how your case dovetailed."

"What else did Leaphorn say?"

Silversmith hesitated. Redbone grinned and picked up the conversation. "Nothin' much, except that some dude named Chee nearly got him killed."

Chee remembered the case. "That was quite a deal. Both of us nearly got killed by a crazed *bilagaana* researcher doing a study on bubonic plague. The guy had a special suit to keep the germs out, and he scared an old lady out there who thought he was a skinwalker."

"I remember that," Redbone said.

"If you have a chance, ask the Lieutenant to tell you about the case of the missing Navajo boy he worked at Ramah and Zuni Pueblo. That was before my time, but it was a classic piece of good investigating. Is he driving out here for the meetings?"

"No," Silversmith said. "We do it all by computer, instant messages, texts, stuff like that."

Redbone said, "Were you involved in the commotion at the high school?"

"No. My wife told me it was a real mess."

"If that bomb had gone off with the lot full of people, it would have been terrible. Lucky that someone would go to all that trouble and screw up the timing."

"Or set it off himself," Silversmith said. "Bam. Maybe that guy who died was our mad bomber."

Redbone said, "So your wife's a cop, too. How do you like that?"

"It's great. She's great. She's really good at what she does."

Silversmith said, "I think it would be too much shop talk and not enough pillow talk. I'd have some trouble with that."

Redbone chuckled. "You're having trouble finding a wife in the first place. You need to figure out how to meet women someplace other than at crime scenes."

Silversmith made a sound between a laugh and a snort.

Chee said, "Anything special at the meeting today?"

"I bet we're going to get guidelines for handling hotheads," Redbone said. "The captain expects a bunch of greenies to roll in from California. Some group famous for getting arrested and claiming police brutality. He's giving us body cameras."

Silversmith said, "The mediation hasn't even started and we're already working."

Chee said, "If that group wants publicity, they're coming to the wrong town. Tuba City doesn't have a television station, a radio station, not even a newspaper unless the *Navajo Times* comes around. If we're lucky, they'll get bored and move on."

"The Internet is everywhere," Silversmith said. "Take a video with your phone, and bam, it's viral even from downtown Tuba City. Of course, this place is kind of famous for combining things that normally don't go together."

"What do you mean?"

"Well, to start with, our Navajo Justice Center, where the meeting is, includes both a jail and space for those Peacemaking meetings so the bad boys get a scolding from their grandmother."

Silversmith had greatly oversimplified Peacemaking, a concept society could use more of. Chee knew the program grew from the belief that families and friends were responsible for one another. If a person abused his wife, stole from a neighbor, or otherwise failed to follow the Navajo Way, his inner circle called him on it, challenged him to do better, and gave him a way to make amends and get back into harmony that did not involve jail time.

"And think about this." Silversmith paused for effect. "Tuba City, one of the biggest towns on the Navajo Nation, is named for a Hopi who became a Mormon."

Chee laughed. "You know we call it Tó Naneesdizí. Tuba City is only the English name. But I see your point. The mediator, the different delegates, and the protesters should be right at home here."

Someone had propped open the door to the meeting room with a wooden wedge. The room looked as drab as Chee remembered. Beige walls, industrial gray carpet, florescent lights, no windows.

The kind of space a person wanted to spend as little time in as possible. The brown metal folding chairs, some slightly bent at the seat or wobbling unevenly on three of the four legs, added to the sense that information would be disseminated quickly so life could resume.

Chee, Redbone, and Silversmith took the last seats in the prized back row. Officers from other jurisdictions: uniforms from the Havasupai people, a woman with Hualapai tribal law enforcement, Coconino County sheriff's deputies, and even a couple of men from the Arizona Highway Patrol began to fill the room. Right before the captain stepped up to the podium, Chee saw Dashee enter by a side door and lean against the wall, followed by a blond man in the dark suit and perfect haircut that marked him as FBI.

Chee had met the officer in charge of the Tuba substation, Captain Bernard Ward, but didn't know him well. Ward passed around a brief agenda.

"Ladies and gentlemen, I'm going to show you a video sent by the FBI about Save Wild America, one of the groups coming to protest. Agent Jerry Cordova, whom some of you know, had planned to attend, but he's working on a fatal car bombing at Shiprock, which may be connected to the meeting here and the protest. We are joined today by two other FBI specialists from the domestic terrorism unit and representatives from the Arizona Department of Public Safety counterterrorism."

Ward directed a round of introductions, then motioned to an officer to dim the lights. The video unfolded on the screen in the front of the room. It showed a protest in Yosemite, demonstrators going limp, taunting police, spitting, and several officers losing their cool. Except for the scenery in the background, it wasn't pretty. It lasted about ten minutes and gave Chee an idea of what to expect.

"Cordova asked me to read you this." The captain put on his glasses and looked at a sheet of paper on the podium. "'The group that you will be dealing with has been in court many times on charges of ecoterrorism, destroying government property, arson, and other crimes. They've also brought numerous suits against law enforcement, federal, state, and local authorities. They don't play nice. In response, we need to be careful and professional.'"

Captain Ward put the paper down, took off his glasses, and looked at the officers.

"From our perspective, the bad thing about this meeting is the timing. From the media perspective, it couldn't be better because, except for basketball and Thanksgiving, nothing much happens in November. People who like to protest have time on their hands. Reporters in Phoenix and Flagstaff looking for news can trundle up here to make life interesting, even if most of them don't know what the hell is going on."

Chee thought about that. The idea that the Navajo Nation might allow development—some sort of tourist resort—on its land near the Grand Canyon had been brewing for years, through many elections for Navajo Nation president. If the project, or some facsimile, eventually managed to win approval of the Tribal Council and got the president's OK, the decision would certainly end up in court. Before the tribal government could reject the idea in total or express some openness to modified alternatives, everything would be considered, debated, amended, and reconsidered. It had taken eons for the Grand Canyon to form, and in Chee's opinion, any development or permanent end to the possibility of development that might be in the wind operated on that same timetable. But outsiders viewed the situation as urgent.

The captain said, "Maybe there won't be any trouble, but plan for the worst, hope for the best, that's my philosophy."

Then a secretary passed around white cards with instructions on how to handle protesters and keep violence from accelerating. The title read "Planning and Managing Security for Major Special Events: Guidelines for Law Enforcement." Chee skimmed the points.

- Do not take comments made by protesters personally.
- Be patient with your fellow officers and commanders.
- While law enforcement must meet its duty to protect people and property during mass demonstrations and protests, it can never do so at the expense of upholding the Constitution and First Amendment–protected rights.
- Use of equipment or weaponry should be restricted to limited situations that clearly justify their use.

He skimmed the rest of the list. Good ideas, but nothing he hadn't heard before.

Captain Ward told them that the delegates would enter and leave the meeting from the rear of the building and that the audience would use the front door and be screened with the Justice Center's metal detector and directed to the meeting room. Chee would do what Largo had already told him—keep a close eye on the mediator and provide security for the Navajo Nation president, who would officially welcome the delegates later in the week as his schedule allowed. In other words, he was a glorified bodyguard.

Chee and Dashee ordered an early lunch off the menu at the Tuuvi Cafe, a restaurant run by the Hopi tribe. The café occupied part of a gas station/convenience store complex that sold tourist hats and T-shirts, snack food, drinks, and DVDs. The business included video rentals and an attractive Hopi arts and crafts outlet in another part of the building. Dashee knew everyone who worked there.

Chee had met Dashee on one of his first assignments, a situation that started with sabotage to a windmill and ended up involving drug smuggling and murder. He couldn't have done his job without Dashee's help.

Chee ordered the Tuuvi taco, a plate-sized piece of fry bread topped with juicy pinto beans, shredded cheese, chopped lettuce and tomato, and a whole roasted green chile. Dashee ate the Hopi stew, a bowl of soft hominy spiced with chopped green chile and a bit of meat. The food arrived quickly, served by a plumpish girl with a lopsided smile.

The taco tasted as good as it looked. Chee took several bites, then put his fork down. "So how has life been treating you?"

"Can't complain 'cause nobody listens." Dashee patted his lips with the napkin. "How about with you? I heard you almost got to be a movie star."

"Not quite. I got sent to Monument Valley and wrapped up with a film company making a movie about zombies, and it turned out to be an interesting case, but nobody offered me a role. So what's new in Moenkopi?"

Dashee looked puzzled. "New? Nothing, same as always. That's how we like it."

Chee said, "I heard the Mormons want to set up some kind of monument there in honor of Lot Smith."

"Who?"

"You know, the soldier, the big man in the Mormon settlement, the Circle S Ranch guy with a houseful of wives and kids? The one Atsidí killed for shooting his sheep way back when."

"Oh, that. Nothing decided there yet. But before we get into religion and politics, well, I need a favor." Dashee cleared his throat. "I've got to tell a family to move some livestock."

"A Diné family." Chee said it as a statement, not a question. Many Navajos had been displaced when a court ruled that they had to leave land they had long considered theirs. Some observers believed the problem wasn't the Navajo or the Hopi, but coal companies that wanted to mine Black Mesa, where the families lived. The US Congress had passed the relocation act, and, agree with it or not, it was an officer's job to uphold the law.

Dashee rested his fingertips on the edge of the table. "They're the Bitsois. Mainly the mother lives there, although the children and grandkids show up to help. She only speaks Navajo, or at least that's what she claims when I try to talk to her. That's why I need some help."

Chee cut another bite of fry bread moist with beans and chile. Not the healthiest thing on the planet, but why argue with delicious and warm? The room was warm, too. He slipped off his jacket and hung it on the back of his chair, all the while pondering his answer.

"Don't you guys have a cop who speaks Navajo?"

"He's on leave." Dashee took a spoonful of his stew. "I don't wanna be the bad guy, but I have to do my job. You know how that goes."

Chee did know. Sometimes, it really was a matter of someone not speaking English. Sometimes, it was a case where the person knew some, but not enough to serve in complicated conversations. Sometimes, the language issue bought time to figure out a complicated situation.

"We Navajos don't have any jurisdiction there. That's your turf."

"If you could come with me, well, I think it would make it easier on the family. I don't want to arrest anybody, and having you along to explain things would help."

"Two cops show up at the place instead of one? Yeah, that always helps people relax."

Dashee chuckled. "I figured you'd be out of uniform, sort of a translator, explaining the situation to Mrs. Bitsoi and whoever else of the family shows up."

Chee let the conversation sit as he finished his meal. "When do you need to do this?"

"Soon. Maybe in a day or two. After the protesters get tired." Dashee grabbed the bill. "I'll get this."

"Trying to bribe me?"

"Nah, if I wanted to sweeten the deal, I'd ask you to the Niman dances." In June, Hopi people living away from their ancestral villages returned to help with the event and visit relatives and friends during the sixteen-day Niman ceremony.

Chee smiled. Dashee invited him every year, but either he or

Bernie always, always had had to work. It had become a joke between them. Whatever the day, something happened in Navajoland that kept them from the Hopi mesas. The last time, Dashee said he'd surprise Chee with the date and hope for the best.

The dances, held at the summer solstice, celebrated the departure of the Katsinas, Holy People of the Hopi, for their summer home on the San Francisco Peaks. Chee knew the mountain as Dook'o'oslíid, one of the four sacred mountains that defined the Navajo world and home of Talking God.

Dashee pushed back his chair. "Think about it, will you? I've got to go to the Hotel Hopi to stay warm with our delegation until the session starts. You working out there in the cold?"

Chee nodded. "Only until the mediator arrives, then I'm inside as a bodyguard."

"I thought you drove him to town last night."

"I mean from the hotel. His clan sister is bringing his dress-up clothes and she'll give him a lift to the Justice Center."

"I bet he was nervous as a one-eyed cat after the explosion."

"You'd lose. He was calm and collected. Bernie said he was upset about his car, but not especially worried about some jerk trying to kill him."

He watched Dashee make his way across the street, Highway 264, the route to the Hopi Mesas. The other road at this intersection, US Highway 160, marked an informal boundary between the Hopi reservation and the Navajo Nation that surrounded it. Highway 160 stretched up to Colorado and east to Missouri, but in Chee's mind, this was its most interesting corner.

He called Palmer to check on him and learned everything was fine. Katie had arrived without incident and would drive him to the session in about half an hour. Chee noticed a missed call from Bernie and listened to her voice mail. She had a couple days off and might come to Tuba City. He called her, but her phone went right to message. "Great," he told the electronic voice. "Can't wait to see you."

He walked back to the Justice Center. A few people had gathered outside the building, some bundled up in hats and coats and others less warmly dressed. He noticed a handful of Indians in the mix but didn't see anyone he recognized. They all had assembled by the main entrance and piled their professional-looking signs on the sidewalk near the front doors: "Save the Confluence," "Love the Grand Canyon," "Ban the Resort," and "Developers = Exploiters." He wondered if they were from Save Wild America. He assessed the group, looking for a leader. No one stood out.

"You have to step back, folks, and put your signs somewhere else. You can't block the entrance."

A potbellied man came up to Chee. "We have a right to protest."

"You do. But you have to move back so people can safely get into the room for the meeting. We don't want anyone tripping over one of these sticks. That doesn't do any good."

"Did you make up that rule about the sidewalk?" The man wore a short-sleeved shirt. His nose and the tops of his ears had reddened from the icy wind.

Chee memorized the face. "It's a safety issue and common courtesy." Looking at the protester made Chee happy he had his jacket. "Where are you from, sir?"

The man looked surprised at the question. "That's none of your business."

Wherever the man lived, Chee thought, it fell short on good manners. "Well, welcome to Navajoland."

"Why do you care where I live?"

"I figured you could be from someplace where it doesn't get very cold. You might want to put on a hat to protect your ears from frostbite." It was too warm for frostbite, really, but Chee wanted to make a point.

The man said nothing.

"Those signs need to be off the sidewalk so someone won't fall over them." Chee was tempted to add, *And lighten up while you're at it.*

The man nudged the pile of signs with his foot, moving them barely to the edge of the sidewalk.

About ten minutes later, an Arizona Highway Patrol car pulled up with a couple of men Chee had seen at the meeting. As discussed, they would take charge of the building's front entrance and help the Navajo cops with parking lot security.

The taller man, Officer Albert Anderson, turned his back to the civilians and spoke in a low voice. "Are these the activists the captain was talking about?"

"I don't know." Chee nodded in the direction of the man standing by the signs. "That guy in the short sleeves has an attitude problem."

Anderson exhaled. "So, we're off to a good start."

His partner, Dan Rivera, said, "At least it's not snowing."

"Not snowing yet, anyway." Anderson zipped up his coat and turned to Chee. "Any bigwigs here yet?"

"I don't know. They're parking by the back doors and assembling in a room there. Palmer wants them to come into the hall all together."

"A grand entrance," Anderson said. "I can hardly wait. How come this meeting is here instead of Phoenix, where it's warmer?"

"The Navajo Nation thought you guys needed a road trip. The site for the potential resort is only half an hour from here, and Palmer plans a field trip at some point."

More vehicles began to trickle in. Mostly Navajo and Hopi people now, he noticed, along with a few non-Natives and Indians whom he couldn't pigeonhole. A handful of new faces joined the protesters. Most of the folks headed inside, and Chee considered that himself. He could stand in the atrium and watch for Palmer without freezing his toes off. But he'd be inside for hours once the meeting started. Best stay here and soak in some sunlight. He'd give Palmer another few minutes and then call him again.

He heard the rumble of a vintage Volkswagen engine. The pumpkin-colored camper van he had visited in the hotel parking lot last night found a spot along the side fence. After some minutes, a man emerged wearing sunglasses, a parka, and a brown knit hat pulled over his ears. He walked to the pile of signs and stopped, talking to the men there. He was carrying something. Something white. Not a gun, Chee thought. At least not a gun like any he'd ever seen.

Then a black limousine pulled into the lot and slowly rolled up to where Chee stood. The driver lowered the window and stopped. "Where is the entrance for the delegates?"

Chee walked toward him. "Head on around the back and use the door there. You'll see another Navajo cop like me. You can park there, too."

"I'm just dropping off my clients, but thanks." The man wore a cap like chauffeurs in the movies. Chee noticed two men in suits in the backseat. One of them leaned toward him.

"Does the session still begin at two?"

"That's what the schedule says." Chee knew from experience that Indian Country meetings started when they started, when the time was right regardless of what the agenda suggested. He wondered how Palmer would handle the inevitable discussion over that.

Then he heard an amplified voice. "This is Bebe Durango. Save Wild America to the front. Hustle up now."

Chee turned toward the noise. The device the man in the brown hat had with him was a bullhorn. People sitting in the cars climbed out and headed toward the front of the building and the limo.

The passenger in the limo who had asked Chee the question said, "Let's get out of here," and rolled up the window. Before the big car could move, Durango appeared, blocking the way. He put the bullhorn to his face and started to yell.

"Shame, shame, shame on Canyonmark." He bellowed it out. The chant became a mantra. Other protesters joined, surrounding the car, waving their signs. The driver inched along, the crowd swarming around the car.

Just as Chee began to think he should do something, the Arizona

Highway Patrol officers moved in. Anderson and Rivera stayed calm and professional, and most of the protesters moved back so the car could pass. Chee radioed Redbone, whom the captain had posted at the delegate entrance. "A black limo, a man with a bullhorn, and a bunch of protesters headed your way. Everyone seems calm enough now."

"I hear them. A few protesters are back here, waiting for the car."

Bebe continued yelling at the limo. He and the sign people followed the car out of Chee's sight.

As Chee headed to the front doors of the Justice Center, a young Navajo man, short and slim in jeans and boots, walked up to him.

"Yá'át'ééh, Officer."

"Yá'át'ééh."

"Do you know if Mr. Palmer is here?"

"I haven't seen him yet."

"But he's supposed to be here, right?"

"You bet. He's the guy running the sessions. What do you want with him?"

"Oh, we know each other from way back. I'm hoping to talk to him for a minute or two before the meeting begins. Thanks." The young man pulled the hood of his sweatshirt up over his ears and walked past him through the big doors and into the building.

Chee stood in the sun, enjoying its faint warmth on his face. He liked the contrast to the frigid November air. The man with the bullhorn must have put it down, because he didn't hear the shouting anymore.

People continued to arrive. Some greeted him with a nod and looked slightly familiar from his time working at the local substation. Most of the people he remembered vividly wouldn't be at the meeting, he thought. They were in prison.

A pickup truck pulled into the lot and drove close to the front doors. He noticed an attractive Navajo woman sitting tall behind the steering wheel, her hair pulled into a ponytail. The passenger door opened, and Aza Palmer climbed out wearing new jeans, black boots with a shine to them, a Pendleton jacket, and a cream-colored cowboy hat. He looked more like a rancher than a lawyer, Chee thought, and the look was probably the perfect persona for the people gathered inside. He carried the black leather briefcase he'd had in Chee's unit over his shoulder with a strap.

"Hey there. Good afternoon," Chee said.

"*Yá'át'ééh.*" Palmer waved at the truck as it left. "My clan sister, Katie. I'll introduce you next time." He looked around the parking lot. "Not many protesters."

Chee said, "Most of them are around back, chasing a limo."

"A limo?"

"One of them recognized the developers inside."

"You'd think those people would try to blend in with the common folks a little better to limit the antagonism, wouldn't you?" Palmer turned toward the building. "Let's go in. I want to check the setup of the space and see if I can tell what the climate of the room is."

"All the heating is centrally controlled. So are the lights. State-of-the-art."

"I meant, is the audience curious, angry, restless, worried? Who wants to make a scene? I know some of these people have come a long way, given up their weekend because what happens with the resort, with the Grand Canyon, matters to them. The delegates and I get to practice listening. That's a great skill to hone for the sessions to come."

"How many people will you let talk?"

"All of them who'd like to, but I might have to impose a time limit." Palmer moved the briefcase higher on his shoulder and started for the building.

Chee said, "There was a young man here who wanted to see you."

"That's interesting. He didn't have a suicide vest, did he?" Palmer grinned.

"Not that I noticed. He went inside."

They walked together through the big doors and down a tiled hallway, the heels of Palmer's boots clicking against the hard floor. He was slightly taller than Chee, but they fell into an easy cadence. Palmer moved like a man with a mission, as though he looked forward to serious work ahead.

Chee ushered him to the head of the line of people waiting to go through the metal detector. "Excuse us, folks."

Palmer gave his bag to the guard, took off his smooth black leather belt with the sand-cast silver buckle. He put his hand to his bolo tie, a piece of turquoise framed with a thin band of silver at his throat. "Do I need to take off my bolo and the jacket?"

The guard looked at the string tie with its silver tips. "It will be fine. Any keys or metal in the jacket pockets?"

"No."

"No gun or knife?"

"Nothing." Palmer walked through the metal detector without setting off the alarm. The guard inspected the bag and belt, handed them back, and turned to the next person in line to repeat the process.

The building was new, part of the big judicial complex the tribe had constructed over the last few years. Chee had been inside before for hearings, and he liked it, a place to be proud of.

Mediation, as Palmer had explained it last night, was similar in some ways to the Navajo's long-established Peacemaking process. But in Peacemaking there was no neutrality. A family matriarch might be the facilitator, and she had an interest in the outcome: getting her clan members to shape up. Unlike a mediator, she would offer suggestions for solving the problem.

Chee led him to the meeting room, a large, bright space filled with conversation. The door to the hallway had been propped open to make it easier for people to come in. The audience section, already half full, contained an interesting assembly, Chee thought. Men in cowboy hats and shirts with pearl buttons, women in tailored suits, Hopi people looking serious in their best outfits. A scattering of Navajo men in their best jeans and matriarchs wearing velvet blouses and silver necklaces, perhaps including a classic squash blossom and armfuls of turquoise bracelets. Weathered *bilagaana* men in hiking boots, probably Forest Service, National Park, or Bureau of Land Management retirees, he thought. He noticed Indians who didn't look Diné or Hopi, maybe Havasupai or Hualapai, two other tribes with a direct and compelling interest in Grand Canyon issues. Behind the audience seats and off to one side, a uniformed Coconino County deputy had positioned himself against the wall near a microphone installed for audience comments.

After surveying the room, Palmer walked onto the stage, put his bag on the table, and studied the delegate seating arrangement, a set of narrow tables covered with white cloths and positioned in a semicircle, facing the audience. A podium with a microphone stood to the left.

He turned to Chee. "This will do for now."

"I can get someone on the staff to rearrange it if you want a different setup."

"It will work for introductions and audience statements. When we reach the time for the delegates to talk and listen to each other privately, we'll create a circle."

Chee looked at the folding chairs onstage. "Who will be here? I wasn't expecting such a large group."

Palmer counted them off on his fingers. "We've got Native delegates from five tribes. The Forest Service, the Park Service, the developer, the Grand Canyon Protectors, representatives from the EPA, and the Arizona Department of Environmental Quality." He listed a few more groups Chee had never heard of, then opened his black leather bag and extracted a folder. Chee watched him take from it a couple of sheets of white letter-size paper, which he placed on the podium. Then Palmer pulled out some tent-shaped signs made of heavy white paper with each person's name and agency.

"Want me to put those on the table?"

"No, I'll do it. I'm considering where people will be sitting today. Relax, Sergeant. I'll let you know if I think someone else wants to blow me up again." Palmer walked to the podium. "I'm going to stand here, read over my notes before we start, and collect my thoughts for a few minutes."

"Can I get you anything?"

"How about a bottle of water?"

"Sure."

Chee had never been a bodyguard before. The closest he'd come was escorting prisoners to jail or to court. He'd never liked that much either, but it was more exciting than watching people come into an auditorium while Palmer silently read notes. He looked into the audience for the young man who'd wanted a word with Palmer but didn't see him.

He had no idea where to get a bottle of water, but he figured he could find someone who could help with that. In the hallway he saw a county sheriff's deputy talking to a group of people in Save Wild America T-shirts. Everyone looked peaceful; he didn't interrupt.

He walked toward the entrance, checking the alcoves for vending machines along the way without success. He asked the security guard about it.

"There's a machine down the hall to the right," he said. "But I don't think there's water in it. Just sodas."

The guard was wrong. Ever since the Navajo Nation had increased the tax on soda and junk food, vendors made an effort to stock machines with healthier choices. Bottled water took its place alongside the colas, diet drinks, and root beer.

Chee found change in his pocket, just enough for a bottle. As he was heading back to the meeting room, he felt his phone vibrate.

Bernie said, "Hi. How's Tuba City?"

"Quiet and cold," he said. "What's new in Shiprock? Anything on the bombing?"

"Yes, actually. The man in the parking lot died and the feds already ID'd the body."

"Anyone we knew?"

"No." She saw no reason to say the name of the dead man and Chee didn't ask. "A witness I talked to saw another person hanging out, looking suspicious. That guy—or maybe it was a female, too dark to tell—didn't match the description of the victim but might have something to do with that bomb."

"Ah, a homegrown conspiracy," Chee said. "I bet Cordova loves that."

"Shiprock is buzzing with agents and investigators. Acronyms I never heard before."

"Same here in Tó Naneesdizí."

"Have you talked to Dashee?"

"He bought me lunch. He wants me to help him with a job involving some trespassing livestock." Chee summarized the details. "I told him I'd think about it. I'm not sure how involved this bodyguard stuff will be."

"Guess what? I got a call from Palmer's ex-wife."

"Did she call to confess?"

"You're funny. She said she was worried about him. I went to high school with her."

"Were you friends?"

"Not exactly. Lona liked boys, and I liked basketball."

"I'm glad you like this boy now. Did she say anything relevant to the bombing?"

He could tell by the silence that the question caught her off guard.

"I'm not sure," she said finally. "I figure the bomber targeted Palmer, but the feds won't say for sure yet that it even was a bomb. Maybe the bomber wanted to damage the school or make a statement against basketball and picked the BMW because of where it was parked."

Chee laughed. "Clever, Manuelito. Evading the question by

challenging my assumption. I guess that means you forgot to ask her. Did she have murderous tendencies in high school?"

"I don't think so. But she and Palmer fought a lot, breaking up, getting back together."

"Sounds like high school. Speaking of Palmer, I need to return to my babysitting job. Catch you later."

In the minutes he'd been looking for water, people who had arrived too late to get a seat had gathered in the hall outside the meeting room. Officer Rivera stood straight, shoulders back and legs apart, talking and stressing his points with his hands, unsmiling. Chee knew the pose, designed to forestall arguments. Closer, he caught the last of what Rivera was saying: ". . . can't sit on the floor or the steps. All the seats are filled, and the fire marshal set the limit for occupancy. When and if someone leaves, someone can come in."

The man in a red T-shirt with a Save Wild America logo scowled. "That's not fair. This is supposed to be the session for public comment. You guys should have found a bigger room, but hey, these sessions are always rigged anyway."

The officer said nothing.

Red Shirt said, "We'll stay here in the hall until that guy Palmer agrees to let us talk."

The officer said, "You can stay as long as the noise out here doesn't disrupt the meeting and as long as your people don't block the flow of the traffic."

Red Shirt turned to Chee. "I saw you talkin' to him. Tell him he needs to come out here and listen to what the real people have to say about the development."

As he entered the room this time, Chee noticed a second person onstage. He stood facing Palmer, who sat at the long table for the delegates. He was of average height, made taller by his hiking boots. Chee couldn't see his face, but noticed that he wore a vest over his fleece jacket and a cap. He moved closer to Palmer, pointing at him with an extended index finger, a rude gesture in the

Navajo world. Chee noticed the startled expression on Palmer's face and sensed the man's anger even before he caught the end of what he was shouting: ". . . good-for-nothing jerks." Then he saw the man reach toward his vest pocket.

Chee leapt over the top steps onto the stage. "Police. Put your hands where I can see them. Step away from Mr. Palmer." The man glared at him, then stepped to the side with a string of obscenities.

Palmer rose and took a step toward the man in the cap. "It's OK. Easy on him. Easy there."

Chee wasn't sure if Palmer meant the "easy" for him or Cap Man.

Cap Man spit out the words, "It's a sad state of events when a person can't express an opinion without police harassment."

Palmer turned to Chee. "I know Mr. Blankenship. He's one of the delegates. I met him on an earlier mediation for another resort. You can back off, Sergeant. It was just a discussion."

Knowing someone didn't guarantee the person wouldn't harm you. In fact, Chee had seen the opposite too often "I was watching you. I could tell he was angry and I saw him reach for something." Then he gave Blankenship his best "don't mess with me" look.

The man scowled back. "I was going to show him something from my billfold. You got a problem with that?"

Blankenship extracted a smooth brown leather wallet, opened it, and pulled out a small photo. "I wanted him to look at this."

Chee glimpsed at a photo of a group of people standing outside along a river. Blankenship held it close to Palmer's face. "That's what I've been talking about. You've got the power, man. Make a difference. Let the river live."

Blankenship massaged his arm where Chee had gripped it. "What you just did, jumping to an assumption there, is why law enforcement has a black eye these days."

Palmer said, "Let it go. The officer was just doing his job."

"His job isn't to terrorize people, last I heard."

Chee said, "Go outside, sir. Calm down. Get that temper under control."

"You're the one who lost it. You're just another empty-headed cop." Blankenship stomped down the steps and out the back door.

Palmer sat down again. "Thanks for the water. I'm going to get things started here in a few minutes. It would be best if you left the stage."

"Why?"

"I plan to open with a little talk about trust and the value of cooperation. Having a cop standing behind me contradicts that. It says either that I am afraid of something or that you guys, the police, are worried about me. Either way, it's the wrong message."

Chee said, "After what happened last night, Largo and the chief are worried that someone will try to hurt you and disrupt the meeting."

"What did happen last night?" Palmer raised his shoulders toward his ears, lowered them. Exhaled. "Something exploded and destroyed a car that happened to be mine. That might have nothing to do with the reason I'm here today."

Chee shook his head. "Until the captain tells me otherwise, I've got a job to do. I'll stand over there against the wall at the edge of the stage where I can watch you and the audience."

Palmer sighed. "We'll try it for today." The mediator walked to the podium, set down some papers, sipped the water, and adjusted the microphone. The noise in the room quieted with anticipation.

"Good afternoon, everyone. I know we're running late and I will get started in a few minutes. The delegates are assembling in the next room. Thank you for your patience." Then Palmer left the stage and Chee heard the sound of a door opening and the thud of it closing again. He knew Silversmith and Redbone were back there, keeping an eye on things, but Palmer's absence made him nervous.

Chee stood against the wall, keeping track of how long the man was gone and studying the audience for signs of trouble.

The people seated in the room seemed mellow. Good. He allowed himself to unwind a fraction of a turn and the fatigue in his muscles and behind his eyes reminded him that he'd had a long day yesterday followed by an early morning.

Just about the time Chee began to worry, Palmer returned to the stage. Behind him came the delegates. Palmer shook hands with each of them, one by one. He had arranged the representatives alphabetically by their own names, not by the entities they represented. They entered in that order and sat at the table behind tent signs identifying them with who they represented in smaller print below their names.

Interesting, Chee thought, and clever. Was it a subtle reminder that they could think for themselves beyond the groups they represented? He recognized some of them. He knew the three Navajos: the tribe's director of development, the head of the historical preservation division, and an elder from the Bodaway Chapter House, the closest local Navajo government unit to where the development might be. He also had met one of the Hopi delegates, a distinguished leader from the Bear Clan. He recognized the developer's representatives from the earlier encounter with the black limousine in the parking lot, but most faces were new to him. It looked like a fine array of bigwigs. A great place, he thought, for a group with violence in its toolbox to make a statement.

In the background, Chee heard the pulse of a siren. An ambulance, he knew. And from the growing intensity of the wail, it was coming his way.

7

Bernie had awakened before dawn. She went for a long run along the San Juan River, noticing the thin layer of ice along its banks where the shallow water lingered. The dead cottonwood leaves wore a coat of frost that added a gray sheen to their faded yellow. At sunrise, she said her prayers to welcome the day.

> *With beauty before me may I walk.*
> *With beauty behind me may I walk.*
> *With beauty below me may I walk.*
> *With beauty above me may I walk.*
> *With beauty all around me may I walk.*

When she arrived at work Largo told her that Cordova wanted her to set up the appointment with the victim's grandmother, planned to meet her at the substation, and hoped to leave for the woman's house as soon as possible. She'd never known an elderly lady who slept in, so she called the number Largo supplied. Not only was it working, but a weathered voice answered. Bernie identified herself as a police officer and asked to speak to Mrs. Nez.

"Go ahead." The old lady responded in Navajo.

"I have some news about your grandson and some questions to ask you, Grandmother. An officer from the FBI and I would like to come and talk to you this morning."

The phone seemed to go dead; then the woman said, "Come now." She gave Bernie directions to find her home.

Cordova updated Bernie on the investigation, noting that he hadn't learned anything about the boys who had fled from the gym, that Byrum Lee, the medic, had a clean record, and that Mr. Franklin and the security guards in the Chieftain Pit had all been of great assistance. Initial research confirmed that a bomb—a homemade device, possibly detonated with a cell phone or rigged to ignite with the start of the engine—had caused the blast. He wanted to drive, but Bernie persuaded him to ride in her unit, arguing that she knew the way and that the Navajo Police department's SUV had the clearance needed for Mrs. Nez's road.

"Just make sure we get there alive, Manuelito. I've heard about your driving."

"What?"

"Never mind. A confidential informant. Let's talk about the interview. Horseman's last address was with this lady?"

Bernie said, "Yes. I'll break the news to her in Navajo."

"You didn't tell her he was dead over the phone?"

"Of course not. After that, I'll try to switch to English if she's comfortable with it. If not, I'm the translator."

"Right. Good." They talked through a few more details and then he looked at his phone. "I've got a signal. I have to make some calls."

She tuned out his conversation and considered the job ahead of them. She dreaded having to announce death. She'd done it before, mostly in the case of missing people whose bodies turned up long after they had wandered away, often victims of dementia or too much alcohol. Usually, the family was saddened, but not surprised.

Cordova put his phone down.

"I've got news. A player with Save Wild America, a guy who had been arrested for setting a bomb in California but released on parole, has been tracked to the protest at Tuba City. We'll have him under surveillance there while we see if there's a link to the Shiprock case."

"Wow. That's great."

"I don't know about great, but it's something. Here's something else I've been wanting to tell you. I've been reassigned. I'm going to Michigan."

"Really?" She wasn't too surprised. With a few exceptions, most of the FBI guys who came to work felonies on the Navajo reservation left for more prestigious assignments after a few years. "What will you be doing there?"

"Still Indian Country cases, but a whole different environment and more opportunity for advancement."

Bernie had lots of questions. She waited to see if Cordova would save her the trouble of asking them.

He said, "You know, when I first got here, I thought I'd been sent to the third world. I couldn't see much except the poverty, the misery. That's one of the problems with this kind of work. We never get a call that says everything is great. Come on over because the people here love each other. But now, well, now I can find the beauty here, too."

He moved his hand toward the windshield, waving at the clear turquoise sky and the tree-covered mountains on the horizon, motioning to include the expansive, arid landscape and a cluster of horses nosing for food. "I mean, not just the geography, but the people out here. It's interesting. You Navajos, the people from VISTA, volunteers on a church program wanting to make things better. The optimists who work at the public health clinics or come out to teach.The grisly old desert-rat dropouts and the Navajo grandparents who barely speak English, bragging about grandkids who have gone to college. You know, Manuelito, I might miss this. I might even miss you, Chee, Largo, and the rest of the crew."

"You think so? You'll have to come back for vacation. Spend some time at Canyon de Chelly, take a jeep trip, hike down to White House Ruin and buy some necklaces from the kids there." Bernie slowed the SUV. "See that windmill up to the left?"

"No. Wait. Yeah."

"That's where we turn for Mrs. Nez's place. She told me it's down in the wash from there, but she didn't say how far."

Cordova said, "I heard a rumor that in Michigan they have house numbers and street signs. That could take the adventure out of finding a witness."

"You'll be bored."

The windmill had a metal water tank at its base. Tumbleweeds gray with time clustered against the broken fence of an empty stock pen. A propane canister and a supply of neatly stacked wood sat next to Mrs. Nez's little house. On the other side, someone had parked an old red-and-white Ford pickup. The brilliant November sunlight might lull a person from elsewhere, like Cordova when he first got to Navajoland, into assuming that the day was warm when in fact the temperature might only reach freezing before the sun started to sink again.

They saw the woman standing in the doorway even before Bernie turned off the engine. The lady seemed big-bosomed in a denim jacket that fit snugly over a collection of sweaters. She wore a skirt that reached the ground and a paisley scarf over her thick gray hair. She motioned them to come in.

Bernie zipped her khaki Navajo Police Department jacket. Cordova took off the seat belt and buttoned his long black coat. "Let's get this over with. If she starts to ramble, bring her back on topic."

"Sometimes these elderlies are lonely. They want to talk, get a sense of us strangers, before they say anything that relates to the case." Was white society all that different? she wondered.

"Whatever. Just don't let her go on all day."

Inside the house was only slightly warmer than outside. They kept their coats on, and the lady stayed bundled in her layers.

Bernie introduced herself again, this time formally in Navajo. Mrs. Nez reciprocated. Bernie switched to English and introduced Agent Cordova in the mainstream American way, with his job title. She noticed that he did not offer to shake hands with the old lady. Good, Bernie thought, he's learned a few things out here. Mrs. Nez had not invited them to sit, so they stood.

Bernie said in Navajo, "We have something to tell you about your grandson."

Mrs. Nez stared at the floor.

"I am terribly sorry, but a man was killed by an explosion last night in Shiprock. The FBI checked his fingerprints, and based on that we know he is your grandson, the one who shared this house with you."

She stopped talking to give Mrs. Nez time to digest the news but Cordova rushed to fill the silence. "The FBI identified the man killed as a person named Richard Horseman."

Mrs. Nez shuddered.

Bernie scowled at Cordova. He might have been FBI, but he wasn't an expert on how to get information from Navajo grandmothers. The names of the dead should remain unspoken; whatever evil remained from the dead one would come when it heard itself called.

Mrs. Nez raised her head and stared toward the window. Her voice shook as she spoke in English. "How do you know it was him?"

Cordova cleared his throat. "The FBI keeps a file of prints of people who have been arrested for certain crimes."

"Prints?" Mrs. Nez looked at Bernie.

Bernie spoke in Navajo. "Your grandson's fingerprints were in that file because he had been arrested before for a felony, a big crime. We came to tell you what happened because he listed your house as his most recent address."

Mrs. Nez did not respond.

Cordova said, "Because of the circumstances during which

your grandson sustained his fatal injuries, I need to ask you some questions about him."

Mrs. Nez remained still and silent. She looked deadly pale.

"Please sit down, Grandmother." Bernie spoke softly in Navajo. "I will help with this interview to make sure the FBI man knows what you are saying and that you understand what he asks."

Mrs. Nez waved her hand toward a couch covered with a frayed brown bedspread. Bernie sat, and Cordova did the same. Mrs. Nez took the chair across from them.

Cordova started with an open-ended question, asking the grandmother to tell him about the young man.

Mrs. Nez leaned back. The old woman took so long to answer that Bernie wondered if she had fallen asleep with her eyes open. Finally, she started to speak in Navajo, stopping periodically so Bernie could translate.

She began the story when her grandson was a small boy and came to live with her because his mother drank too much. He liked sports and art, she told them, and she detailed his school achievements. He wasn't good at reading but he went to classes for a while at Shiprock High School. He moved away after that to get a job in Albuquerque with a relative who ran an auto repair shop. But his plan didn't work out so he came back to Shiprock to help her.

Mrs. Nez stopped talking.

Cordova said, "Is that it?"

"I'm thinking." The impatience in her voice reminded Bernie of Captain Largo on a terrible day. The old woman paused a bit longer and then resumed the story.

Since he'd been back, her grandson had lived with her on and off, mostly coming to her house to sleep and eat. He sometimes spent a few days with a girlfriend. Her grandson was handsome. He had two jobs, and besides that, he helped her with wood for the stove and bought groceries for them when he could. He used to buy beer, but he stopped drinking. He took her to the clinic for her appointments and picked up her medicine.

"He's a good boy. That's what I have to say."

Cordova jotted a few notes. "Tell me what he did last night."

Mrs. Nez began to speak before Bernie could translate.

"He came home, we ate dinner and talked. He told me he was going to the big basketball game and that he would stay somewhere else that night with the friend who picked him up."

"Do you know the friend's name?"

"I didn't see who drove up, but it could have been the girlfriend."

"What's her name?" Bernie heard the irritation in Cordova's voice.

"He calls her Sonnie."

"Do you know Sonnie's last name?"

Mrs. Nez shook her head.

"Do you know where she lives?"

"Over there in Farmington or maybe Bloomfield."

Bernie said, "Do you know who her family is?"

Mrs. Nez switched back to Navajo. "She's a *bilagaana*. From Boston or Vermont or someplace like that. She told me but I forget. She talks funny. She works as a secretary for one of those drilling companies."

Bernie translated. Cordova frowned. "The explosion last night destroyed a car that belonged to a man named Aza Palmer. Did your grandson ever mention a man by that name?"

Mrs. Nez hesitated, and Bernie translated. The woman shook her head.

"Did he ever go to any meetings about environmental issues? Stopping development, things like that?"

Mrs. Nez waited for Bernie to translate, then responded. "I don't think so. He goes to those meetings to help people keep beer away."

Cordova glanced at his notes. "Did he have a computer?"

The old lady gave Cordova a wry look. "Too expensive."

"Did he ever make anything that blew up?"

She sat quietly for a few moments, then rose, went to a shelf by the window, and came back with a small carving. She switched to Navajo. "This is what he makes. He carved this for me." She extended it toward them, a palm-sized wooden image of an eagle. Bernie noticed the fine workmanship; Cordova barely gave it a glance.

"Can I see Horseman's bedroom?"

Mrs. Nez looked puzzled. Bernie clarified in Navajo, "He would like to see where your grandson sleeps and where he keeps his belongings."

Mrs. Nez indicated the couch where they sat with a twist of her chin. "He sleeps there. He has clothes and things in that closet by the window."

Cordova rose. "May I take a look?"

Mrs. Nez nodded. Cordova opened the closet door, and Bernie watched him take a step back in surprise. The pungent stench of mothballs escaped and mixed with the aroma of wood smoke from Mrs. Nez's stove. Bernie had grown up with the smell and would have been surprised if Mrs. Nez hadn't used them as well as natural cedar to protect her rugs.

From where she sat, Bernie could see that, like the rest of the house, the closet was neat. A large rug rolled into a cigar shape filled the single shelf. The floor had a pair of white athletic shoes, insulated boots, and a small gray suitcase. A few shirts, jeans, and a padded camo jacket hung from the clothes bar.

Bernie asked, "Are you sure your grandson never talked about Aza Palmer?"

Mrs. Nez had been watching Cordova unzip and rezip the empty suitcase. She said, "My grandson never mentioned that name."

Cordova said, "Was R—"

Bernie caught his eye and glared. How many times did she have to tell him?

"Um . . . was your grandson interested in the Grand Canyon?"

"He never talks about that. Never been there yet."

"What about the proposal to build a new resort? Did he speak to you about that?"

"No."

Cordova rejoined Bernie on the couch and leaned forward toward Mrs. Nez. "Officer Manuelito and I are almost done here. Is there anything else you wish to tell us about your grandson?"

She turned to Bernie, switched to Navajo. "He's a good boy. He helps me here more after we had the ceremony for him. I don't know why he got hurt. I don't know what I will do . . ." Her voice cracked and she turned away.

Bernie translated, giving Mrs. Nez a moment to compose herself.

Bernie noticed Cordova glance at the keys on the counter. "I need to inspect the truck," he said. "Is it locked?"

Mrs. Nez didn't respond.

Bernie shook her head. No reason to lock a vehicle out here.

Cordova rose from the couch. Bernie followed. "*Ahéhee'*. Thank you for your time, Grandmother. We may be back in touch with you if additional questions arise." She conveyed her sympathy to Mrs. Nez and left a business card, although she doubted that the grandmother would ever call.

When they were outside, Cordova said, "I'll take a look at the vehicle. Be right back." Bernie climbed into her unit, started the engine for the heat, and watched him disappear behind the house and emerge on the other side after a few minutes. He slid in, put on his seat belt.

"Did you learn anything?"

"Nothing suspicious in the cab or the bed. I didn't see a bomb-making studio outside there either."

Bernie turned onto the bumpy trail of a road.

He said, "It would be nice if Mrs. Nez knew more about the girlfriend. Sonnie in Farmington. Not much to go on there. You think the old lady was truthful about that?"

"Most grandmothers I know would have more information, but she seemed to be talking straight there. But she's lying about something. Well, maybe not lying, but not telling the whole truth."

"Probably about Horseman being a good boy. What makes you—"

His phone buzzed, and he held up a finger and answered.

"Sure. Absolutely. We just finished with the grandma." A pause. "The standard 'how could my angel be involved.'" And then, "Oh really?" He ended the call.

Bernie said, "Was Mrs. Nez helpful to you?"

"Yeah. I doubt that Horseman had anything to do with the bomb. He was a petty crook, considering driving off with an expensive car at the wrong time."

"If he was going to steal the car, why didn't he? Why did he just linger there?"

"Maybe he wanted to wait until the game was nearly over so he wouldn't stand out from the crowd. Maybe he reconsidered the heist while thinking about his sweet Granny? If the bomb was triggered by the ignition, he's dead because he was dumb enough to pick the worst possible car to steal. If it was triggered by a cell phone somewhere, then we've got a new layer of questions.

"So while you and Sam check for potential witnesses, I'm going to look into those e-mail threats. I'm sure this is tied to the mediation. Whoever did this knew there would be extra security at the meeting, so they planned the attack for Shiprock."

Bernie nodded. "At the game, just the rent-a-cops."

As they headed back to the substation, the clouds moved away from the sun. Tsé Bit'a'í, the volcanic monolith of Ship Rock that gave the town its name, stood bathed in the welcome late-fall light. The formation had many different personas depending on the season, the time of day, the weather. Today it looked formidable and imposing, a sacred guidepost in the Navajo cosmos. Diné stories of the Hero Twins' journey to make the world safer mention the huge stone landmark rising from the desert floor as the place of both bloody murder and wise compassion. She relished the gift of being born Navajo, part of such a special place.

Cordova removed sunglasses from the inside pocket of his coat and put them on. "You know, I'm going to miss these views when I get to Michigan. That, and the sunshine."

"What's Michigan like?"

"Good hunting. Good football. Lots of water—the Great Lakes. They have a bunch of colleges. Trees everywhere and a lot more towns and people. You ever heard of Detroit, Ann Arbor, Battle Creek?"

She ignored the question. "Do you have friends there?"

"Not me, but my wife's college roommate lives in Wyoming."

"Wyoming? Chee and I want to go to the rodeo in Cheyenne next summer. Are you heading up there before you leave?"

Cordova chuckled. "I meant Wyoming, Michigan. It's near Grand Rapids. You never heard of it? Just like I never heard of Sheep Springs until I came out here."

They drove awhile, and then he said, "What do you think Mrs. Nez was lying about?"

"I don't know, but it has something to do with her grandson's past."

"She glossed over the past. OK, here's what we know. Horseman was arrested for car theft, which probably means he stole other vehicles before getting caught. Rookie Sam discovers Horseman's burned body at the blast site. You and I visit Horseman's house. There's no evidence of bomb making, no sign that he knew or cared a thing about explosives or knew Palmer. You with me so far?"

"Yes." Bernie kept her eyes on the road.

"OK. Granny says an unknown friend, maybe the girlfriend, picked him up to go to the game even though he has a vehicle and that he's a good boy. But she knows he's *not* a good boy. I think Horseman's a guppy in the shark pond. I'm moving on to the big fish."

Bernie thought as she drove and Cordova went back to his phone messages. She wanted to believe what Mrs. Nez told them about Rick turning his life around. But, in her gut, she knew the old lady had a secret.

8

When all the delegates were seated, Palmer walked to the microphone to officially open the session.

"Welcome, everyone. *Yá'át'ééh*. I am Aza Palmer and it is my pleasure to be here on this important day. I will be mediating this series of meetings to help resolve issues surrounding a proposed development for an area of the Grand Canyon at the confluence of the Little Colorado and Colorado Rivers, adjacent to the national park."

He switched to Navajo and gave his "born to" mother's clan as Irish and German and his "born for" father's side as Towering House Diné. He detailed his Navajo grandparents' lineage, then moved back to English.

"I am honored to have an opportunity to help these delegates come to agreement about an issue that will affect not only all of us in this room but also many generations to come.

"Before we proceed, the elders have requested that our session begin with a prayer. I ask you all to please stand."

Palmer stepped back from the microphone. The Hopi Bear Clan man wearing a starched white shirt, new blue jeans, and freshly polished cowboy boots rose from his seat at the table. The other delegates and the audience stood. Chee felt his phone vibrate, but ignored it as he bowed his head. The elder began speaking, whisper soft at first and then a bit louder. Chee absorbed the spirit, rhythm, and music of the words, even though he couldn't understand the Hopi. The wail of the ambulance provided an odd background.

The Hopi prayed long and hard. Palmer thanked the elder for the blessing, and moved back to the podium. "I will briefly explain how the mediation process works. After that, the delegates will speak, each taking no more than five minutes. Then I will open the floor for comments from the audience. We seek your input today."

Chee glanced around the room. The audience was paying attention, not restless yet, although he noticed a few studying their cell phones. He hoped the worst thing that happened today was booing. He'd love to agree with Palmer that his services were superfluous.

Palmer said, "Mediations are done in private, with the resolution or lack of success announced later. But because of the tremendous interest in the possible resort, the delegates want to hear your ideas today before their work begins. Everyone at the table also has pledged to listen to every other delegate with respect and attention. When I look at the faces of the men and women around this table, I see commitment. People who want to do the right thing."

The men and women at the delegate table did look serious, Chee thought. They looked worried, in fact. News of the bombing had spread throughout Indian Country as fast as a dust devil, and the police presence must have underlined the reality of the threat. If the Shiprock incident inspired these folks to work hard, settle the multitude of issues that surrounded the possible resort, and go home, it well might be an example of good springing from evil. He wondered if any delegates or anyone in the audience had been at the Shiprock game. He'd ask Bernie about that.

Bernie? Chee checked his phone and her text made him smile. He replied: *Miss you too.*

Palmer spoke articulately and with conviction. He had shed the quiet persona Chee had seen on the drive to Tuba as easily as he had changed clothes. Chee had noticed the same sort of transformation in Lieutenant Leaphorn when they had worked cases together, from a silent, self-contained listener to something bordering on charming, cajoling a subject into cooperating.

Palmer closed his notebook. "The delegates will now introduce themselves. I will welcome the speakers by reading the brief biography they put together for today."

Palmer called the name of the elderly woman representing the Hualapai and read what she'd written about herself. She had a red folder in her hands. Palmer lowered the microphone so she could be heard. She greeted the audience in what Chee assumed was the Hualapai language. Then she switched to English, talking about the importance of the Grand Canyon as the place of the creation of the universe, the site of the tribe's ancestral origin and their spiritual homeland.

Chee wondered if pure randomness accounted for her being first or if Palmer had stacked the deck. The delegates paraded to the microphone, said their bit, and sat back down. A diverse group of people, he noted, most of them thoughtful. The session dragged on.

The delegate from the Havasupai Nation, the youngest of the negotiators, was at the podium now. He referred to some note cards and, like the Hualapai representative, talked about the Grand Canyon's profound importance: "We act as though we humans own the planet and that everything on it is for sale. That isn't true. The world is not a marketplace but a holy place. My goal is to help keep the canyon and the land that surrounds it sacred."

The delegate from the US Forest Service took the stage. He spoke with the jargon of an insider, talking about mitigating environmental impact and responding to concerned stakeholders.

The word *stakeholders* shifted Chee's thinking to those metal platters that held a nice piece of beef. He pictured a thick steak, grilled crisp salty outside, juicy with the first cut of the knife. He'd buy some steaks to barbecue as soon as he got home.

He forced his attention back to Palmer, who jotted notes as the man in the green uniform droned on, his voice soft enough to soothe a restless two-year-old at naptime. Three of the delegates looked like they had drifted off, and Chee's own eyelids were growing heavy.

Then his phone vibrated again. He pulled it from his pocket. Bernie. He responded to her call with a text . . . *Will get back to you at the break.*

After Mr. Forest Service finished, Palmer announced a twenty-minute recess. The delegates left through the stage door, but Palmer stayed at the podium. Chee saw the young man who had asked him about the mediator earlier come onto the stage through the side door. Palmer glanced up, startled.

Chee moved forward, on alert. Palmer stepped away from the podium to face the man, hands extended palms up. The young man headed back toward the side door. Palmer dropped his notes, grabbed his black bag, and hurried after him.

Chee raced to the stage and then to the delegate waiting room, searching fruitlessly for Palmer. He took the door that led outside.

Palmer was lighting a cigarette. The young man stood across from him, staring at the ground. If they had been involved in conversation, they weren't talking now.

Chee approached. "Everything under control out here?"

"Chill, Sergeant. I'll be in when I finish this cancer stick." Palmer exhaled smoke as he spoke. "Give us some privacy. This is absolutely none of your business." The expression on the younger man's face reminded Chee of a harshly scolded puppy.

Chee stood by the door, upwind from the cigarette smoke, aware of the jagged energy between the men, of the discomfort and awkwardness in the exchange. He was ready to intervene, and hoping he wouldn't have to.

He called Bernie, hoping to hear her voice, but she didn't answer. He left his usual message: "Just wanted you to know I'm thinking of you. Everything is OK here. Call when you get a chance." Chee watched the younger man kick at the dirt a couple of times, then storm off. The mediator crushed the cigarette butt under the sole of his boot and glanced at Chee. "Aren't you cold and bored out here?"

"What were you and that young guy doing? The bomber is still on the loose, and you're a target, man. Don't put yourself at risk."

"No need to fret. No explosives involved except a few choice adjectives. Like I said, give me some privacy once in a while. I'll have to fire you if you keep breathing down my neck. Don't worry so much."

He resented Palmer's attitude and his words left Chee uneasy. Whenever someone told him not to worry, that usually meant there was something to worry about.

9

As the delegate statements continued, Chee noticed the people in the audience growing quieter. He wouldn't have been surprised to hear someone snore. If those in attendance had expected fireworks after last night's uproar, they must have been disappointed.

Then the big doors that led to the hallway opened with a screech. The person at the microphone, a woman representing Arizona's Office of Tourism, stopped in midsentence. Many of the audience, startled by the sound, turned toward an embarrassed-looking Cowboy Dashee.

Chee took a step toward him, and Dashee motioned with his chin toward the hall. Chee eased the door closed.

"A lady was raising a ruckus outside and then collapsed by the front door. She says she won't get up until she can come into the meeting. Maybe you could talk to her."

"What about Silversmith or Redbone? Or the Arizona Highway Patrol guys? I'm supposed to keep an eye on Palmer."

Dashee reached into his pocket and handed Chee a card. "She gave me this when I told her she had to leave. Whatever she wants, I thought you might like to keep it in the family."

Chee saw the official Navajo Public Safety logo and the police crest along with the station number in Shiprock. The name read "Officer Bernadette Manuelito."

Dashee said, "I'll babysit for you."

"What else do you know about this lady?"

"Well, when the guard told her the meeting was full, she started yelling and then beating on him. That's when he called me."

"Was the guard hurt?"

"Only his pride."

"I'll see what I can do." He put Bernie's card in his pocket.

A small crowd of demonstrators and latecomers had gathered at a respectful distance to gawk. Chee made his way to the uniformed man who squatted next to a Navajo woman on the pavement. The guard told him the woman was Mrs. Nez. When he wouldn't allow her into the meeting, she argued with him and then collapsed.

Chee lowered himself onto his heels. She was a gray-haired lady wearing traditional Navajo garb—a blouse of deep red velvet ornamented with three silver-and-turquoise pins. She had a sand-cast concho belt at the waist of her long skirt and a wide silver bracelet on both wrists. She looked pale, he thought, pale and shaken.

"Grandmother," he said in Navajo, "they say you aren't feeling so well."

She looked at him, then quickly away. "My heart." She put her hand on her chest.

Chee said, "We can call the ambulance to take you to the hospital, where the doctors can give you medicine to help you feel better."

"That *bilagaana* pill won't do no good. You help me stand now and we will go into the meeting." She looked him over. "You're a strong one. Pull me up."

Chee said, "Have you had anything to eat or drink today?"

She shook her head. Chee motioned to the guard. "Could you please bring this lady some water?"

The guard came back with a bottle of water and a bag of peanuts and gave them both to Chee, who nodded his thanks.

The woman pushed herself to a seated position with a little grunt. She looked at the guard. "You go on now." She spoke in Navajo, and her gesture reinforced her words. "Bother somebody else. This man is the one I want to talk to."

Chee started to hand the woman the water, then pulled back to twist the cap loose first.

The woman put the bottle down next to her without taking a drink.

"Why are you here, Grandmother?"

"I need to go to the meeting to give somebody something. But that man over there"—she glanced toward the guard at the metal detector—"he told me I couldn't do it. Help me up."

Chee hesitated to put his hands on an elderly stranger, both because of fear of hurting her and the ingrained Navajo sense of personal privacy. "Can you stand if I give you my arm?"

She nodded.

He stood, and she gripped his forearm with her right hand, clinging to him for balance as she pulled herself to her feet. After a moment she took a shaky step forward. "Let's go."

They wobbled along until Chee could usher her to a wooden bench in the hallway.

"Please sit a moment, Grandmother, and talk to me." To his relief, she complied, using him to steady herself and settle onto the seat. She sipped the water. He sat next to her and offered her the peanuts, but she declined with a wave of her hand.

Chee said, "The room is full. No one can go in. Every seat is taken."

"What about you." It was a statement, not a question. "You got a uniform."

"Why is the meeting so important to you?"

She reached into a pocket of her voluminous skirt and pulled out a white envelope. "I have this."

Chee noticed that someone had written "Mr. Blankenship" on the outside. He recognized the name, the delegate he'd tangled with in the meeting room before the session opened.

"What's inside?"

She shrugged off the question. "My grandson left this."

Chee said, "Why didn't he come with you?"

"He could not." Chee heard the catch in her voice and then silence. Diné grandmothers didn't show their emotions, especially to strangers.

"Are you sure that meeting is full?"

"Yes, ma'am. Absolutely."

The woman studied the floor for a moment or two. Then he felt a cold, bony hand squeeze his arm again. She held the envelope toward him.

"You take this." She put the envelope on the bench and slid it toward him. "Give it to this man in there. Promise to do this for an old woman. Then I can go home."

Chee noticed that the flap was tucked, but it wasn't sealed. "I'm not sure it's safe for you to drive, Grandmother."

The woman took another sip of water. She gave him a look that reminded him of the sharp rebuffs he'd received from his own *shimásani*. "I am going to my sister's house when I leave here. She's out past the dinosaur tracks, not too far. She's waiting for me now."

Chee picked up the envelope and put it in his jacket pocket. "I will make sure this goes where it should."

She studied his name tag. "Sergeant Jim Chee. Your Little Father was the singer, the one who married Blue Woman?"

"Yes, ma'am." His uncle Frank Sam Nakai, his mother's brother, was known as his Little Father in the Navajo system of relationships. He had died a few years ago. With his passing, Chee had put his own training as a *hataali*, what some people called a medicine man, on hold.

The woman nodded. "He did the ceremony for my grandson.

After that, the boy promised he was done with drugs, with glue, spray, all that. He returned to the Navajo Way."

Chee listened. He'd seen too many young lives destroyed by sniffing glue and hair spray. Cheap highs lethal to brain cells.

"Help me up. I have to go."

They walked to her vehicle, a classic red-and-white Ford pickup. The woman now moved more steadily.

"You promise you will deliver that envelope?"

"I will."

"I need two more things before I go. Do you have the card from the lady policeman?"

"Here it is."

She slipped it into her skirt pocket and smiled at him for the first time. "Remember those peanuts?"

"Yes, ma'am."

He reached into his pocket and gave her the bag. Then he opened the truck door and she hoisted herself up into the driver's seat. He closed the door and waited until the truck started before he returned to the meeting, past the protesters outside and the crowd in the hallway waiting for a vacant seat in the room.

The door to the room screeched again, and people turned to look as Chee entered. Dashee leaned against the wall by the foot of the stairs that led the stage. His friend looked sleepy, Chee thought, and that meant nothing had happened worth getting excited about.

10

Bernadette Manuelito could be patient when she had to be, with her mother for instance, or with a stressed-out crime victim. But she preferred action, movement, doing something, not wasting time waiting. Her tolerance for boredom was as thin as the paper-like *piki* bread the Hopi made.

She had called Leaphorn, left a message, sent an e-mail. Since she couldn't reach him, she decided she'd stick with her plan to drive to Window Rock to see the Lieutenant and Louisa. Even before she got Largo's message that Leaphorn wanted to talk to her, she'd wanted to talk to him.

On her drive, she called to check in with Mama and Darleen. Her sister answered the phone.

"So what did you find out?" She could hear the smile in Darleen's voice. "Is CS a criminal or what?"

Bernie said, "Gosh, I haven't had time to check."

"The Cheeseburger's there because of that Grand Canyon development, a big meeting, right?" Darleen didn't wait for her response. "CS wants to go up and check it out. He heard that resort could harm some sacred sites, threaten endangered species, and do other bad stuff. He wants to make a video about saving the Grand Canyon or something. Cool, huh?"

Darleen talked about her classes. She didn't mention the friends she liked to go drinking with, Bernie realized. Was that because sister wasn't hanging with them now? Or because Darleen knew how Bernie felt about her partying? After they hung up, Bernie realized that she hadn't asked about Mama.

LOUISA CAME TO THE door and invited her in. The Lieutenant's housemate looked better, more rested than when Bernie had seen her last, and they chatted a bit at the kitchen table.

"Nice of you to stop by. Jim's not with you today?"

"He has an assignment in Tuba City because of that big meeting about the Grand Canyon."

"I love the Grand Canyon, don't you?" She didn't wait for Bernie to answer. "Joe's in his office, looking forward to helping you with whatever you're working on. Would you care for some tea?"

Louisa's tea, brewed from an allegedly health-promoting herb Bernie had never heard of, had an aroma that reminded Bernie of sweat socks begging for a trip to the laundry. Lemon and honey couldn't do much to make it better. Bernie had grown up drinking what her family called Navajo Tea. Mama gave it to her when she had an upset stomach. Louisa's tea was enough to give her a tummy ache.

"No, thank you." Bernie extended her water bottle. "I'm all set."

"I know you need to talk about police business. I'll make some tea for us. I'll bring you both a mug with lemon and honey when it's ready. You go on now."

"Oh, please don't worry about that. I can't stay long at all."

"No trouble." Louisa turned on the burner. "You get your business done."

The Lieutenant was sitting straighter than when she'd last visited. Returning to work had helped his recovery from the head wound more effectively than any prescription or therapy.

He glanced up from the laptop when she entered his office and motioned her to a chair, patting the seat with the palm of his hand. She watched him at the keyboard, specially modified to type in Navajo, obviously absorbed in something. He finished what he was typing and turned to her.

"*Yá'át'ééh.*"

His speech had improved slightly, but communication both through the computer and face-to-face was easiest for him in Navajo. That was fine with Bernie. Although he'd spoken English for decades, now it posed a challenge that created a roadblock in resuming his work as a consultant with non-Navajos who had used Leaphorn's crime-solving services in the past. Louisa could speak a few words of Navajo, and understood more. Bernie had noticed that they seemed to communicate effectively on a nonverbal level.

She talked about her family and Chee's Tuba City assignment for a few minutes; then Leaphorn changed the subject. "Tell me about the explosion."

She looked down at her hands, assembling her thoughts. "I was the first cop on the scene. The feds think the man killed in the explosion—" She stopped. "Did you know about that?"

Leaphorn nodded.

"They think he was collateral damage—a would-be car thief in the wrong place. They've moved on to radical environmental types who made threats against the mediator. But the more I think about what I saw, about the dead man, the more questions I have."

Bernie glanced out the window at the porch. She remembered the red hummingbird feeders Louisa hung there that drew the *dahetihhe*, small bits of flashing feathers with voracious appetites. The constant activity buzzed on from late spring until the end of summer. Now the porch looked empty, quiet.

She said, "What if I tell you everything I observed out there, step by step as it unfolded, and about the interview with the dead man's grandmother?"

Leaphorn nodded, swiveled his chair away from her, and picked up the laptop sitting on his desk. He turned back ready to type, focusing on the screen. She felt more comfortable speaking to the top of his head.

She started with the scene inside the gym, the sound of the blast, the glow of the burning car, the smell of the fumes, the discovery of the victim, the boys who ran, the medic who helped, the arrival of the fire truck, other cops, and, ultimately, Cordova. She painted the picture as vividly as she could. Leaphorn's fingers moved sporadically on the keyboard as she spoke.

She explained about the follow-up interviews, the lurking person with the dark hoodie, and the man in the brown jacket—perhaps the man the rookie found on the asphalt—sitting in the car. "The feds identified the body as a guy with an arrest record for car theft, but nothing like bombing or murder." She told Leaphorn the dead man's name. She summarized the interview with the grandmother, Cordova's unsuccessful search for bomb materials at the grandmother's house, and Horseman's lack of ties to the organizations on the FBI's list. "His grandmother told me he had turned his life around, but she lied about something."

Leaphorn stopped typing when she fell silent. She noticed that he had closed his eyes, and the way the sun illuminated his smooth face. She said, "What do you think?"

He opened his eyes. "First, what are your questions?"

"Let's see. If Aza Palmer was the intended target, why did the bomb go off before he got to the car? What about motive? I guess that should be the first question. Why would someone want to kill him? Cordova believes it's linked to the mediation, but Palmer is a lawyer, and he told me he had enemies." Bernie took a sip from her water bottle.

"More questions?" Leaphorn sounded like a patient father coaching a slow child.

"If the victim was the bomber, why did he die? If the dead man wasn't the bomber, why was he outside instead of watching the game? If the attack is tied to the mediation, why not blow up the car there?" Bernie leaned back in the chair, then sat forward again. "Oh, I forgot to mention that the mediator's ex-wife called the station and I talked to her. She wanted to know if Palmer was injured."

Leaphorn raised his eyebrows.

"She seemed genuinely relieved that he wasn't hurt. She said they were friends."

He nodded and glanced at his laptop. "Dark sweatshirt?"

"The witness thought it was blue." Bernie related as many details of Julie Pahe's story as she remembered. "I don't know how to track that guy and, well, the feds have moved on."

Leaphorn rested his chin in his hands, the pose she'd noticed he used when he was thinking. He spoke in Navajo. "Interesting. Interesting and complicated. The dead man puzzles me. Did Palmer know him?"

"I'm not sure."

Leaphorn said, "I'll see what I can find out about the man who was killed."

Bernie heard footsteps in the hall and then Louisa arrived with tea and some store-bought cookies. "I remembered that Joe and I have to go to his therapy appointment in about half an hour. I'm sorry I didn't think of it before now."

"I need to leave soon anyway," Bernie said. "I'm off work today, so I'm heading off to Tuba City."

"Have some tea first. It will give you energy for the road." Louisa handed them each a steaming cup and passed the plate of cookies. Bernie took a bite of a pink wafer, as crisp and flavorless as Styrofoam except for the ultra-sugary white filling. She hoped it might ease the shock of the tea. It didn't.

Louisa said, "I heard about the bombing. They said someone was killed. Was it a police officer?"

"No. It was a young man."

"Anybody you knew?"

"No. Thank goodness. I met his grandmother, Mrs. Nez, when I drove out to give her the news."

Leaphorn put his cup on the table, the tea untouched. "Nez? Where does she live?"

Bernie explained.

"Do you know her?" Louisa asked.

Leaphorn shrugged.

Bernie was acquainted with at least a dozen Nezes; her mentor surely had met even more. Nez was as common a surname in the Navajo world as Johnson or Nguyen or Garcia outside the reservation.

Louisa started to chat, as white people do. Bernie's mention of Tuba City and the possibility of a visit to the Grand Canyon stirred Louisa's own girlhood memories of a mule ride from the rim to the Colorado River.

Bernie managed to make the cookie last through half a cup of tea and most of the story. When Louisa offered her more, she found the polite opening to say good-bye. She had to talk to Palmer about the dead man, connect the dots, and she wanted to do it face-to-face. More than that, she missed her husband.

The Toyota cruised along Arizona 264 toward Tuba City. She turned on the radio, didn't like anything she heard, and turned it off. She was ready for a few hours of quiet. The Lieutenant had promised to e-mail her any insights he had on the case; it made her happy to know she had his help.

She stopped at Keams Canyon to get a Coke, to stretch her legs, and to chat with the manager of the complex, a trading post that now included gas pumps, a café, a grocery store, and a gallery featuring some fine Hopi art. She loved the scenery here at the border of Hopi and Navajo territory, the big rocks, the scattering of piñon, juniper, and Siberian elms leafless in the dark days of early winter. She took a deep breath of the fresh cold air and glanced out toward the Hopi mesas. Life was good.

Inside on the bulletin board she saw a green flyer, a call for protesters to rally at the Grand Canyon development meeting in Tuba City. It looked like the ones she had seen at the Shiprock gym. At the bottom was the logo for Save Wild America, a picture of the Grand Canyon with smokestacks at the bottom. Odd, she thought, since the proposed development was a luxury resort.

She took her Coke with her and cruised up the highway, past the Hopi High School, Polacca, and the road that climbs to the First Mesa villages of Hano, Sichomovi, and historic Walpi. She passed the handmade signs for in-home artist studios, the junction with Highway 87, which headed south to the interstate, and drove on to Second Mesa. She cruised through Shongopovi and stopped at the Hopi Cultural Center restaurant for a bowl of *nok qui vi*, the tribe's equivalent of mutton stew. It had hominy instead of potatoes and lacked the carrots and onions Mama always put in hers. She figured the Hopis must like it, but next time, she'd go back to her regular choice, a hamburger.

She remembered a funny story Chee had told her about the time he started a fire here in an effort to flush out a bad guy, nearly burning down the cultural center without the sanction of the Hopi authorities or Captain Largo. Not her husband's finest hour, but he solved the crime.

The dining room stood relatively empty, only two other tables occupied. The Hopi women at the table closest to hers discussed the meeting in Tuba City energetically enough that she could listen without feeling like a spy.

"I'm glad they brought in a mediator. Even though he's Navajo, at least he's a Native," the one with the blue blouse said.

"You know the developer is underwriting everything, even though the Navajos are the ones who set it up. You think a person doesn't know who signs his paycheck?" Her companion wore a wide silver bracelet in the classic Hopi overlay style, a bear-claw design cut into one piece of silver topped with another and then soldered together.

"Aren't you the cynical one." Blue Blouse patted her lips with a napkin. "The delegates, even ours, agreed on him. They could have opted for somebody else, but they thought this man had the integrity to do a good job. Give him a chance."

"I hope that's right. And I hope they come up with a plan that protects the sacred places. I don't care what else the developer and those Navajos do out there."

Blue Blouse laughed. "Yes, you do. You'd like your boys to be able to live closer. A resort out there would bring some jobs for everybody. You remember Michael's girlfriend? The one from Third Mesa?"

"Sure. Did she finally get a job?"

"Not exactly but . . ."

The women talked on. Bernie added some salt to her stew and took another bite. She didn't disagree with the women's observations on the resort, but she didn't know all the intricacies of the argument. Until the attack on Palmer that had drawn her in, she had been only peripherally interested. Not that development at the Grand Canyon wasn't an important topic, but it had been under discussion since she was a girl, one of those issues that never got resolved and never went away.

On the way back in the car she checked her phone for messages. She'd turned it off at Leaphorn's house out of courtesy and, she now realized, forgot to turn it back on. When it powered up, she noticed two missed calls from Chee.

She sent a text: *Surprise! Leaving Second Mesa now. See you soon.* She called Leaphorn to thank him, got no answer, and remembered that the Lieutenant had his therapy appointment. She didn't leave a message.

The Hopi villages were islands of Pueblo culture surrounded by the vast Navajo reservation. In a region known for long views and empty country, the arid and rugged Hopi mesas elevated landscape to a fine art. Navajo families and their sheep spread out over landscape like this; the Hopi people clustered together like bees in a hive. Many hives, actually, linked by shared ceremonies that brought the people of the mesas together.

She remembered Cowboy Dashee telling her that the gods had given the Hopi their sacred mesas because they didn't want life to be so easy that the people forgot to pray. Indeed, the dry land made farming difficult. In the old days during the growing season the men of the Pueblo hiked down to the fields to tend their corn and then back up again each day to their homes. The ancient ways were fading, but many Hopi still farmed. The old village of Walpi, which some said was the oldest continuously occupied city in the United States, still had no indoor plumbing or electricity. Tribal members who wanted less isolation and difficulty lived elsewhere.

Dashee, Chee's friend and now hers, had invited them to dances here. Someday, she told herself, she'd come up here to hear the drums and see the ceremonies.

She heard her phone buzz and reached over to extract it from the backpack on the seat next to her. It was Sandra from the office. She thought about ignoring the call for a split second, then picked up the phone and put it on her lap on speaker.

"Hey there."

"Hi, Bernie. Where are you?"

"In Hopiland, on my way to Tuba City. I'm surprised you got through. What's up?"

"A woman called for you, said it had to do with the bombing. I told her the rookie and the feds, mainly the feds, were working on that, but she said she needed to talk to you personally. She sounded upset."

Policy was for dispatch to contact off-duty officers only if they thought an urgent message could not wait until the person returned to work. Sandra conscientiously refused to divulge personal phone numbers, but had trouble deciding what defined *urgent*.

"Who was it?"

"Wait, I've got it here. Lona Zahne."

"Let me have her number."

"I'll text it."

Bernie slowed as a truck loaded with firewood pulled out in front of her. "What else is happening back there?"

"The rookie has been talking a lot to Cordova. He's all puffed up, like he's personally made a breakthrough in the bombing case or something."

"A breakthrough?"

"Oh, I'm just guessing. But I did hear that the feds identified somebody from the pictures you or the rookie took. Some bearded guy in the background looks kinda like someone wanted on some other bombing case."

"Wow. That's great. Thanks."

"Be careful out there." Sandra ended the call.

If there had been a breakthrough, Bernie wondered why Largo and Cordova hadn't kept her in the loop. As the only two women in the Shiprock substation, Bernie and Sandra had a solid working relationship based on mutual respect. They didn't make a big deal of it, but they watched each other's backs.

The road climbed to Third Mesa and past some dry springs, then slipped down into the Moenkopi Valley, a sleepy place, gray now without the summer's blessing of green cottonwoods and cultivated fields. Past Moenkopi, the Hopi tribal government had constructed the fancy Hotel Hopi, with a swimming pool and meeting rooms. She'd read that future development plans included a marketplace/fairground in the empty lot just beyond the hotel.

She was curious about the meeting and if Chee had adjusted to his unwanted assignment as bodyguard. And she wanted to call Cordova and talk to him about the person who had shown up on the video or the photos she—or the rookie—had taken. But first, she decided, she'd check into the motel.

That's when the trouble started. The young man was polite but firm.

"I can't give you a key to that room without Mr. Chee requesting it. Company policy. Sorry."

Bernie frowned. "Let's call him. He can authorize it over the phone."

The clerk dialed a number and let it ring.

"Sorry, he's not in the room."

Bernie felt her patience growing thin.

"Of course he's not. He's working. Can you call his cell phone?"

The clerk looked at the registration information on the screen again. "He's a cop, huh?"

"Right. Me, too."

He looked at her skeptically, but dialed the number and left a message for Chee to call the motel. "Well, that didn't work. Why don't you just come back later?"

"No. I'd like to talk to the manager."

"I can ask him to call you soon as he gets in, or you can come back in a couple of hours and talk to him. You're welcome to wait in the lobby until we get this worked out."

Bernie settled into a well-worn chair and called the number Sandra had texted for Lona.

Lona didn't bother with pleasantries. "Why didn't you tell me about the man who was killed by the car bomb?"

"You asked me about Aza Palmer and I told you he wasn't hurt. The bombing is an ongoing federal investigation. I don't remember if the man had died yet when we talked."

Lona's irritation had transformed into audible sorrow. "Why did you keep it a secret? I thought we were friends."

Stay professional, Bernie told herself. "Calm down. I didn't have the identity of the victim when I talked to you." She took a breath. "I didn't know he was dead, and how could I have guessed that it would matter to you?"

"He was my relative. The son of my younger sister."

"I'm sorry. I'm sorry for your loss."

"But why is *he* dead, and Aza's still alive?" Lona stopped talking. Bernie heard her blowing her nose. She came back to the conversation more composed. "I can't believe he's gone and just when he'd turned his life around. He wasn't an angel, but he had no reason to try to kill Aza even if he could have figured out how to build a bomb. That guy was an artist, not a chemist."

Bernie said, "The FBI man who went with me to talk to Mrs. Nez doesn't think your nephew was linked to the bombing."

"Thank goodness." Bernie heard Lona sigh. "I shouldn't have lost it with you. I'm shocked and frustrated by all this. And angry. Sorry."

"Don't worry about it. Can I ask you something?"

"Sure." Lona sniffed. "Go ahead."

"Do you know why your nephew would have been out there when the bomb went off?"

"How would I?"

"I don't know. I'm trying to make sense of this."

Another sniffle. "I'm glad you're working on this, Bernie. I remember watching you during those basketball games. You were the one with the most determination."

"I was the shortest one out there. I had to be determined."

"If anyone can find out why my nephew is dead, it's you."

After Lona hung up, Bernie went back to the registration desk.

"No callback yet." The young man winked at her. "Next time, you ought to tell your boyfriend you're coming."

"Next time, you ought to keep your opinion to yourself. Where is the meeting about the Grand Canyon development?" Bernie knew she sounded irritated and she didn't care.

"Oh, that." The clerk gave her directions.

She walked outside into the cold, switched on the car's engine, and drove to the meeting. She thought, It's a good thing driving while grumpy isn't illegal.

11

Joe Leaphorn awoke from his nap clearheaded and with a mission.

He grabbed his cane and went to his office, thinking about Bernie and her drive to Tuba City but mostly thinking about the questions she asked. She'd given him a challenge.

Back before he retired, he'd seen the cool gray eyes of advancing technology racing toward him and backed away as fast as he could. He resisted buying his first telephone answering machine, one of those with the little tapes he could erase until they got so scratchy he couldn't understand the messages on them. He'd learned what he had to know about computers and nothing more when the Navajo Division of Public Safety in Window Rock brought them in. He couldn't help noticing how technology had changed the face of law enforcement, making it easier to search records and keep track of details that could lead to solving crime. And when they went down for unexplainable reasons, computers made it nearly impossible to do what used to be called paperwork.

After he'd left his job as a police detective and begun his work as an investigator and consultant, technology moved ahead even faster. Officers drove units with cameras to record their encounters with the world. In some parts of the country, cops wore body cameras. Maybe it was good, Leaphorn thought, or maybe it was a distraction from the heart of police work, people helping people to make the world a little safer.

Back when he'd first become a cop, nobody thought of suing anybody, especially not on the reservation. And no one sued the police. No one had a lawyer except the big-time politicians who got caught spending the tribe's money as they shouldn't.

He'd resisted having a computer in his office at the police headquarters, but he knew he was swimming upstream. Once he got used to it, he liked it as long as it worked and didn't lose things. When he retired, the chief let him buy it, saying it was obsolete. He made a place for it in his home office, and it had worked fine. Even though Bernie and Chee thought the machine belonged in a computer museum, he was content. With anything electronic, his philosophy was: "If it works, leave it be."

But now, because of getting shot, he had a new computer: smarter, smaller, faster, friendlier. To his surprise, he loved it. If his brain hadn't been hurt, he would have argued with Louisa about spending the money. He would have stayed loyal to the dinosaur on his desktop. But she didn't ask. She bought it for him as a gift.

Louisa. Her support after his accident had been vital to his recovery. But she still fussed over him, babied him, and did things for him he could have done for himself. Her kindness felt suffocating. He avoided arguments by keeping quiet, and when she barraged him with questions he'd remind her that he wasn't one of her interview subjects.

He walked to the filing cabinet. When the department decided to move its files onto computer storage, around the time he was considering retirement, he asked if he could have the paper folders with some of the cases he'd worked.

"Take what you want," the chief told him. "It saves us the trouble of shredding them."

So Leaphorn had a collection of the more intriguing and complicated crimes he'd solved and criminals and situations he'd found especially interesting or puzzling. He added a few unsolved cases that had baffled him, the department, and the federal agencies that had been part of the team. A file that had something to do with a Mrs. Nez and a boy named Horseman hid in the cabinet somewhere.

He had organized the folders by case number at the station, and he kept them that way. The older files seemed the best place to start. Because of the changes the bullet had made to his brain, those well-established memories were the most vivid. Leaphorn didn't go back to the beginning of his career, but to a time when he might have encountered the man who was now dead. He pulled a handful of manila folders from a section of the collection that ought to coincide with the early years of Horseman's life. As good a place to begin as any.

He took as many as he could comfortably carry to the table in the center of his office and thumbed through the stack. Reviewing them stirred memories of troubled souls who had lost their bearings and of men and women who convinced him evil was real. Unlike Jim Chee, Leaphorn was a skeptic when it came to the world of the spirits and witchcraft, but he had seen time and time again how those who forgot the wisdom of their grandparents became lost souls. He remembered another man named Horseman from a different clan and another part of the reservation whom he'd encountered early in his law enforcement career. Luis Horseman had knifed a man in a fight in Gallup, fled the scene, and ended up a corpse with his mouth stuffed with sand, allegedly killed by a shape-shifter.

The files he glanced at made him feel nostalgic for the old excitement of the job and relieved that he didn't have to deal with the dual stress of the life-threatening danger and the ever-shifting politics that came with police work. Navajoland, like the world in general, had grown more violent.

He finished reviewing that batch of files and went back for another.

After only an hour, he found what he'd been looking for. Mrs. Nez's name turned up in connection with a domestic violence case. The file was slim, but the details he had included brought the incident back to his recollection as clearly as if the boy had been standing next to him.

Leaphorn remembered how the case opened. He'd seen a child walking along the side of the road. Nothing unusual about that. In Navajoland, people walked, children among them. But the boy wore only one shoe and held out his tiny thumb, trying to hitch-hike. When the car got closer, he saw that the child's dirty face was streaked with tears.

He offered the little boy a ride in the patrol car. Leaphorn re-called that he persuaded the shy, scared youngster to climb in by showing him how to turn on the light bar. The child smelled of sweat and cigarette smoke. His dirt-caked pants had a broken zipper. Leaphorn asked the boy if he'd like an apple he'd saved from lunch. After he ate it, the child spoke for the first time, saying thanks and asking if Leaphorn could turn on the flashing lights one more time.

The boy, who said his name was Ricky, was heading to his grandmother's house to let her know that the baby wouldn't stop crying and his mother had fallen down. "I'll check on your mother," Leaphorn remembered saying, and he drove the boy home. Leaphorn found a woman passed out and smelling strongly of beer—nothing he hadn't seen before—and a baby whimpering. The woman looked as though someone had beaten her, and beaten her more than once. He remembered Ricky ignoring his mother, as if this state of affairs were common, picking up the baby, and asking Leaphorn if he please had another apple, one for his brother.

What happened in the ensuing years to turn that sweet boy into a casualty discovered at a crime scene?

Leaphorn usually kept his work to himself, not sharing the details with his dear wife, Emma. He liked to leave the cases at the office. But the sight of Ricky's unconscious mom and the little boy's efforts to comfort his hungry baby brother left a residue of sadness. When his wife asked what bothered him that night, he'd told her.

"I left the boy with the grandmother," he remembered saying. "The baby went to the hospital."

Emma put down the book she'd been reading. "Someone should be helping those little ones." She asked Leaphorn for the boys' names and the grandmother's and for their address. The Horseman boys became one of her projects.

Once a month, she sent Ricky and his little brother funny cards with a dollar bill tucked inside. Leaphorn suspected she did other things for the boys, good deeds he wasn't aware of. Perhaps because they'd had no children of their own and because Emma's only sister had never married, the brothers had held a special place in his late wife's heart.

Leaphorn set the folder on his desk. He thought about that polite, hungry little boy and the thin crying baby. How many lives had been ruined by alcohol and domestic violence? Too many. Bernie said the FBI identified Rick Horseman's burned body through fingerprints taken when he was arrested for car theft. But he suspected Horseman's troubles had started long before that.

The Lieutenant didn't like loose ends and things that didn't make sense. They gnawed at him, like beetles slowly eating through the soft wood under the bark of a piñon tree. If he could figure out why Rick Horseman was standing close to the bombed car, he would know why he was dead.

Leaphorn pushed himself to standing. He would follow up on the mystery of this dead young man for Emma's sake. For Emma and for Bernie. And he knew just where to begin.

He took a few minutes to compose a note for Louisa, who had gone to her book club meeting, laboriously shaping each letter because of the problems the bullet had created between his brain and his right hand. He placed a notebook in his shirt pocket, slipped on a jacket, found his gloves, and took his truck key from the hook by the door. Then he walked out to the driveway and his pickup. He climbed in, using the steering wheel to help pull himself up, and put his cane on the passenger seat.

He had driven the truck last week, the first time since his accident. Louisa, passenger and copilot, watched his every move while trying not to act nervous. Today, it felt good to get out of the house on his own, and even better to be working on a case again. The department had given him a couple little jobs since his injury, things someone else could have handled, as a goodwill gesture. This was different.

He drove carefully, a mile or two under the speed limit, making his truck one of the slowest vehicles on the road in Window Rock. He pulled into the parking lot at the Navajo Nation Department of Family Services. The daughter of an old colleague worked here, and if he handled things just right, she'd do him a favor. As he approached the entrance, he realized that it might have been smart to make an appointment. Oh well. He had time to wait if he needed to.

The building, like many official government offices on the reservation, needed a facelift. He went to the front desk and wrote the name of the woman he wanted, Maryellen Hood, on a page in his notebook and then "I have trouble speaking."

"You need to see Maryellen?"

He nodded.

"Can you wait, sir? I'll see if she's available."

Leaphorn nodded again.

"Can I tell her your name?"

He reached into his pocket for his billfold, extracted a card, and handed it to her. The woman looked at it, looked at him again, and disappeared with the card and his note.

He made his way to a chair and took a pen from his pocket. While he waited, he made a list of what he knew already about Rick Horseman and his mysterious death. The list was short.

After about ten minutes, a slim Diné lady invited him into a small office with a window that offered a glimpse of the arid landscape of Window Rock. She motioned him to a padded folding chair on one side of a table cluttered with papers, books, and folders. She cleared off a place in front of him and one across the table for herself.

"Lieutenant, what a pleasure. My father used to talk about you all the time and I've always wanted to meet you. I heard about that crazy woman who tried to kill you. I'm glad you're doing so well."

He said the Navajo word for father with a question in his voice, and Maryellen understood. She shared news of her father's retirement and his renewed interest in volunteering and home improvement projects.

When the right time came, Leaphorn tried to tell her what he wanted, first in Navajo and, when he realized she didn't comprehend, in English.

Because she still couldn't understand, he laboriously wrote down his request and supporting information in bullet points: the approximate date he'd called social services; the location of the home where he'd found the intoxicated, injured mother and the crying baby; and the names Ricky Horseman, as the child he'd transported, and Marie Nez, as the woman who had claimed the boy.

Maryellen frowned at the note. "I doubt that we still have the specific information about that family, that case." She tapped a manicured nail on the sheet of paper. "That was a long time ago. And besides, you remember, I'm sure, that case records are confidential. I'm sorry I can't help you. But it was an honor to meet you."

He could drop it now, he thought. Go home. Eat the dinner Louisa would fix for him. Relax. Watch TV. But he remembered Emma addressing those envelopes in her small, precise handwriting. He remembered Emma's smile as she showed him the cards—a frog that sprang out when the card opened, a fire truck with a ladder that expanded. He wondered if the grandmother gave the boys those cards, if the grandmother used the money to buy something for the kids. In any case, sending them gave Emma pleasure.

He looked at Maryellen's shiny fingernails. "Shiprock bomb."

"You think this might be connected?"

Leaphorn nodded once.

"I don't know how these records could have anything to do with that, sir, but you're the detective."

He said, "Important." And then a word he didn't use much: "Please."

She wrinkled her brow and looked at the desktop a moment. "How is the best way for me to follow up with you?"

He moved his fingers as if he were typing and then pushing a button.

"I don't . . . Oh, wait. Is it easy for you to e-mail?"

Leaphorn nodded. Not easy, but easier than trying to speak English or laboriously print the letters.

She looked at his card again. "Is this your correct address?"

He nodded.

She said, "I can't promise. I'll see what I can do."

Maryellen walked the few steps to her desk. She opened a drawer and removed a purse the color of buckskin. She unzipped a pocket, took out a small flat case, opened that, and reached for a card. She handed it to him.

"This is the best way to contact me."

He noticed that the e-mail was a private address, not the official one for business, and that the name printed on it was *k'aalógii*. Butterfly, not Maryellen.

She said, "I saw pictures of that explosion on TV. The boy you're asking about, did he die at the scene?"

Leaphorn wasn't sure if Horseman's name had been released by the FBI, but he knew how the game worked.

He shook his head and said, "Later . . . ," this time with a finger to his lips.

He didn't realize he'd left his cane in the waiting room until he got to the car. He went back for it with a spring in his step.

12

Bernie drove to the Justice Center. The parking lot was nearly filled with cars, trucks, and SUVs, but she found a place for her Toyota near an old pumpkin-colored VW camper that reminded her of something from the '60s. November's pale sunlight provided a little extra heat, and she always tried to park her car where it caught the rays in the winter. She could have walked from the motel, she realized, and a walk would have calmed her.

She noticed the protesters, a remarkably energetic group despite the lack of attention they were drawing. She spotted the big white truck with a television station logo on the side; weekends were notoriously slow news times except for traffic accidents and DUI arrests. She wondered if Palmer and the delegates would allow the cameras inside.

As she walked toward the courthouse, a man with his gray hair in a bun handed her a "Save the Grand Canyon" flyer.

"There's no more space in the meeting room, sweetheart. You can stand in the hall, but you can't see or hear a thing from there." He wore a windbreaker, and his cheeks were red with cold. "I don't like the way they shut us out."

"Who shut you out?"

"The cops, the developers of course. The National Park Ser-vice, the tourism vultures, the greedy Indians . . ." He stopped, and Bernie realized that he had figured out she was an Indian. "Uh, did you know they have the Navajo council in their pockets? Hopis, too."

"Really?"

He tapped the flyer. "Read that. It will open your eyes."

The man moved closer, and Bernie could tell he wasn't as old as she'd initially thought. "Even though it's cold, we're safer out here. I heard that there could be a bomb inside."

"A bomb?"

"Boom. Like the one at that high school the other night that killed that protester. I saw it on TV."

She was almost at the building's doors when she heard someone walking up behind her. Moving quickly.

"Miss. Excuse me."

She turned. A man in a dark coat and a hat that covered his ears smiled at her. He had a camera. "Jack Rightman, KOAX. How about a comment on the meeting?"

"I haven't been there yet."

Bun Man trotted up to Rightman. "I've got something to tell you." When Rightman turned away, Bernie walked into the build-ing. One of the Arizona officers in the lobby opened the door for her.

"If you are here for the meeting, all the seats are filled, ma'am." He was dark and muscular. About her age or maybe a touch older.

"I'm Officer Manuelito, Navajo Police. My husband's the Navajo sergeant who got assigned to keep an eye on the mediator."

"Albert Anderson." He extended his hand toward her. "Chee's here, babysitting Palmer, in with the delegates. If you want to catch him at the break, they use the stage exit." He smiled. "You know, I made you for a cop. I noticed how you handled yourself with that wacko out there. If he'd tried to pull anything, you could have held your own."

"That man strikes me as mostly talk, but he mentioned a bomb threat. Did you hear anything about that?"

"Nope. But you Navajo cops are running the show. I'm here because I could use the overtime." Anderson shifted his weight from heel to toe and back again. "I heard about that incident in Shiprock. A huge arena crammed full of spectators? That could have been a whole lot worse. Do the feds have a suspect?"

Bernie said, "I don't know." If Cordova had learned something, she thought, he hadn't shared it with her.

Anderson said, "You might mention that bomb talk to the honcho in charge, Captain Ward. Head on down the hall and take the steps."

Bernie found Ward in conversation with a man dressed in overalls. She introduced herself and mentioned the bomb rumor.

Ward grimaced. "That story has been going around all day, and so far it's just talk. We haven't had any phone calls about a bomb, but the feds here are on the alert, doing what they do."

Bernie realized that, as far as she knew, the explosion at Shiprock had come without warning. If she'd been in Captain Ward's position she would have reacted with the same skepticism, but the chaos she'd experienced in the parking lot gave her a different perspective.

The captain said, "Chee ought to be in the meeting room doing his impression of a bodyguard. You know where that is?"

"No, sir."

He gave her directions.

She went inside and stood against the back wall, trying to look inconspicuous while hunting for her husband. The room was about half filled, some people seated, studying their phones or chatting, others standing at their seats or in the aisles. Onstage, she saw people she assumed to be the delegates, but not Palmer or Chee.

She spotted a tall, thin man in a white cowboy hat in the aisle about halfway toward the stage. It took her a minute to come up with the name: Lee Something? No, Something Lee. She walked up to him.

"Mr. Lee, I never got a chance to thank you for staying with the injured man and helping with the traffic situation after the explosion at the high school. *Ahéhee'*."

She could tell from his expression he didn't remember her.

"I was the officer in charge for a while out there. Bernadette Manuelito."

"Howdy. Sorry I didn't recognize you. You look shorter when you're not working." He chuckled, then turned sober. "Did that guy make it?"

"No, he died at the hospital."

Lee took off his hat. "He was banged up pretty bad. Any ideas yet on what caused that explosion?"

His short joke still grated on her. "Not that I've heard. The feds are in charge of the investigation."

He nodded. "What brings you here, ma'am? I mean, Officer?"

"My husband has an assignment, so I thought I'd give him some company. How about you?"

"Mr. Gardner, the delegate representing Canyonmark." Lee put his hat back on, making it easier to talk with both hands. "He wants me to do some contracting work if the project is approved and told me about the big powwow here. I'd never met him in the flesh. So I figured I'd mosey on out here and say hello. I wanted to find out about the hubbub over the hotel, or resort, or whatever the heck the plan is before I sign on to work with him. Did you see those demonstrators out there?"

"I did. There are quite a few groups here. I didn't expect so many different viewpoints."

Lee adjusted his shirt cuffs. "The worst are those self-righteous guys like Blankenship, the man who represents the commercial rafting organizations. Those folks are only concerned about themselves. That man is a liar, and a cheating son of a gun. Before he opened his raft business, he was an organizer for one of the wacko groups that want the world to go back to 1890 or something. My sister gave that bunch money she couldn't afford to and, of course, she didn't get it back even when they had to close because of fraud. He's a—"

She heard the chime of a cell phone and saw Lee pat his shirt pocket.

Bernie said, "Do you know when the session will reconvene?"

"Well, the mediator said they'd start up again in ten minutes and now it's been twenty. Excuse me, Officer. I've got to take this. If you'd like a seat, you can have mine." He indicated a place in the second to last row on the aisle.

The delegates had filed back on stage, with a portly, balding man in a dark suit arriving last. Palmer headed to the podium. He seemed older than he had at the game, perhaps because, instead of a basketball jersey, he wore dress-up clothes. He hung his Pendleton jacket with turquoise in the design on the back of a chair and she noticed his fancy western shirt with pearl buttons.

A few moments later, Chee came striding across the back of the stage. He looked tired, she thought, tired and worried. Palmer readjusted his microphone and turned it on. "Welcome back, everyone, and please be seated. We'll get started with public comments." He gestured to the two stands with the microphones in the back of the room, arranged so the speakers would be facing the delegates, and explained the rules for commenting. "I invite anyone who would like to address the panel or myself to please approach the mics."

Bernie watched Chee watching the audience. He was tense. She kept her eyes on him, admiring his good looks and wondering what troubled him.

Then the creak of the door behind her caught her attention. She turned to see the TV man enter the room carrying a large black duffel bag. He began to unload and set up equipment, a tripod, power cords, and more she didn't recognize.

Onstage, Palmer was summarizing. "I ask that everyone act with respect, including respect for those with whom you disagree. Stick to the topic. Mention your most important points first, in case you run out of time.

"Speaking of time . . ." Palmer held up a card with the number thirty on it. "I will raise this when you have thirty seconds to complete your remarks." He held up a second that read "Thank you." "When you see this, your time is up and you need to sit down." Palmer glanced at the people who had assembled at the back of the room. "The lady in the blue T-shirt, please introduce yourself, tell us if you are speaking on behalf of a group, and make your brief remarks. Then I will call on the man with the red tie at the second microphone."

The woman mumbled her name and gave a rambling talk about the importance of the Grand Canyon as a place where city people could enjoy the night sky without light pollution. The cameraman stopped the video.

Next came a man in a button-down shirt with a fish-logo tie who identified himself as a member of Swim Free, a group dedicated to preserving habitat for an endangered fish, which he named in Latin. Because the fish could not speak for itself, he said, he and his organization protected its interests as they related to planning for and construction of the resort. He began a discourse on the interconnectedness of nature that sounded to Bernie remarkably like something her grandmother might have said.

Palmer held up the sign with "30."

Mr. Swim Free talked a little faster.

She saw Palmer's hand move to the "Thank you" sign. Then, suddenly, the microphone died and the windowless room plunged into blackness. Although she hadn't heard an explosion, the protester's reference to a bomb threat flashed in her mind.

13

Bernadette Manuelito rushed to the back of the room and opened a door to let in more light. Officer Silversmith followed her lead and opened the other back door. The weak afternoon sunlight reflected off the clock, an old-fashioned kind with hands stalled at 2:20.

Palmer went to the podium. His microphone was dead, but his lawyer's voice filled the hall. "Ladies and gentlemen, as you've noticed, we're having some technical difficulties. I'll let you know what's going on as soon as I find out myself. I hope to resume public comment in a few moments.

Most of the audience stayed put. A few made their way toward the exit.

A figure stepped onto the darkened stage from the side entrance. Bernie felt her instinct for danger kick in. She watched Chee step between Palmer and the man, briefly blocking his passage, then allowing the person to proceed to the podium. He looked at Palmer's microphone, checked the connections. Then he fiddled with the light switches on the stage wall. Now that her eyes were accustomed to the dim light, Bernie could tell from the way the technician hunched his shoulders that he didn't know what to do next.

Rightman, the TV reporter, thumped the malfunctioning microphone in the back of the room. "No power here either." His voice resonated in the darkened hall.

The space slowly filled with the rumble of conversation. Power outages were common in the summer, often caused by lightning strikes. In the winter, more rarely, the weight of snow or wind toppling trees against the power lines took out the electricity. November incidents were ususual.

Captain Ward walked into the room toward Palmer and Chee. The people quieted. After a brief conversation, Palmer headed back to the podium.

"Ladies and gentlemen, the entire building has lost power. Building maintenance is at work on the situation, but the captain is unsure of how long the situation will take to resolve. Rather than continuing in the dark—some would say this issue has already been in the dark too long—we will reconvene at nine a.m. tomorrow. If the power is still off here at the courthouse, the meeting will shift to a different location, perhaps the Tuba City Library, and a notice with a map will be posted outside. Thank you."

Rightman focused on Palmer, the light from the camera serving as a mini spotlight.

Since she was already at the back door, Bernie walked toward the exit rather than struggle against the flow of the audience to reach Chee. She nodded to Officer Silversmith. "I'm a cop from the Shiprock station. Need any help?"

"No thanks. Everyone seems pretty mellow and Chee will pitch in if we need him. You're his wife?"

"That's me. Bernie Manuelito." She introduced herself properly with her clans.

Silversmith did the same as he kept an eye on the crowd. "Chee said you were smart, but he forgot to say that you're pretty, too."

She observed the crowd move down the hall and out toward the parking lot. When the room had mostly cleared, she stepped back inside. The stage was empty and she figured that Chee, Palmer, and the delegates had left through the back door. She'd wait in the parking lot, she decided, and she noticed that the idea raised her level of anxiety. First she had watched the Lieutenant get gunned down in a Window Rock parking lot, and then she had seen the aftermath of the car bomb. She swallowed her nervousness and reminded herself she was a cop.

Outside, a group of protesters in Save Wild America T-shirts with the Grand Canyon smokestack design had gathered. She also noticed a well-built but otherwise nondescript man watching her watching them. She made him for FBI. Then she saw a red-haired woman in jeans that hadn't come from Walmart. His partner? The Arizona Highway Patrol officers also were on alert.

The TV reporter stood by his white van, also studying the crowd, in no hurry to leave. She noticed two men in dark suits and ties chatting as they walked. Lawyers or bankers, perhaps, who'd come to speak at the meeting. But they didn't seem quite old enough, and out here even lawyers and bankers wore boots and bolos. Maybe they were Mormon spokesmen who'd come to share their viewpoints on the possibility of alcohol or gambling at the resort. They were dressed for TV, she thought. But they headed to a gray jeep-like vehicle without being accosted.

She had no such luck. Rightman glanced her way, then picked up his equipment bag and walked toward her. "Hello, again. How about a comment now for the news tonight?"

"No."

"Ah, come on. You look like a person who has some great opinions. It's easy, I'll just ask you a question or two, and we're done."

"No thanks." She heard a vehicle honking around the back of the building. "Besides, you don't want that irritating sound in your footage."

She noticed a young Navajo man hurrying toward the cluster of protesters. She watched him pull the hood of his sweatshirt over his close-cropped dark hair and sprint toward the back of the

building, where the honking originated, the area where the delegates parked.

When she first went into police work she gave everyone the
benefit of the doubt. Now, after a few years on the job, civilian
naïveté had been replaced with what she considered a more realis-
tic view of humanity. She ran after the runner.

Bernie found the beginnings of chaos.

A man in a parka the color of desert sand and a hat that made
his head look like it came to a point stood directly in front of a large
black limousine. From the stoop of his shoulders, Bernie estimated
that he was in his sixties or perhaps older. He pounded the car's well-
polished hood with his "Stop Development Now" sign. In addition
to the car beater, a small group of people milled around, some with
signs they'd made on their own, some with the slick-looking Save
Wild America logo enlarged, printed, and stapled to a stick. The
crowd provided an encouraging audience and blocked the other delegate cars from moving forward. The honking only encouraged them.

The driver's-side door of the black limo opened and the driver
got out. Bernie had never seen anyone wear a cap like his except
chauffeurs on television. He approached the angry man.

"Sir, I don't give a hoot about your politics, but get the hell
away from my car. You don't have the right to damage it."

The man with the sign shouted back at him, "You're part of the
problem."

"I'm trying to make a living."

"You're an idiot."

A man in a green jacket stepped forward. "Come on, Bebe. Get
out of the way before you get run over." Instead of cooperating,
Bebe swung the sign. She heard the thunk of impact as Green Jacket's body hit the asphalt. By the time she reached him, the victim
was upright and gripped Bebe by the forearm. Bebe struggled free
and hoisted his sign again.

The driver stood stiffly, his hands clenched into fists. "Get him
out of here before I punch him."

Bernie felt the familiar rush of adrenaline as she stepped forward. "I'm a police officer. You all need to move back so these cars can pass."

"You look like a nosy Indian to me." Bebe attempted to give the car another dent, but he was too far away. The vehicles behind the limo continued honking.

Bernie put muscle in her voice. "Put the sign down. Step away from the car now, sir. Quit what you're doing before you or someone else gets hurt."

Bebe stopped bashing the hood, turned, and swung his sign at Bernie. She took a step back in surprise, avoiding the blow. Green Jacket grabbed Bebe's wrist. The sign dropped as he twisted Bebe's arm behind his back and pushed him out of the line of traffic. Bernie expected Bebe to continue to resist, but Green Jacket seemed to have subdued him.

Officer Silversmith, slightly out of breath, ran up next to her. "Want me to arrest that guy for assault on an officer?"

"No. You've got enough to deal with and his buddies have him under control. But keep an eye on that man."

Silversmith spoke to the driver. "Move your car so the folks behind you can get out of the parking lot, and I'll take your statement and photos of the damage."

The driver turned away. "Forget it. I'll deal with this later. Mr. Gardner is already running late for his meeting in Page."

Some of the protesters had their cell phones out. Bernie hadn't noticed anyone filming the attack on the car, but probably someone had. Silversmith turned to her. "You sure know how to have fun on your day off. Thanks for your help."

The protesters who had been distracted by the car beating came to life as Chee and Aza Palmer left the building. Chee looked grim as he and Palmer walked toward his unit. About the same time she noticed them, Bebe did, too.

"Aza Palmer, this power outage is a hoax to cut off public input. You should be ashamed. Shame. Shame. You're in the back pocket of Canyonmark. Shame. Shame." He kept it up, and the chant of "Shame, shame" spread through the protesters. In addition to Save Wild America, Bernie saw signs that said "Swim Free," "Let the Colorado Flow," "Save the Canyon," and "No to Canyonmark" flashing in a flurry of organized energy. Someone shouted, "There's a Canyonmark flunky," and the group turned its attention to the approaching vehicle, and the line of traffic slowed to a crawl.

Rightman moved in front of Bernie to focus on the messages. The TV attention energized the crowd, and they followed Rightman to a car with a delegate. Bernie walked over to Chee's unit, and he lowered his window.

"Hey there," he said. "I saw you in the meeting room. Glad you made it to Tuba. Sorry I didn't have a chance to talk."

"You were busy. Can I help?"

Before he could answer Palmer said, "I need to get back to the motel to see what I can find out about the power outage and arranging an alternative site before all the businesses close down today. I can't think sitting here." His voice was icy, formal. "With me gone, the situation might calm down."

"OK I'll turn on the lights and siren and we'll cruise on outta here." She heard something she rarely noticed in Chee's voice: irritation.

Bernie said, "My car is on the other side of the building. What if I give Palmer a ride to the motel and keep an eye on him for you. We can cut through the building."

"Watching him is my job."

"Consider me your deputy for the moment. It will make everyone's life easier."

Palmer said, "This is ridiculous. Just let me walk back to the hotel."

"Quiet." Chee kept his attention on Bernie. "If you'd give him a ride, that would be great."

"On one condition." She leaned in toward the unit's open window. "I need a key to our room."

"Oh. Sorry." Chee reached in his jacket pocket and handed her the little envelope with the key and the room number.

Bernie gave Palmer a steel-eyed look. "Come with me. I've got something I need to talk to you about."

Palmer climbed out of the police car, and he and Bernie made their way quickly through the darkened hallways of the Justice Center building and out a side door.

She moved her water bottle from the Tercel's seat, and he climbed in.

She noticed that his knees were at his chin. "You can scoot the seat back with a bar underneath so you'll have more room. My mother usually sits there, and she's almost as short as I am." As she drove toward the exit, she saw Rightman unlocking the white van with "KOAX" painted on the sides. He aimed the camera at them as she sped past.

Bernie pulled onto the street and stopped at the stop sign. She noticed a blue sedan behind her.

"How was the meeting?"

"So far, so good, except for this power failure. Not nearly as hair-raising as what happened at the basketball game. Why are you here?"

"I'm squeezing in a little time with my husband and I have some questions about what happened at Shiprock. I think you know more about the situation than you told Cordova."

She waited for him to respond, but he stayed quiet while she drove to the motel. She pulled into a parking spot in front of the building and turned off the engine. The blue car that had been following them drove past the motel. Maybe it was nothing. The explosion at Shiprock had set her nerves on edge. Palmer took off his seat belt. "The FBI guy asked me a million questions, and I'm sure he told you what I said. I haven't had any great insights since then. Why does it matter to you anyway?"

"They identified the person who died in the explosion, a man from Shiprock with no links to domestic terrorism or, as far as I can tell, to the mediation. I had to give his grandmother the news. She said the young man never mentioned you, but I think she was lying about that."

"No one told me the body had been identified. Who was it? Maybe someone I dealt with as a lawyer."

She hated to say the name of the dead, but she had to. "Richard Horseman."

Palmer slumped back in the seat as if someone had punched him in the gut. "Ricky? Oh no. No. Are you sure?" He pursed his lips and blew out a long exhalation. "Dead? I loved him like a son. We hadn't seen each other since I got divorced and started working too hard. But I never forgot him. I should have—"

He buried his face in his hands. The chill of grief hung in the air. Bernie waited.

After a few minutes, Palmer said, "Let's go for a ride. I've been inside all day with Chee staring at me."

"Chee's just doing his job."

Palmer said, "Yeah, he thinks everyone is out to get me. But I'm alive. Ricky is gone. Why him?"

"That's what I want to talk you to about."

Palmer clicked his seat belt back on. "It's not that far to the Grand Canyon. We could make it to the first overlook while we still have some daylight. We can talk in the car."

"I don't think so. Someone wanted to blow you up. Chee asked me to keep you safe."

"If Chee were here, I'd ask him to take me. You don't want me to hitchhike. Who knows who might pick me up? Another bomber. Come on, Manuelito. It's been a tough day. Play nice. A little fresh air, the world's best view. You might find some inspiration there, too." Palmer sighed. "I need some time, some space to process all this. It's depressing to think of being back in that little motel room. The canyon is why we're all here, you know? The mediation isn't just theoretical. Something real and, well, precious is at stake. Maybe Rick's death did have something to do with the meeting."

She heard a vulnerability in Palmer's voice she hadn't noticed before.

He said, "If we leave now, we can catch the sunset from the deck at the Watchtower. I'm sure you've got your gun in case you need it."

She restarted the engine. "OK. I'll call Chee and tell him the plan."

"Does he know about my nephew?"

"He knows the name of the victim, but not the link to you."

Bernie dialed Chee's number and heard it go straight to voice mail. "Palmer and I are taking a road trip out to the canyon. Catch you later."

Bernie drove southwest on US 160, the highway also known as the Navajo Trail. She and Palmer sat in silence. She cruised past the small assortment of buildings that comprised the outskirts of Tuba City and on southwest into the open country. The sky was a moving collage of white and gray against deep blue, the upper atmospheric winds creating a dynamic pattern. Bernie felt her tension begin to disappear. She loved to drive, especially when the scenery took her breath away.

They passed a homemade sign on the side of the road that announced "Dinosaur Tracks."

Palmer said, "Dinosaur tracks?"

"The Navajo Nation is full of surprises. This area is called Moenave."

"Have you been out there?"

"When I was in high school."

"Are they real?"

"They looked real to me. Dinosaurs used this area as a highway about two hundred million years ago. They say several different kinds of them walked in the mud on their way somewhere and back again. The guys who live around here take you on a little tour. They even show you what they say are dinosaur droppings."

"Droppings? I get an image of littering. You know . . . dinosaurs leaving water bottles, gum wrappers, cigarette butts."

Bernie laughed. "Not quite. It's prehistoric poop. Coprolite."

"Do you know the Diné word for dinosaur?" he asked. "I can't remember it."

"I've heard *na'asho'iiłbahitso*. Giant lizard. That's not a word I use very often." She glanced in her rearview mirror and saw the car she had noticed before behind them again. The driver kept a respectable distance behind her Toyota, but he or she failed at being inconspicuous.

She turned right onto the road indicated by the dinosaur sign. The sedan continued on. After a few hundred yards, out of sight of the highway, she pulled into the improvised dirt parking lot across from a row of small open-air booths where families in the area sold dinosaur tours, jewelry, and souvenirs.

Perhaps because of the cold and the wind, only two of the booths had merchandise. A woman sat in one and a man in the other, both huddled as far out of the wind as they could manage, bundled in coats and hats. The woman had a blanket wrapped around her, too.

Palmer looked out the window. "Where are the tracks?"

"Oh, past the sales booths. The hike to see them takes about half an hour, depending on how much information the guide shares."

"It makes me cold just looking at those people over there. I can pass on seeing the tracks for now. Let's head on to the canyon."

She drove back to the main highway, noticing that the blue sedan had parked at the dinosaur track entrance. She could see a young Navajo man behind the steering wheel. She didn't spot a passenger. She continued beyond the junction for the one-runway Tuba City Airport to the intersection with US 89. Bernie turned south toward Cameron, and the blue sedan followed.

It had been a few years since she had been on this stretch of highway, but she remembered how she loved it. The hills looked like softly sculpted mounds in the afternoon light. The bands of ashy gray, warm tan, striking white, and a touch of iron red marked the northern end of what photographers and geologists called the Painted Desert. The landscape, barren of vegetation but rich in color, reminded her of the hues used in weavings from the Two Grey Hills area, Mama's home territory. The erosion had created a web of shallow crevasses from top to bottom. Navajoland had to be the most beautiful country anywhere, she thought, stretching from the blue mountains of Colorado to this fine desert and beyond.

Palmer intruded on her day dream. "I still can't wrap my brain around the news about my nephew getting killed."

Bernie said, "Do you know why?"

"No idea. We hadn't spoken in years. He was the son of my sister-in-law, who drank herself to death after her other son died as a little guy, from what we think was abuse by one of her boyfriends. No one could prove it."

Traffic picked up on US 89, the route from Page and the cold blue water of Lake Powell to the Grand Canyon. Even in November, Grand Canyon National Park drew visitors from all over the planet, and US 89 led most efficiently to Desert View Drive, the paved road that accessed the rim of the canyon, and Technicolor views. She noticed that the blue sedan stayed behind them. She felt her instinct for danger crank up.

Palmer said, "Have you ever been in the gallery at the Cameron Trading Post? I'm talking about the one in that other building, not the big gift shop."

"Yes. They have amazing things. Prizewinners from a lot of the big Indian shows. Someone told me she saw an old rug my mother made in there. I'd like to see it. Thanks for reminding me."

A few minutes later, she turned into the parking lot outside Cameron Trading Post, noticing that the car did the same.

Palmer looked up from his phone screen. "Good thing we're stopping. I could use something to eat. My blood sugar is low. Diabetes." He started to take off his seat belt.

"Hold on. That blue sedan has been on our tail ever since we left the mediation. I wanted to see if it would keep following us, and unfortunately, it did. The driver parked over there."

Palmer glanced out the rear window. "You realize this is the logical stopping point between Tuba City and the Grand Canyon." She noticed him studying the vehicle. "But I remember seeing the car outside the hotel when Katie brought my things and took me to the meeting. And another time, too, at the Justice Center."

If she had been in her unit, Bernie would have called Sandra and asked her to run a quick plate check so she'd have a better idea of what she was dealing with. In lieu of that, she resorted to plan B. "I'm going to go up there and talk to him."

"You know the whole thing is about me." Palmer grimaced "I'll go with you."

"No. Stay here and lock the doors."

"Are you sure?"

She gave Palmer her fiercest look, then dialed Chee's number and hung up when it went to voice mail. "Keep trying to reach Chee. Tell him where we are and about the car and that I'll call him as soon as I know something."

She touched the holster on her hip and opened the car door.

"Are you sure that—"

She cut him off. "Stay here and call Chee."

She pulled her shoulders back, stood straight, walked to the sedan, and tapped on the driver's window with her left hand, her right on the gun. A young man lowered the window. She showed him her badge. "I'm the driver of that Toyota you've been tailing."

"Oh my God." He slunk back against the car seat. "I didn't know you were a cop."

"Why were you following me?"

"It wasn't you, I swear. I needed to talk to Palmer, and he kept blowing me off. I have to tell him something he ought to know for the mediation. There's some bad dudes out there and I heard—"

"Do you have a weapon?"

"No. No, ma'am. You wanna see my license or something?"

"Definitely."

Like the plates on his car, his license was from Arizona. She handed it back to him. "Come inside with me and we'll talk where it's warmer."

When the young man climbed out of the car, she could see that he was small and lean. He zipped up a blue sweatshirt against the cold.

She motioned to Palmer to join them.

14

The restaurant occupied the back of the trading post, past racks of T-shirts with Kokopelli and petroglyph designs, Navajo- and Hopi-style necklaces made overseas, and vintage glass display cases with the real stuff. The Cameron Post, one of the few on the reservation that had once been run by a Navajo, featured supplies attractive to area residents as well as a wide spectrum of Grand Canyon souvenirs for travelers. The Navajo weaver who frequently demonstrated her craft as part of the post's attractions had already left for home.

Bernie asked for a table for three near the windows facing the Little Colorado. The young man, looking sheepish, followed her and the hostess quietly to their seats. The ambience—the pressed tin ceiling and the huge rugs on the walls reflecting the variety of designs created on the Navajo Nation—gave the restaurant a feeling of times past. Undoubtedly many secrets had been shared here. Appropriate, she thought. A good place to figure out what was going on with this inept stalker.

The hostess offered them menus. After she left, Bernie said, "Mr. Palmer will be here in a minute. Anything you want to tell me before he shows up?"

"Are you really a cop?"

"Officer Bernadette Manuelito from Shiprock."

"No kidding? I thought you were his girlfriend."

"What's your name?"

"Rocket."

"Rocket? No, your real name. Just show me your ID."

He looked straight ahead, then said, "Um, it's Robert."

She glared at him.

"Robert Palmer. I left my wallet in the car, but I can get it if you want."

"Palmer, the same as Aza?"

"Yeah, Palmer like Aza, Arnold, Robert. Lots of us Palmers." He opened the menu. "Are you buying?"

"Are you cooperating?"

He shrugged. "You sure are tough for such a short babe."

Bernie couldn't help but laugh. "You sure are tough for such a short guy."

Robert smiled for the first time. "We gotta be, don't we? We should let the lawyer buy. He has the money."

"Are you related to Aza?"

Robert put down the menu. "We go way, way back, all the way back to his time in Shiprock. Back before he got to be a hotshot."

He stopped talking as Aza approached the table and pulled out a chair. He sat between the young man and Bernie, his only option. Aza picked up the menu and studied it as though he'd never seen one before. Robert stared at the tabletop.

"Enough, you two. Tell me what's going on here." She turned to Robert. "You can start."

But Aza spoke. "I told him back at the meeting I had nothing to say to him. Why don't you just leave me alone?"

"Like you left me and Mom alone, huh?"

"You don't know the half of it. You're so full of judgments and anger, and now you've got the police involved in our private—"

"Wait a minute," Bernie said. "I invited him in. I don't like being followed, and he said he wanted to talk about a plan to disrupt the mediation. I thought we both should hear him out. I didn't realize he was your son."

The conversation paused while the waitress took orders, a Coke for her, a burger for Robert, and a hot beef sandwich for the mediator. The break seemed to have calmed Robert, Bernie noticed, but Aza sat with clenched jaw.

Bernie said, "After the bomb in Shiprock, the Navajo Nation is keeping an eye on Mr. Palmer for his own protection. Robert, acting like a stalker is never cool, but with the mediation and all the security, it could get you arrested."

"Dear old Dad would probably like that."

"I wouldn't like it. You don't know a thing about me. That's my fault, I guess."

"You think?"

Bernie said, "Be kind to each other, you two."

Her comment hung over the table as the waitress gave Bernie a Coke, brought tea for Robert, refilled the water glasses, and left.

"Kind?" Robert leaned back in his chair. "OK. Nice way to blow me off back at the meeting."

"I've reached out to you more times than I can count, and you've ignored me. When you approached me at the session break? That wasn't the place or the time for a father-son conversation. I take my work seriously. Not that you'd know anything about work. If it wasn't for your mom's boyfriend hiring you—"

Robert didn't wait for Aza to finish. "How do you know that? Anyway, I'm not after a relationship with you, dude. I just needed to tell you something and you wouldn't give me a chance, so I tried to talk to you at the hotel, but you took one look and had her, the officer, drive away. Like you're scared of me or something."

"I needed to go for a drive after hearing some bad news. It had nothing to do with you."

The food arrived. Palmer sprinkled pepper on the gravy that covered his roast beef sandwich. "What happened to your glasses?"

"I got my eyes fixed."

"How's your mother?"

"Ask her yourself."

"I'm trying to have a conversation with you, and Lona is one of the things I know we have in common. I'd appreciate it if you'd give me a chance. I know I made some mistakes. Maybe you did, too."

"Mom and her boyfriend just split. Whenever they would fight, she'd compare him to you, and he got tired of it. I guess I liked him better than she did. He's the one who paid for my eye surgery."

Aza continued eating.

Bernie said, "Robert, what do you know about plans to disrupt the meeting?"

Robert swallowed, stared down at his hands. "Let's get this over with. I heard that some of those white-guy protest groups plan to raise hell. The outdoor recreation people, the tour directors, I can't even keep track of them all. They're just interested in their own causes, not the canyon itself. They want to delay the meeting as long as possible. Some of those groups have a lot of money at stake in keeping things the same. They look like the good guys, speaking up for nature and all, but they aren't as bighearted as they want people to believe."

Robert looked up at Palmer from his uneaten burger. "I'm telling you this because you're the main honcho. You run the show. You ought to know what's going on behind the scenes. It's not all peace and joy out here, and some of these guys are bad actors. That's it."

"If I'd known why you wanted to talk to me, I would have been more sympathetic." Aza put his silverware down on his nearly empty plate. "I couldn't deal with any family drama this week because I had to stay focused on the task at hand."

"You're supposed to be the big problem solver, but the way I see it, you just make problems." Robert stood. "That's what I needed to say."

Bernie put her hand on his arm. "Sit down. Tell me more about the plans to disrupt the sessions. Do you have any specifics?"

"I know a guy who got offered a big job working for Canyon-mark, you know, the development group? He said Canyonmark will be hiring a bunch of people if the development gets going. So I mentioned this to someone I met because he looked kinda scruffy, you know, like he could use some work."

Robert took a gulp of his tea. "This guy got all steamed up and started telling me how bad Canyonmark is and that a group he worked for would pay me to act as a sort of spy to help find out what Canyonmark planned before the mediation started so they could raise some hell. It sounded like a cool job—"

Aza put his water glass. "What happened to your judgment to get involved in something like this? What kind of a moron . . ."

Bernie glared at Aza and he stopped talking.

Robert's voice tightened with anger. "You didn't let me finish, Daddy. It sounded like a cool job, but the more I thought about it, the creepier it seemed. I said no."

She could see some resemblance to Aza in the young man, especially in the shape of his nose and the swoop of his eyebrows. "Robert, who was the guy and who did he work for?"

"He just told me to call him Mr. X and he didn't tell me what group it was."

Bernie waited a moment and Robert said, "He had a black beard. Kinda stocky with a suntan."

"Did you hear him or anyone talk about putting a bomb in your dad's car?"

"No."

"I was there right after the bomb went off." She could still smell the burning vehicle, the seared flesh. "It wasn't a joke. People who went to see a basketball game ended up scared. Kids were there and they might have nightmares about this. Besides the man who died, a lot of people had their cars, trucks damaged. People like you."

Aza said, "I just found out a few minutes ago that Rick Horseman died from that explosion. That's why I asked Bernie to take me for a drive."

"Rick? No way! I didn't . . . It's on me." He leaned toward Aza. "But he's dead because of you. This is all screwed up."

Bernie said, "If you know anything that can help, you need to tell me so I can tell the investigators."

"I don't have anything to tell you. I don't know anything about what happened in Shiprock. I've got to go."

"Not yet." Bernie placed her pen and notebook on the table in front of him and opened the book to a blank page. "Give me your phone number and where you're staying."

"That doesn't matter now." But he scrawled something and handed it back to her.

She motioned toward the waitress.

"Would you bring us a box for his food?" She gestured at the untouched meal. Robert said, "I'm not hungry anymore."

After Robert left, Aza Palmer pushed his plate away. "Now you know my family secret. Successful lawyer becomes failed husband, miserable father, and creates hostile son."

Bernie put the burger, the fries, and the little packets of mustard and ketchup in the to-go container. "Before you came in here, did you contact Chee?"

"I told him where we were and that you'd gone inside with my son, who had been following us. He wants you to call him."

"You were gone a long time." She knew Chee wasn't much of a talker.

"Was I?"

She heard him hesitate and wondered if he'd tell the truth.

"Well, I had to check my blood sugar and give myself an injection."

Bernie paid the bill, declining Palmer's offer to chip in for his sandwich. She noticed the five-dollar bill he left on the table in addition to her tip.

THE WESTERN SKY HAD a soft apricot glow, the beginnings of sunset, when they stepped outside and got in the car. She drove past the tour buses and over the bridge that spanned the Little Colorado. "It would be dark before we got to the canyon, so I'm heading back to the hotel."

"I figured." Palmer stretched his legs. "I remembered where else I've seen Robert's car. He was the one who was waiting for Katie and me after the explosion. I didn't recognize him in the dark." Palmer told Bernie the story.

They continued in silence, Bernie appreciating the light traffic. Then she said. "Can you explain what the mediation is really about? Maybe it will help me understand why someone seems to want you dead."

"Do you mind if I condense it and give you the CliffsNotes version. Do they still have CliffsNotes?"

"*Mediation for Dummies* will work. But before that, tell me the real reason you didn't come right in from the parking lot."

Palmer shifted in his seat. "I recognized Robert as soon as I saw him and I didn't want another argument. I didn't want to talk to him, period. I'd had enough conflict for the day. Satisfied?"

"Yes. Thanks."

His tone changed. "OK, here's Grand Canyon Mediation 101. So, the first thing to know is the background of the dispute, and to talk about that, we have to talk a little about the canyon's history."

A traditional storyteller would have started with the forces that created the ancient Vishnu Schist and Zoroaster Granite. Palmer began with the early mining expeditions, the creation of the national park, and the Fred Harvey Company's expansion of tourism. He mentioned the controversy over sightseeing helicopter flights and the idea of building a tramway from the canyon rim to the river. He summarized the Hualapai's Skywalk and its financial problems and pending plans for growth in Page and Tusayan. He explained Canyonmark's proposal to work with the Navajo Nation to develop a resort at the eastern edge of the canyon on tribal land near the confluence of the Colorado and the Little Colorado. He condensed the findings of the environmental impact studies and talked on.

Bernie knew about the shifting viewpoints and differences of opinion about Grand Canyon development among Navajo tribal councilors, presidents, and those families closest to where a resort might be constructed. But she adjusted the heater vents and let Palmer speak.

"So, why the mediation now?"

"Canyonmark's offer got the tribe's attention. Jobs earmarked for the Diné, a percentage of revenue besides money from the land lease, and other benefits. Everyone knows the issue is deep and complicated—like the canyon itself. The Navajo want to hear from all sides before making even a preliminary decision. They want the full picture before deciding how to proceed or if they should. I think that's smart."

"What do you do as mediator?"

Palmer glanced at her. "That's right, you missed the intro at the session when I explained that. I'm like a referee. My job is to make sure that everyone at the table has a chance to be heard and that disagreements remain respectful and opinions don't get presented as fact. I try to keep the discussion on track."

Bernie passed a minivan. Palmer kept talking.

"I expect the sessions will ignite some long-standing animosity between some of these groups, including Natives and the different environmental factions. The federal departments and state of Arizona agencies involved in regulations at the Grand Canyon all have their own priorities. And the private enterprises that make a living from the canyon's visitors—raft trip and scenic flight operators, hotels and restaurants, gift shops—they have varied reactions to any new development. Everyone involved is asked to see into the future. That's tough."

He fell silent and she thought about what he'd said. If all these folks had agreed to discuss the Grand Canyon's future, why would one of them want to kill the mediator? But what about those who had been excluded?

"What does this have to do with your nephew's death?"

"Nothing I can think of."

The landscape looked totally different in the fading light, approached from the opposite direction. She savored its raw beauty all the more because of the humans she encountered behaving badly.

"Amazing country, isn't it?"

Palmer said, "What? Sorry, I was checking my phone messages."

She turned into the motel parking lot.

"It's none of my business, but I think Robert would like to make peace with you."

"You're right. It's none of your business." Palmer opened the car door.

"Wait a minute. I'll walk in with you." Bernie reached behind the seat for her backpack and the box with the burger.

"Don't worry. I'm not going anywhere except to my room."

Bernie grabbed her belongings and locked the car. By the time she reached the lobby, Palmer had disappeared.

She found the room that Chee had been assigned with no trouble, but Chee wasn't there. She washed her hands, turned up the thermostat, slipped off her shoes. She noticed a text from Darleen: *CS & me coming to GC maybe? Stay w u?* She texted back: *Call me.*

She checked for a message from Leaphorn and found nothing.

Disappointed, she stretched out on the bed with the book she always kept in her backpack. But her attention kept drifting back to Palmer and Robert.

What had happened to make that young man so angry? In some divorces, one parent's bitterness toward the former partner infected the children. But Lona seemed to like Palmer. Robert had complained about being neglected, but most children, even if their parents aren't divorced, would like more time with their moms and dads. As she started to read, she noticed her body melting into the bed, the softness folding around her like a cocoon of warmth and peace. She put the book down and closed her eyes.

15

After Bernie left with Palmer, Chee helped Silversmith deal with the chaos in the parking lot. He knew the federal agents were in the mix somewhere, making videos and keeping an eye on things. Meanwhile, the consultants and experts explored the guts of the Justice Center, helping the electrician determine what had created the power outage.

The protesters calmed down after the last delegates came through the gauntlet, packed up, and headed off. No doubt, Chee thought, to prepare for tomorrow's demonstrations. Before he left, Captain Ward informed them that vandalism caused the blackout. Foul play, but not a bomb.

He climbed into his unit and, when he reached for his seat belt, felt the envelope Mrs. Nez had given him. Palmer had explained that all the delegates had rooms at the Hotel Hopi. Chee figured he'd drop it off, then head back to his own room and, he hoped, get there around the time Bernie and Palmer arrived.

But, as often happened in Jim Chee's life, things didn't go exactly as planned.

The Hotel Hopi was beautiful, no doubt about it. From the

outside, it looked something like a pueblo village. Light from the interior filtered out to the street through the glass doors at the entrance and the huge circular window on the second story.

In the lobby, three or four times the size of the trailer where he and Bernie lived, his attention focused on the fire blazing in a fireplace built from stone, careful work that reminded him of the artisans at Chaco Canyon. The flames cast a glow onto the plush couches arranged in a semicircle. Chee noticed the pottery bowls, the elegantly carved katsinas, and the selection of oil and water-color paintings in the classic Hopi style. He walked past the gift shop and a large room with tables, probably for breakfast.

At the registration area, a Hopi man about Chee's age stood behind a graceful swooping counter. He glanced up as Chee approached.

Chee rested his forearms on the desktop. "Hello there. I need to see one of your guests, a Mr. Blankenship. Can you tell me how to find his room?"

"Do you have his room number?"

"No."

"Well, I can't release that information. Hotel policy." The clerk turned back to whatever he was doing, or pretending to be doing, on his computer.

"Would you call and tell him I'm here?"

"You can tell him."

The man sauntered to the end of the counter, picked up a phone, pushed in four digits, and handed it to Chee.

As he listened to the rings, Chee wondered if the clerk's attitude was because he was Navajo and the clerk was Hopi, or because the man had a grudge against the police. Or maybe because he hated life in general.

After six rings, a mechanical voice informed him that the guest he was trying to reach was unavailable. Chee left a brief message with his phone number. He rethought his idea of leaving the envelope for Blankenship at the front desk. He knew the room number from watching the clerk dial and could call it directly next time, or just knock on the door.

Back at the motel, he was pleased to see Bernie's car in the lot and happier still to see her in their room. But Palmer was there, too, sitting in the chair at the desk. He could tell that something was off.

"Hey," Chee said. "So this is why you threatened to fire me. So Bernie could be your bodyguard."

Palmer laughed, an embarrassed chuckle. "I lost my head back there. I didn't mean to snap at you. You were just doing your job. I appreciate your work even though I think I'd be fine without you." He cleared his throat. "It's been a strange day. Bernie can tell you about my stalker."

"The incident you called about, right?"

Bernie nodded. "The man turned out to be his son. I bought them dinner and they had a little talk."

"My kid is a jerk but harmless. But when I got back to my hotel room, the light on the house phone was blinking, you know, indicating that there was a message. Nobody uses those phones, but I picked up the receiver to check and heard something odd." Palmer swallowed. "The caller said my name, waited, and then hung up."

Chee said, "Yeah. Odd. Maybe he was going to leave a message and changed his mind. Or forgot what he was going to say."

"That's what Bernie thinks. But no one except you knows what room I'm in. That's why I registered as Harris."

"Did you recognize the voice?"

"I'm not sure."

"Who do you think it could be?"

Palmer shook his head. "It's a voice I've heard before, but I can't place it. Low, gravely, like an announcer at some sports events. I saved the message."

"Did he sound threatening?"

"Not exactly, but letting me know he knows how to find me seems scary. Or maybe I'm overreacting."

Bernie stood. "I suggested that we switch rooms. He takes this one, and you and I move to his."

Chee said, "So tell me again about the phone call. What else?"

Palmer stood. "Wait a minute. Everyone knows about the mediation and a lot of people know what I look like. There are only two hotels here. If I'm not in one, well?"

"But what about checking in as Harris?"

"That's why it spooked me, I guess. I'm sorry to have imposed on you."

Chee said, "It's my job to make sure you can do your job, but that call doesn't give me much to go on. And just to be clear, you can't fire me because I don't work for you. I work for the Navajo Police."

"Understood." Chee walked with him to watch as Palmer safely entered his own room. "All clear in there?"

"Everything's fine."

Bernie opened the door to their room before he could slide his card in the slot. Chee sat on the bed and started to take off his boots. She sat next to him. "It sounds like you and Palmer got into it."

"I hate being a bodyguard. He ditched me during a break at the mediation, and when I mentioned that he couldn't do that, he said he'd like to fire me. Tell me about Palmer's son."

"He'd never survive as a stalker, too obvious. At Cameron, they were rude to each other and angry. Robert told Palmer some of the delegates have ulterior motives. Palmer knew that already, of course. I think Robert wanted his dad to reach out to him, apologize for things that happened a long time ago. Palmer didn't buy it."

Chee said, "Speaking of relatives, your sister called after you drove out of the Justice Center parking lot."

"Really?"

"She said she and a friend plan to come to Tuba City to check out the session and then go to the Grand Canyon. They might be here tomorrow."

"Unless she changes her mind."

"Right. That's happened."

"Did she say which friend? She left me a phone message, but . . ."

"A guy with a strange name. CSI? Wait. It was CS without the I. CS? Country Sizzler? "

"What did she say about him? Are you going to give me any more information on the dude?"

"Oh, so you haven't met him yet." Chee sat a little straighter. "Well, I might tell you what I know. Or maybe not. It depends on how well you can bribe me."

He reached for her, and she felt good in his arms, warm, strong, and soft in the places where soft matters. He loved the texture and the smell of her long silky hair, the way her kiss made him forget everything except wanting to kiss her again.

Then, at a most inconvenient time, he heard a chime. Not his phone. Not Bernie's. The interruption was coming from the desk, electronic music based on a Native flute melody. Reluctantly, he left his lovely wife and picked up Palmer's forgotten phone.

"Hello?"

"Who's this?" The voice on the phone sounded young, male, and irate.

"You called this number. Who am I talking to?"

"Robert. Is Mr. Palmer there?"

"No, but I can give him a message."

"Why do you have his phone?"

Chee repeated himself. "Can I give Mr. Palmer a message for you?"

"Is he paranoid or something?" Robert didn't wait for an answer. "Tell him to call me. He's got the number."

"Will he know which Robert?"

"His son. Tell him it's urgent." The phone went silent.

Chee walked back to the bed. "Robert said it was urgent for Palmer to call. You met the guy. Do you think urgent could wait?"

She sighed. "Call Palmer on the room phone and let him know Robert called and that his cell is here."

He punched Palmer's extension into the old telephone console on the desk. It rang a few times and then went to a generic message. He hung up. "Did I tell Palmer to ignore the phone?"

"Not at all. You told him not to be paranoid, but in a nice way."

Chee looked at her and picked up Palmer's cell phone. "Remember where we were. I'll be right back."

He went across the hall and knocked on Palmer's door. No answer.

He knocked again. "It's Chee."

Then he came back to Bernie.

"That was quick."

" He didn't answer. I have a key to his room."

She got up out of bed. "Give me a minute. I'm coming with you."

"What if he's in the shower or something?"

"I'll wait in the hall. This doesn't seem right."

This time, she did the knocking. "Palmer. Palmer? It's Bernie. You in there?"

Chee slid the plastic key card into the slot. A small green light flashed, and he pushed the door open.

16

The room resembled the one she'd just left except that the photo over the bed showed a different view of the Grand Canyon. The door to the bathroom hung open, and even with the light off they could see that it was empty. Palmer's black bag sat on the bed, the laptop on the desk.

"Did I tell you what happened at the mediation?"

"Sort of. I noticed that you looked grumpy in there."

"When Palmer gave me the slip, I reminded him that whoever had blown up his car was still on the loose. He accused me of over-reacting and whined about how he deserved his privacy." Chee clenched his jaw. "But I still have to babysit the man. To make it worse, I have to guard him even after the session, at a reception tomorrow. You know how I hate that kind of thing."

"I know."

"You can come. There's a buffet involved. Keep me company."

"I'm the one person who dreads that social stuff even more than you do."

"Please?"

"Let me think about it." Then she noticed the blinking light on the room phone perched on Palmer's nightstand. She picked up the receiver and followed the recorded instructions for message retrieval. One new, one saved. She put the phone on speaker and played the fresh one.

A male voice: "Aza Palmer. Now that I have your attention, are you ready to do the right thing? Time is running out. You know how to reach me."

Chee said, "Did that sound like a threat to you?"

"Yes."

She pushed the button again. The saved message had the same voice saying only "Aza Palmer."

"I guess he was lying about not knowing the man who made that phone call."

"I have to find him."

"I'll come with you," Bernie said. "Something about that voice sounds familiar."

Chee raised an eyebrow. "Really? That's interesting."

"I can't place it, but it will come to me."

They headed down the hall.

Bernie said, "I'll get my backpack and my weapon. Let me use Palmer's phone to call Robert. Maybe he knows something."

"I'll check around and meet you at the unit."

Chee learned that the desk clerk had been in the back, focused on the day's report, and hadn't noticed a tall man in a white shirt and Pendleton jacket leave the building. He scanned the hotel parking lot, hoping to find Palmer smoking a cigarette. No Palmer, but he noticed the Volkswagen of Protest was back. This time, Bebe Durango had parked near the entrance, farther from the building. If his dog barked, maybe no one would complain. Bebe was standing at the open side door.

"Officer?"

He wanted to ignore him, but maybe he'd seen Palmer. "Sir?"

"Come over here a minute."

Durango disappeared up the step and inside the vehicle, leaving the door ajar. Chee saw a table stacked with newspapers. The inside of the old camper was neat and well organized. He climbed the steps, noticing that the dog hadn't barked. He wondered why, and what the old man wanted.

"I need to thank you and the other cops, especially the lady, for trying to keep things calm out there. I forgot to take my medicine this morning, and when that happens, I get riled up. I'm glad nobody arrested me, you know, took me to the slammer."

Chee smiled. He had never heard anyone say that. "No need to thank us. We were doing our jobs. Have you seen Mr. Palmer out here recently, smoking or something?"

"I might have." Bebe stroked his chin with the knuckle of his index finger. "There was a tall man in a colorful jacket over by the building. A pickup came and he climbed in. I couldn't say for sure it was him, or what he was smoking."

"What color was the truck?"

"It was a light one. White, maybe, or gray. I don't know if it was a Chevy or a Ford or a whatever."

"Thanks." It could have been Katie, he thought and flashed back to earlier in the day when the mediator arrived in a truck. He remembered silver.

Bebe said, "What time and where is the meeting tomorrow?"

"As far as I know, the session will start back at the Justice Center at nine." Chee turned to leave. "I'm glad your dog calmed down."

"Oh, I'm sure that stinker is barking his head off somewhere. My friend Bruce took him so he won't have to spend the day in the camper while I'm out working to save the planet."

Chee drove his unit to the entrance, arriving as Bernie left the hotel. She'd brought his jacket from their room, he noticed with relief, and was wearing hers. The backpack was on her shoulder.

"The man in the VW says a guy in a colorful coat left with someone in a truck a few minutes ago."

"Well, that narrows it down to about half the vehicles in the county. I'll call Robert while you drive." Bernie retrieved the phone from her pack and turned it on. "Darn. Password protected. Any ideas? I need four of something. Numbers, letters, symbols, combinations."

"What about the year he was born?" Chee said.

Bernie made a few estimates. None of them worked.

"Try 2–4–6–8 or 1–3–5–7. Something easy, you know."

"I've got an idea." Bernie fiddled with the phone. "I'm in."

"What did you use?"

"S-C-23."

"My wife, the genius. Why that combination?"

"I remembered his jersey number. You know what they say: 'Once a Chieftain, always a Chieftain.' I put in the S for Shiprock."

"You remembered it from high school?"

"Not really. He had the same number at the alumni game. What now?"

Palmer's most recent missed call had a 480 area code—that wasn't Shiprock, or even New Mexico. Maybe Phoenix. She dialed and switched to speaker.

"About time you called me."

"Robert, this is Officer Manuelito. Do you know where Mr. Palmer is?"

The line was silent for a moment. "No friggin' idea. You told me you were keeping track of him."

She waited for him to say something else. "I called because I wanted to talk to him about my mom, get it? That's all. It was something personal, not police business. If you find him, tell him to call me. And give him his phone back."

He hung up.

Chee said, "If Bebe is correct, it sounds like our man left willingly. Maybe he arranged for the truck to pick him up. Maybe the man on the phone came for him. Did you remember where you heard that voice on his message machine?"

"No. Not yet anyway."

"So, let's look for a white pickup while we figure this out."

"What's Palmer's clan sister Katie's cousin's last name?"

Chee paused. "I don't know. She sped away after she dropped him off this morning, and he said he'd introduce me later."

"I'll check his recent calls."

Chee cruised the streets near the hotel while Bernie searched the phone.

"No Katies. He must sort by last name. "Here's an Austin with a 505 prefix from yesterday. Think that's her?"

"It sounds like a name for a rich guy from New York."

"I'll try it anyway." She dialed with the phone on speaker.

Bernie heard the phone ringing four times, then the message: "You've reached the service department at Premiere BMW. Mr. Austin and his staff can't take your call, but we love your business. Please leave a message and . . ." She hit the end call button.

Bernie found three more recent calls, last names only. She called all three. Two were answered by men who didn't know Palmer or Katie. The third was a generic electronic voice. Since women sometimes use that feature for security, Bernie left a message with her cell number.

"That didn't work very well."

He squeezed her hand. "If Palmer is with Katie, he's probably safe. If the man we heard on the phone picked him up and took him out somewhere to blow him up, he's in serious trouble. If he'd only . . ."

Bernie said, "If he had his phone, we could just call him. I wouldn't be surprised if he left it behind on purpose. Do you think you should tell Largo or Captain Ward or the feds about this?"

Chee shook his head. "Let's keep looking."

They drove for a while with no luck, and then Chee stopped in front of the Hotel Hopi. "I remembered that I need to drop off something."

"What?"

"It's an envelope for one of the delegates."

"I'll go in with you," she said. "Maybe I'll get an idea while I'm waiting."

Bernie settled into a chair in the lobby.

Chee noticed that the man he'd spoken to earlier was still behind the desk. The clerk glared at him but dialed a number. The phone rang three times and then a voice said, "Blankenship."

"It's Sergeant Chee. I've got something for you."

"What is it?"

"An envelope that a person who came to today's meeting wanted me to give to you."

The voice on the phone said, "I can't come to the lobby now. Can you leave it at the desk?"

"No, sir."

"Why not?"

Chee turned his back to evade the desk clerk's obvious eavesdropping and lowered his voice. "I'll walk it over to you. No problem."

"Who's it from?"

Chee took a breath to reduce his growing impatience. "An elderly Navajo woman named Mrs. Nez. She said her grandson left it for you. She drove three hours to get to Tuba City."

"I don't know any old Indian ladies with grandsons. Bring it to the session tomorrow, and I'll pick it up. Have a good evening."

"THAT WAS TOO QUICK," Bernie said. She saw the frustration on his face.

"The guy was there, but he asked me to bring the envelope to the session tomorrow."

"How did you get involved as an errand boy for this grandmother? I know, you just can't say no to an old lady."

Chee smiled. "Actually, it's your fault. This lady had one of your cards. She gave it to Dashee, and he forwarded the job to me."

"That's interesting. What's her name?"

"Mrs. Nez."

Navajoland had hundreds of women named Nez. "What did she look like?"

Chee described her.

"She's the grandmother of the man who was killed. That's why she had my card. I went with Cordova to give her the news."

He pulled the envelope from his pocket and opened it. Without removing them, he showed Bernie three one-hundred-dollar bills.

"Holy smokes. That's a lot of money."

"Mrs. Nez said the envelope was from her grandson. When I asked why he didn't deliver it himself, she wouldn't answer."

Bernie looked at the name on the outside. "Because the grandson is dead. Mrs. Nez never mentioned the money. Where did he get this, and why did he want Blankenship to have it?"

"Call Cordova and tell him about this."

She dialed his number and left a message.

Then they sat, staring at the fire, deep in thought.

"I don't understand why a poor Navajo man would give three hundred dollars to a guy like Blankenship. What do you think?"

Bernie pushed her hair behind her ears. "Cordova asked Mrs. Nez if her grandson had ever been to the Grand Canyon, ever talked about it, and she said no. And today's situation, the way Palmer gave us the slip, doesn't feel right either. Why would Palmer mention a message that obviously upset him, but lie about knowing who it was from?"

Chee moved a little closer to her. "My best guess is that the call was something personal, something embarrassing. My job is to protect him as mediator, but he obviously doesn't believe that carries over to his private life."

"Maybe he didn't recognize the man at first, a voice from the past or something. And then, after the second call, he clicked on who it was."

"And he called whoever it was on the room phone and arranged for the pickup?" Chee glanced up at the muted TV behind Bernie, noticing two newscasters behind a big desk and then a commerical.

"I heard that voice when I worked the bomb scene, but I talked to so many people that night, I can't place it. Palmer grew up in Shiprock." She shrugged her shoulder. "I don't think the threats on Palmer are connected to the mediation at all. I think it's personal. Somebody from his past."

Chee caught the end of a pain-reliever ad and then the resumption of the evening news. "Hey, look what's on TV."

She glanced up.

"That's footage from when the meeting let out." Chee leaned closer. "There's Dashee."

"Look, there you are."

Chee winced. "I look like a skinny teenager."

"I'd call it lean and handsome."

"There's the guy with the sign bashing the black car."

Bernie leaned forward. "One incident of violence and that's what gets on TV."

They watched a few more moments. A man came up and stood next to the big couch, watching, too.

"Just like TV to miss the whole point," he said. "Did they explain what the meeting was about?"

"I don't know," Chee said. "The sound is off."

"They probably didn't," the man said. "Everyone oversimplifies issues like this. That's why the mediation was a good idea. Too bad the guy in charge is in the back pocket of the developer."

Chee said, "Are you sure about that?"

The man tugged at his ear. "I don't trust him." The report on TV switched to something happening in Phoenix. The man walked toward the elevators.

Bernie said, "So what now?"

"I need to find Palmer. Let's do some more driving."

"If we don't spot him, let's go back to the hotel and see if he's returned. If not, we can look in his black bag and in the room for something that might help locate him."

Chee reached in his pocket for the car keys.

17

Aza Palmer looked at the wrinkled face framed by the long gray braids. He'd made a mistake climbing into the old pickup with the dent by the passenger door. He should have told Mr. Duke no. Pressed him to come inside the hotel to talk. But he knew how hardheaded the guy was. Better to just get it done with.

"How long will this take?" Palmer took a drag on his cigarette, feeling the warm smoke in his throat, in his lungs. Exhaling slowly, savoring the sensation.

"As long as you want, once we get there. We don't have very far to go."

The old man cruised like a local, avoiding the potholes as he drove through town and then east on gravel roads. Palmer finished his cigarette and added it to the ashtray, a convenience he didn't find in new vehicles. The one in Duke's truck was half full of filters.

Palmer had been standing outside the hotel, smoking and thinking about poor dead Rick and wondering why Robert had grown so angry. He heard the truck approach, heading toward the entrance overhang. But it passsed the motel's front door and continued straight ahead, to where he stood. He'd felt a surge of adrenaline.

The driver lowered the window. "Are you Mr. Palmer, the leader for the meeting about the Grand Canyon?" The voice was the man on the phone.

"I'm the mediator, if that's what you mean."

"Hello, sir. I'm Denny Duke. I'm a councilor with the San Juan Paiute. You heard of us?"

"Yes, of course. I recognized your voice on the phone. I got your letters and your voice mails."

"I got your answers. I didn't like them much, and that's the truth. I need to show you something."

Palmer told Duke that he was totally occupied with the mediation, asked him to make an appointment.

Duke interrupted. "No, sir, no. I need you to see something tonight. It's connected with the big meeting." His distinctive voice had a low, smooth, rhythmic cadence.

"Tell you what. Go get what you want to show me and bring it into the motel. It's warm in there. We can sit in the lobby."

"No, sir, that won't work. You'll be glad you came with me, but we need to go now."

"I can't do it. I'm out here enjoying a smoke and then I've got to get back to work and later try to catch some sleep. Like I told you on the phone." He kept the nervousness out of this voice. Duke was too aggressive, too persistent.

"Your job as mediator is to be fair, right?"

"Yes, correct."

"Well, you can't be fair until you see this. I promise you, you won't regret it. I'll haul you right back here—I give you my word on that. I'm an old Indian with a bad knee and a beat-up truck. Why are you worried?"

Palmer faked a smile. "Oh, maybe because someone killed my nephew and blew up my car and because whoever did it is still out there."

"I'm sure sorry about that, but it wasn't me. Come on now. We could have already been there in the time you spent jawing. It's warmer in the cab here than out there." The old man grinned, showing what remained of his front teeth.

"Just let me finish my smoke."

"You can smoke in the truck. Mother does it all the time."

The decision was made to exclude Duke's band of Paiutes from a seat at the table for several reasons, the most obvious of which was the band's small population—fewer than five hundred tribal members. The mediator had invited them to submit their views in writing and to sit in the audience. He hadn't noticed Duke in the crowd today, but he could have overlooked him with everything else going on.

Palmer said, "You know, a Navajo cop got assigned to be my bodyguard. He'll give me grief if I don't ask him to ride along."

"Nope. This has to be just between us. Come on, brother. You won't regret it."

Chee got on his nerves and this old man seemed harmless. Interesting, even. In the research he'd done to prepare himself for the mediation, Palmer had learned a bit about the San Juan Paiutes. He'd found nothing about a cultural inclination toward kidnapping or murder. So he walked to the passenger side, pulled the heavy door open, and climbed in.

He noticed the rifle on the rack behind him. Even though almost every pickup in Indian Country had a weapon on a rack, he felt his stomach tighten.

Duke cruised through Tuba City and out past the town's lights and pavement without conversation.

Palmer knew that this branch of Paiutes had a 5,400-acre reservation, an island inside the boundaries of Navajo Nation. The name of the band came from the San Juan River, which bordered their territory and which they, like the Diné, held sacred. The band had a distinct language, although some tribal members also spoke Navajo, Hopi, and English. They were known for their baskets;

many of the wedding baskets used in the traditional Diné marriage ceremony were created by San Juan Paiutes.

Palmer glanced out the truck's windows into the black night. "Are we going to your house?"

"No, sir, we're driving to my mother's place. She's the one who can tell the story and the one who keeps it safe."

"How much farther?"

"We're almost there."

The truck turned onto a rutted road and bounced over a cattle guard. The road became a track through the sandy soil. Palmer saw the beam from the headlights reflect off the dried vegetation between the tracks and heard the plants scratch the truck's undercarriage. He looked through the windshield into the velvet evening, no human-made light in sight. That reminded him of the flashlight on his cell phone and that he should have at least called Chee.

He patted his jacket pocket for his phone, then checked his shirt and pants. No luck. He felt around the truck seat.

"Whatcha doing?"

"I think my phone must have fallen out of my pocket."

"I'll help you hunt it up when we stop. Those things don't do nothin' out here in the sticks anyhow unless you're lucky. The radio in here used to work. I don't know what's gone wrong with it now." Duke banged on the radio with the palm of his hand and turned the round knob. Palmer heard a click but nothing else. "Getting old like the rest of us."

Duke slowed for a pair of bony horses caught in the beam of his headlights as they meandered across the road. Palmer stared out the windshield beyond them into unbroken velvet night.

"Do the people who live out here have electricity?"

"Not a bit, except a few who got generators. Mother gets by with her heating stove, kerosene lamps, and candles. She has water now, so I don't have to lug it out for her no more. She usually goes beddie-bye by now, but she said she'd stay up till we got there."

They stopped in front of a house, and the truck lights illuminated gray cinder block. Palmer noticed a butterscotch glow seeping through a gap in the curtains.

Duke turned off the engine, then reached over to the passenger side and opened the glove box. Palmer saw a thin beam of light and heard the rustling of paper as Duke grasped a small black flashlight. He clicked it on. The beam flicked along the bench seat and then moved to the floor where it illuminated dirt and a cracked floor mat. "I don't see your phone, sir. You wanna try?"

Duke handed him the light. Palmer opened the door and shone the beam along the side between the seat and the door and along the floor and under the seat. No phone, but he found a small silver earring and handed it to Duke along with the flashlight. The Paiute had the rifle in his right hand, barrel pointed to the ground.

"Mother's been missin' that. She's waiting to meet you, sir. Let's go on in. I'm sure sorry about that telephone, but it don't work good out here anyways."

Duke was shorter and a bit younger than Palmer had assumed. He moved fluidly, the strands of red yarn tied to the end of each gray braid swaying. As they walked toward the house, Palmer noticed a trailer, or maybe it was an RV, parked away from the dwelling. Stepping into the house was a journey back in time. Even in the dim light, Palmer noticed that the little home swelled with handcrafted touches, from the stone floors to the wooden furniture to the baskets, weavings, and pottery. A large drum, its hide top well used, sat in a corner beneath a curtained window. He inhaled the subtle spice of cedar drifting up from the fire in the large black stove that stood in the middle of the room.

The house reminded him of other Indian homes, modest on the outside, rich with tradition, family, and memories inside.

An elderly woman, a smaller, rounder, more stooped version of Duke, acknowledged his presence with a sober nod and wordlessly offered him a place at the wooden table. Spread out before him, Palmer saw a yellowed map, hand-drawn and elegantly illustrated, like no map he had ever seen before.

"This is what we needed you to come look at." Duke leaned the gun against the wall and joined Palmer at the table. "Mother wanted you to see this now so you will understand why nothing can be built here." He moved his hand to cast a shadow over a section of the map where, Palmer speculated, the Colorado River and the Little Colorado came together. The spot sat at the map's center.

Palmer stood for a better look and studied the map for a long time, admiring the depiction of mountains, rivers, canyon walls, bears, elk, deer, and mountain lions. "It's beautiful. Can you help me understand what I'm seeing?"

The old woman spoke for the first time. "You are Navajo?"

"I am."

She settled into the stuffed armchair and arranged the pink blanket over her lap. "I will tell you." Palmer knew a story awaited him.

Her English, even more than her son's, had a slow, lilting, songlike rhythm. She started with a story of the love of a Paiute leader for his wife, a woman who died too soon. The profound depth of the leader's grief stirred the heart of the God Taavotz. Taavotz promised to show the leader that his wife was happy in the world of spirits, but only if he could put his grief aside during their journey.

The old woman stopped speaking and looked at Palmer. Then she held her hand over a place on the map, a spot near the center marked with a graceful golden swirl. "This is where they came. Does your heart want to hear more?"

Palmer had listened to stories like this before, elaborate tales of sites so sacred that their existence benefited not only the people who knew their history, but everyone on the planet. He had never seen a map like the one on the table, which made the story more concrete. The map looked as though several Holy People had created it over a long span of time. "Please go on. I am honored that you would tell me this story."

"Because Taavotz is a strong, strong god, he forged a trail in solid rock, a deep path through the holy mountain that guarded the spirit world. The leader followed this long, rough road. Then, where the trail met the river, he beheld his wife. She couldn't see him, but he realized that she lived happily now, free from pain, free from sorrow, free from worry. The leader's heart lightened and he followed the trail back to his homeland. Then Taavotz poured water into the path as a blessing to the earth and its people. See here?"

The woman moved her hand over the map, along the course of the Little Colorado River, southeast to northwest, stopping at the junction of the Colorado. "Taavotz told the leader to warn the people that the river would swallow them if they tried to visit the spirit world before their time. And so it is." Palmer heard the tone of her voice darken. "It is wrong to disturb the spirits. Anyone who does this will bring great suffering to the world. The ancestors deserve a happy rest. That way they can send prayers to keep the world safe, prayers for all their children, even for you Navajos. Prayers for everyone. What would happen if they are disturbed? What tragedy will come to us?"

Palmer noticed the tears on her cheeks reflected like gems in the candlelight.

After a while, the woman said, "Our ancestors speak through us now. They ask us to tell you that there are many things, important things, that can't be measured by reports and computers, by people from Washington or Phoenix. They remind us that there is more to being human than making money. I know you are not Báyóodzin', not one of our people, but you are an Indian. I hope you understand this in your heart of hearts. In the end, we are all relatives."

Palmer's throat felt tight. "You and your son should come to the meeting tomorrow and tell the delegates how you feel."

The woman shook her head. "We should not speak of such sacred things to outsiders, but we prayed and learned that we should bring you here. That's why I decided to show you this map and to tell the story."

Then the woman started to chant, softly at first and then with more power. Duke stood and used the drum to reinforce the rhythm she set. She closed her eyes, and Palmer saw how the Paiute words she sang erased the lines of worry and smoothed her forehead. When she finished, she looked toward Duke and he helped her to rise, then went to the woodpile and stoked the stove. She studied Palmer with her sharp dark eyes. "We, my son and I, are peaceful people; we know that isn't true of everyone who honors this place and its story. You be brave and be careful."

Duke said, "Can I help you with anything, Mother, before we go?"

The woman shook her head and then turned again to Palmer. "Do your best to save this sacred place."

Palmer shoved his hands in his pockets and followed Duke to the truck. The chalky wisp of a moon and an abundance of icy stars shone in the deep black sky. He heard the music of a coyote in the still, frigid air. *Ma'ii*, the wise trickster, challenging him to make sense of what he'd just experienced.

Palmer said, "Where did that beautiful map come from?"

"No one alive today can remember that far back. It's a treasure, and my mother is the one who tends to it. That's about what I know."

"How does your tribe honor that holy spot?"

"We don't talk about that outside of our own people." He put the rifle back in the gun rack and started the truck. The heater fan blew cold air onto Palmer's legs. "Some of our folks are angry as hell about the development those Navajo big shots are talking about. They blame you, sir, because they think your meetings give the project life."

Palmer thought about defending himself, arguing the point as they headed away from the house into the darkness. Instead, he thought about the story, the map, and the message from *Ma'ii*.

18

"You're making me nervous." Bernie muted the game on TV—the Arizona Cardinals playing some team on the football field. "You told the clerk at the desk to call you when Palmer shows up. You left a message in his hotel room. We drove around looking for him. What else can you do? Stop beating yourself up. What happens next is up to Palmer."

He saw her eyeing his untouched half of the burger.

"Go ahead," he said. "I'm not hungry."

"You sure?"

He marveled at Bernie. She could live on Cokes and burgers, with an occasional break for her mom's mutton stew and fry bread. She'd eat corn, squash, and green beans when he cooked them, but left to her own devices, she'd live vegetable-free. She was slim, he decided, because she had the same metabolism as her mother. Mama and the hummingbirds.

She took a bite of his dinner. "Don't worry about Palmer. You've done all you could."

"I'm not sure about that. I'm longing for the day when I never have to think of Palmer again. Did you hear anything from the Lieutenant about the dead guy?"

"No. I sent him an e-mail, but he hasn't responded yet. I hope that means he's busy working on the case." Bernie moved closer to Chee. "What would the Lieutenant do in a situation like yours?"

"He would have told Largo to find somebody else for bodyguard duty. Unlike me—the guy who gets the chump assignments."

"Stop it. You're a first-class cop. People take advantage of your good nature sometimes, but you don't come in second to anyone. Largo appreciates you."

"Yeah, because I'm easy to manipulate."

"No, because you're a kind man and a great officer." She put down the burger. "You've had a long day with lots of stress and you've hardly slept since you started this assignment. Give yourself a break."

He stared at the silent television, then sat up and slipped off his boots and stretched out on the bed next to her again.

"You're right. Palmer manages to push all my buttons. To rattle my cage."

"He's a burr under your saddle."

He grinned. "Yeah. A fly in the ointment."

"An itch that needs scratching."

"A thorn in my side."

"An ant at the picnic."

"A weed in the corn patch."

"A sandstorm at a powwow."

"A coyote in the sheep pen."

"A bug in your ear."

"He bursts my bubble."

She laughed. "I can't think of any more. You win."

"So, do I get a prize?" He snuggled closer to her.

"Hmmmm. We'll have to see about that."

They heard a noise. A chime. Then again. Palmer's phone.

Chee padded over to the desk, disgruntled. The screen said the call was from "UNKNOWN." If it had been his own phone, he would have turned it off.

"Hello?"

He heard Palmer's voice. "Chee, why are you answering my phone?"

"You left it in my motel room. Where are you? Bernie and I drove all over looking for you. We've been worried sick."

"Calm down. I'm out in the parking lot. I thought I must have dropped my phone out here."

"Come inside and I'll meet you in the lobby. I've got a message for you, too."

"I'll be there in a minute," Palmer said. "I just have to give my companion back his phone."

Chee put his boots back on. Then he slid Palmer's phone into his pants pocket.

"Want me to go with you?"

"No. This jerk is my personal headache."

Bernie turned the television sound on. "You might want your jacket. You never know what will happen."

"Right."

He grabbed his gun from the dresser as he left.

Palmer wasn't in the lobby, of course, so Chee went outside to look for him. The clouds, which could have kept the temperature at the frigid average for November in northern Arizona, were gone. What little heat the day had stored had disappeared into the pool of blackness. He zipped his jacket. The stars shone with exceptional brilliance and the cold air invigorated him.

Chee spotted Palmer standing against the building. He seemed to be studying the orange camper van.

Palmer glanced up. "I didn't think you'd be so quick. Want one?"

He noticed Palmer's half-consumed cigarette. "No."

Palmer breathed out a cloud of smoke. "So you had a message for me?"

"Yeah. Your son called. He said it was urgent, and that was a while ago."

"He ignores me for years and now everything is urgent. Anything else?"

"Yeah, I've got another message for you. Grow up. Get over yourself. No more of this cat-and-mouse stuff. I'm doing my best to do my job, which is to keep you alive for the mediation."

Palmer took a long drag and stared at his cigarette. "I've quit dozens of times, but the old habit comes back. These things are more dangerous than anybody out there." He stared out into the parking lot. "Chee, I know this started when Katie dropped me off at the station, but it should end now. The police presence at the mediation sends the wrong message—not just you but the whole posse. I'm calling the captain first thing in the morning to get him to call off the dogs. What's his name?"

Chee told him. "You should call the chief, too. This was his idea."

"I will."

"Where did you go, anyway, without a car?"

Palmer took another drag on the cigarette. "A headman of the San Juan Paiutes picked me up. He came by in his pickup, said he had to show me something important. So I went with him. I explained that you had the bodyguard assignment, but he said you weren't welcome."

"Was he the one who called you?"

Palmer affirmed it with a nod. "Denny Duke. He took me to his mother's house, and they showed me something beautiful they thought was relevant to the mediation. Then he brought me back here, no harm done. You've got nothing to worry about."

"Did you really think it was a good idea to go off in secret with some guy who has something at stake in the outcome of the meeting?"

Before Palmer could respond, Chee heard a noise across the parking lot. He noticed the lights blazing inside the VW camper and Bebe Durango standing by the open door.

Durango noticed him noticing.

"Hey, Sarge, come here for a second."

Chee didn't like being shouted at. He waved at him, meaning, *When I'm done here.* He turned back to Palmer. "So you disappear with the guy who threatens you over the phone. Did Mr. Duke make any more threats?"

Palmer ground what was left of his cigarette into the asphalt. "He warned me that some of the other Paiutes think I'm stirring up trouble because I'm the mediator. That's the extent of it." He shoved his hands into his jacket pockets. "The only business we have left is for you to give me my phone."

Chee extracted Palmer's phone and handed it to him.

"I'll call my son now about his urgent need to speak to me, and I'll call your bosses in the morning. The signal is better out here."

"It works fine in the lobby, too." Chee said. "Go inside and I'll be there in a minute."

Palmer started to argue, then thought better of it, turned, and walked toward the motel's entrance. Chee waited until he disappeared, then trotted to the camper van.

Durango opened the door before Chee could knock and started talking.

"I heard a rumor that the power will go out again tomorrow and every day of the mediation. A power failure, get it? It's a symbolic statement about the failure of the power of the people to stop the development. You watch for this." He rudely pointed a finger at Chee. "I'm giving you a heads-up so you can plan a little. You seem like a nice guy for a cop."

"Anything else I should know?"

Durango eyed him cautiously. "You should know that this Palmer guy isn't the straight shooter, goody two-shoes he says he is. He did a mediation in Redondo Beach that is still being sorted out. If you need something to do, check that out. And check out the Mormon Mafia around here, too. I heard they plan a lawsuit to keep alcohol and gambling out of the canyon."

"Mormon Mafia?"

"If you don't know what that is, well, you ought to. Good night."

Chee walked back to the motel, wondering if Durango had inside information about the electricity and if some LDS representative would show up to speak tomorrow.

Palmer stood in the center of the lobby. He looked pale, stricken. "What's wrong?"

"I called my son—no answer, of course. Then, just as I was planning to go inside, a cop called me. He said Robert had been in a car wreck. An ambulance took him to the hospital in Flagstaff."

Dramatic disaster clung to Palmer like a bad stench, Chee thought.

"The officer gave me the number of the hospital. I'm going to call and see if they can tell me how he's doing. Rocket was alive when the ambulance got to him."

"Rocket?

"Rocket—that's what his mother and I used to call Robert. A nickname because he was such an active little kid. I haven't used that name for him in years. We had our differences, but . . ."

Palmer raised his hand and spread his fingers, as if to signal defeat. Chee had a lot of questions, but he waited to see if the man wanted to tell him anything else first. The lights in the room seemed too bright, Chee thought, the space too big and public for this conversation.

Palmer said, "Robert's mom always bragged about his driving. He's never had a car accident as far as I know, not even a scraped fender. What happened out there?"

"Do you recall the name of the officer you talked to?"

"Breen, Green, Dean, something like that." Palmer shrugged. "I was more focused on the message than the officer's name."

"I think I know who you mean. I'll call him while you call the hospital."

It took only two tries to reach Officer Clyde Skeen of the Arizona Department of Public Safety.

"I responded to a single-car roll over near Red Mesa. The driver went down an embankment. Clear road, no traffic. Maybe he fell asleep. Who knows? No signs of alcohol or drugs at the crash, but speed may have been a factor." Skeen cleared his throat. "Lucky for him, a car came by headed the other way not too long after it happened and noticed the headlights."

"How badly was he injured?"

"Bad, but he had on his seat belt, and that may save his life. That and the other driver calling 911. Why all the questions?"

"The injured man's father is the mediator for the Grand Canyon summit, the guy whose car blew up. He's here in Tuba with me now."

"So what are you doing in Tuba? I thought you were assigned to the Shiprock district?"

Chee explained.

"You know, Chee, some guys get all the luck." Skeen cleared his throat again. "I noticed some scrapes on the driver's side of that car. Might be that someone forced him off the road."

"Maybe." It was an area worth investigating, Chee thought.

"Yep. Or maybe we've been watching too many car-chase movies."

Palmer had settled himself onto the lobby couch. His head was in his hands.

Chee sat next to him. "What did the hospital say?"

"Not much. A nurse told me Robert is in intensive care, and she took my number. Intensive care? That's not good."

"It means he's getting all kinds of help." Chee remembered visiting the Lieutenant on that high-tech ICU floor at the hospital in Santa Fe. The staff, along with some prayers, brought him back from the threshold of death. "Do you want to me to drive you down to Flag?"

Palmer patted his shirt pocket where the cigarettes lived. "I'm no good in hospitals. Too much waiting. I never know what to say. The nurse gave me a direct number to the unit where Robert is so

I can check on him. We're not close anymore. And what could I do, anyway?"

Chee nodded. The few times he'd been a hospital patient, he just wanted to be left alone. "Does his mother know?"

"The officer said he called her first because Rocket had her as his emergency contact."

"I'm sorry this happened. Let me know if I can do anything to help you."

"Did the officer tell you about the wreck?"

Chee explained. "He said it looks like speed may have been a factor, but not alcohol. He noticed some scrape marks on the side of the car."

Palmer said, "Do you think this has anything to do with the mediation or with me?"

"I don't know." After a moment, Chee said, "We need to go to bed. I'll give you a ride to the Justice Center in the morning."

They walked down the hall. Chee checked Palmer's room and said good night.

"Hey, Chee?"

"Yeah?"

"Thanks for making that call."

Chee slid his key card into his own room's door slot and saw the green light flash. Bernie had fallen asleep, but she awoke when he gently eased himself into bed next to her.

19

Joe Leaphorn couldn't stop thinking about Richard Horseman. Little Ricky. A sweet child born with the odds against him. When Emma got sick, because of the damage the tumor did to her brain, she began to lose track of the boys. Her cards for them remained unsent, forgotten, like so many other things she'd once loved and enjoyed.

He recalled their last conversation, before she went in for the surgery that was supposed to restore her brain but instead took her life.

He sat with her in the surgical waiting room, just the two of them. She squeezed his hand and said, *"Ayóó anííníshní,"* and then again, "I love you." He remembered the tone of her voice, fear and hope intermixed.

He said, "I'll see you in the recovery room."

But she didn't recover. And despite his focus on work, despite colleagues who reached out to him, and the support that came from Emma's family, he hadn't recovered either. After so many years, the gaping wound had scarred over, still raw underneath.

The week after Emma died, he found a pile of cards for the boys in her dresser. He stamped and mailed the cards she'd sealed and addressed. Then he put five dollars in the others, signed them with her name, and mailed them, too, one a week for as long as they lasted.

He'd kept working full-time after that for a while and then switched to contract work. Louisa, a college professor studying comparative spiritual beliefs among the Native people of the Southwest, had come into his life and befriended him. Her companionship helped keep loneliness at bay. At least most days.

Immediately after Emma's death he'd taken on the case of a missing woman archaeologist because he knew Emma would have wanted him to do that. Now, for her sake, he would find out why a boy she had loved and cared about had grown up to be the first person in the history of Shiprock killed with a car bomb.

He thought more about Horseman. Leaphorn kept the little notebooks he used to jot down facts and questions about his cases as an officer and a detective. When he cleared out his desk at the station, he thought about tossing them, an old man's memories of his better days. But something made him save them, and often in his consulting work he was glad he had. Perhaps he had made some entries about the boy's family, or his situation, something he might have forgotten now that would help him help Bernie.

He opened the lower drawer of his desk, reached toward the back, and felt the stacks of old notebooks sandwiched together with a thick rubber band. He pulled them out. He had bundled groups of five years together and written the beginning and ending dates on a slip of paper with each pile. He had at least one notebook for every year. Some years, if crime was rampant or the cases he investigated especially complex, he'd started a second book.

He found the notebooks that should bracket the years he guessed he might have encountered the boy and slipped off the rubber band. He'd seen the child on a warm day, so he started by reading his entries from June, then moved to July. His notes sparked the memory that it had been a refreshingly slow period for crime, before meth made its debut in Navajo country. He scanned entries about cattle rustling, illegal liquor sales, and runaways. He reviewed calls about husbands and boyfriends beating up on wives and girlfriends. The journal recalled lost tourists, stolen vehicles that relatives had allegedly borrowed, dogs killing livestock, UFO and shape-shifter reports. But he saw nothing about a scared boy walking down the road for help.

He thought back to the scene again and remembered the way the light had fallen. It didn't seem like the August sun, so he went to his notes for May, year by year. If he came up empty, then he'd look through September. But there on the twenty-seventh of May, eighteen years ago, he found the reference. Mostly, it was as he recalled it.

Noticed a child along the shoulder of the road. Pulled up next to him. He was limping because he only had one shoe. He was crying, sobbing. He had on an oversized wristwatch with a green dial.

He had forgotten about the watch. His notes indicated that the situation at the house was worse than he'd recollected. He had recorded the name and age of the woman who lived there, Naomi Horseman, 23, and the boyfriend who lived there, too, but, she said, was away working. Leaphorn had also made a note of the children in the house: Richard Horseman, 4, and Harris Horseman, 1.

The woman had old bruises on her face and neck and a freshly swollen eye. She wouldn't say what happened, but when I asked if her boyfriend had hurt her, she didn't deny it.

He heard Louisa's steps approaching and stopped reading.
She spoke from the doorway to his office. "The news will be on in a few minutes."

He nodded. They watched the national and then the local news on television together every night before dinner.

She put her hand lightly on his shoulder. "You're awfully quiet and busy today."

"Fine."

He waited for her to leave before he read the rest of the entry. It seemed like an invasion of the family's privacy to review his notes with another person in the room.

The woman said her mother often kept the children. The grandmother, Mrs. Nez, had no phone, so after the ambulance left, I took Richard to her place and she agreed to care for him and asked about the baby's condition. She told me she was angry with her daughter and the daughter's boyfriend for neglecting the boys.

He skimmed his description of the neat house and ramada, the sheep pen, the hogan.

He had written: "Case referred to Social Services." This is where Butterfly's notes would help him understand what happened next.

He heard the familiar theme song of the evening news, closed the notebook, grabbed his cane, and went in to be with Louisa.

The most interesting thing on the news was the report on protesters at the Grand Canyon meeting. The announcer talked about them with footage of an elderly white man in Tuba City using a protest sign to beat on the hood of a big black car until fellow protesters strong-armed him away. He saw Jim Chee in the background. Chee, he recalled, had a knack for being in the exact spot where trouble might be lurking.

Louisa said, "I wonder if those people had anything to do with the explosion? What do you think?"

He shrugged. He was pleased that nothing happened in Tuba City that would embarrass the Navajo Nation. Or, if something like that had happened, television hadn't captured it.

The reporter said that one of the Tuba City protest groups had been linked to ecoterrorism in the past. They showed the footage of the destroyed car in the Shiprock gym parking lot and noted the ongoing FBI investigation. The reporter said the feds had identified the dead man as Richard Horseman, 22.

Leaphorn's cell phone rang twice during dinner. He itched to answer it, but he and Louisa had an agreement: no calls during the news or at meals. She had baked meat loaf with mashed potatoes and gravy, one of his favorite dinners, but he wasn't hungry. His mind kept replaying the scene with the boy. He was missing something, but what? How could those two random events be connected?

"You usually like my meat loaf. Is something bothering you, Joe?"

"Thinking."

"So you're working on a case?"

He nodded once.

"Are you helping Bernie?" She didn't wait for his response. "Let me know if I can do anything. I'd be glad to make calls for you. Whatever you need."

"Guh." He meant to say "good," but he could tell she understood.

When they'd finished dinner, Louisa cleared the table and carefully pulled out the large board with a half-finished jigsaw puzzle, a scene with mountains and multicolored wildflowers. She liked it when he found the pieces to create the picture and said the three-dimensional thinking helped his brain. He considered it a tedious waste of time, but not as big a waste of time as arguing with her. His lady friend meant well, he knew, but she didn't understand what went on inside his head. No one could unless they'd had damage to their brains. If they were like him, they didn't want to talk about it even if they could.

"We're half done with this one. What's left is harder."

He walked to where she had the puzzle ready and waved his hand.

"Working," he told her. "Bernie."

"Are you sure?"

He nodded.

She smiled. "By the way, I picked up a copy of the *Albuquerque Journal* when I was out. I left it on the living room table for you."

He picked up the paper and took it back to his office. He hung the cane on the extra chair, and sat down with the files and his notebooks. He looked at his phone. The first message was from Maryellen Hood. When he'd first come home from the hospital, he had trouble remembering how to use his cell phone. Now it was second nature. He'd even learned to text.

She'd said, "Check your e-mail," and then, "Be careful, sir. There were some rough players in this case."

He tapped the computer screen, it came to life, and he went to his e-mail. He scrolled past notices from AARP, Sacred Wind phone service, the latest newsletter from the retired police officers association, and ads for products that embarrassed him. He found a message from Butterfly. He clicked on the subject line: "For a friend of my Dad."

Maryellen had typed:

Lt. Leaphorn,

    The files I found are attached. The ones before the earliest date you see here are paper only, stored offsite and not accessible to me. Please delete these when you are done.

He moved the mouse to the symbol of a paper clip and clicked. An icon that looked like a manila folder drifted to the bottom of the screen. He kept clicking as prompted, thinking how much easier it would be to open a real file and thumb through pages.

The information looked like photocopies of a series of typed sheets dating back two decades. As he had suspected, his encounter with the sad little boy was not the Horseman family's first experience with law enforcement or family services. Nor was it the last.

The social workers' reports told him that Ricky's mother had been arrested for drunken driving that resulted in child endangerment, battery on a household member, and child neglect. Periodically, the children were monitored by Navajo Social Services. One entry documented the arrest of a man identified as Naomi's boyfriend for child abuse.

Leaphorn read on. It looked as though young Ricky did better after he went to live with Mrs. Nez. The reports were boring, perfunctory. Then something happened and a security guard at a Farmington grocery had detained Horseman for throwing rocks at cars. He found that the grandmother complained about the boy's "attitude of disrespect" and reported him as a runaway several times. Another in the parade of caseworkers wrote that the boy had dropped out of high school and moved back to live with his mother, who had just been released from prison.

The final file Butterfly had sent was a note that Rick Horseman had been arrested in Gallup after a shoplifting incident that involved video games. He was seventeen. There was no juvenile record of arrest for involvement in gangs, drugs, or violent crime.

Leaphorn thought about it. Sometimes puberty alone activated the switch that made boys go crazy for a few years, especially young males growing up in challenging circumstances without male relatives to guide them. Maybe that was what had happened to Horseman. Then Richard Horseman aged out of the system and reporting from the Navajo Social Services stopped. Ready or not, Richard Horseman was legally an adult.

All in all, Ricky grew to manhood with some struggles, but not a hopeless case.

He had asked Largo to check the file on Horseman for him, and he'd noticed the captain's e-mail when he was scrolling for Butterfly's message. Largo had written: "One report on Horseman as an adult. Two years ago, he was arrested on suspicion of car theft, but charges dropped for technical errors. Nothing pending." If the captain couldn't find anything more, it wasn't to be found.

At the police station, he'd used his map of Navajoland with colored pushpins marking unsolved crimes with special designations for burglaries, rustling, bootlegging, drug cases, and homicides. It helped him make sense of things, see connections. When he retired, he'd left the map there, but he still liked the idea of mapping crime, diagramming relationships of criminal acts to the varied geography of Navajoland and among the people involved in the cases he was working. Instead of a map now, he used the printout of Bernie's bullet points to organize his thoughts. He printed the note Bernie had sent him earlier and reread it.

She had written:

Possible reasons for Horseman's death

1. He was hired to plant the bomb by someone who wanted to hurt Palmer and blew himself up by accident.
2. He came to watch the game and just happened to be in the parking lot by the car when it exploded.
3. He was planning to steal the car when the bomb went off.
4. He knew there was a bomb in the car and wanted to remove it.
5. Palmer knew him, sent him out to get something from the car, and he triggered the bomb.
6. Someone wanted to kill Horseman and used Palmer's car as the means to do it.
7. Some combo of the above.
8. None of the above.

Leaphorn's brain expanded the speculation. A fancy BMW might have offered more temptation than Horseman could resist. Perhaps he stole cars on assignment. The FBI, using their fancy equipment and extensive bureaucracy, had ruled out the possibility that Horseman was a bomb maker and found no link between him and any terrorist group. Maybe while he stood there, contemplating the heist, he discovered that the car was unlocked or jimmied his way in, never suspecting that there would be a bomb there. Maybe someone hired Horseman to put the bomb in the car and he'd accidentally made a deadly mistake. He leaned back in his chair and noticed the newspaper Louisa had picked up. The Shiprock bombing was on page three. He glanced at the photograph of the bomb scene, studying it closely. It captured emergency responders at work. In the background he saw an officer in a Navajo Police uniform talking to a man in a red shirt. He didn't recognize the officer, but he figured it must be the rookie Bernie had mentioned. He looked for her in the photo but didn't spot her. He'd have to tease Bernie about that, accuse her of hiding from the camera.

Leaphorn went back to work with Butterfly's files. This time, he read more closely, noting the progression of incidents involving either overt neglect or profound maternal ignorance. He read about male friends of Rick and Harris's mother who showed up briefly in the reports, most of whom shared her problem with drugs and alcohol. None of them seemed interested in the boys. One social worker commented that a son-in-law of Mrs. Nez was a "positive influence" on Rick and paid some medical bills for baby Harris. Another outlined the grandmother's efforts to get social services more involved in helping the boys' mother. Each caseworker added more observations and theories. Meanwhile, the home situation grew worse for the boys.

He found: "Harris is severely underweight and small for his age, failing to thrive. Richard's growth continues in the normal range."

And then in the next report: "Harris has missed developmental milestones and shows signs of FAS and possible abuse. Richard is gentle with and concerned about the younger child."

Leaphorn knew FAS, fetal alcohol syndrome, cursed the child of the mother who drank—usually these women were alcoholics—with a variety of conditions, including retardation, hyperactivity, heart problems, tremors, and seizures. These babies were vulnerable to abuse, too, because they were hard to parent, hard to love.

He read about Harris's scheduled evaluations and missed appointments. Then he read: "On a visit to mother's house, a friend found Harris unconscious. He was taken to hospital by ambulance and died the following afternoon."

Leaphorn looked up from the computer and rubbed his eyes. He thought about Emma, sweet Emma, and how she'd sent cards to little Harris not knowing the youngster had died. He barely remembered the baby, a little crying person in a house of despair and sadness. Even though it happened years ago, the child's death—and especially the thought that an adult who should have cared for the baby might have contributed to it—troubled him. Now, both boys, two lives that could have made a difference, were gone.

He sent an e-mail to Largo, knowing the captain sometimes worked late, asking if the FBI had come up with anything else on the bombing and Horseman's involvement. He missed the days when it was easy for him to walk down the hall and ask for what he needed to know, or when he could pick up the phone and assume the person he called would understand him.

Leaphorn stood, noticing the stiffness in his back, took his cane, and went to the kitchen. He would have enjoyed a cup of coffee, but since there was none and he didn't feel like making some himself, he opted for water. Louisa had left the puzzle on the table and was reading in the living room. Or, rather, dozing in her favorite chair, a book on her lap. A good woman, he thought. A good woman, indeed. He didn't understand what she saw in him, but he didn't understand women anyway. He would ask her advice on this, he decided. Before his injury, he'd enjoyed talking to her about cases he worked. She had good insights. It was time to talk to her again.

When he limped back to the office, Largo had already responded. The FBI had identified the kind of bomb it was, the sort detonated with a cell phone—not with the vehicle's ignition. Other than that, they weren't saying anything, except that the investigation continued and that Rick Horseman "was not a suspect at this time."

20

Bernadette Manuelito liked routine. She cultivated habits to keep herself from wasting time on what she considered minor issues—when to go for a run, what to have for breakfast, where to buy gas for her car, what day to do the laundry. Her theory was that this saved space in her brain for more important items. She pictured the brain as a living computer with only so much room on the hard drive. When it got too full, it started to delete things. She was explaining her idea to Chee, who supported the "take life as it comes" approach. They'd started the discussion because she said being away from home and her regular schedule made her a little antsy. He muted the sound of the football game on the big-screen TV in their motel room. "The way I see it, the brain resembles a balloon with ideas floating around inside. Most of us keep it barely inflated and have room for more than we imagine. When I was studying to be a *hataalii*, I realized that I could learn the songs, learn the paintings, learn the correct ways to do complicated things I thought I'd never understand. The more I learned, the more I could learn. My balloon brain grew. I visualized the colors and the shapes of the sand paintings. I heard the rhythms of the chants in my dreams. I would remember one part, and then the next part and the next came to me."

"Breath, the wind of life, that's what makes a balloon grow and that's what supports our spirits. You can keep your computer brain."

"If your brain is like a balloon, at some point it might get too full. Pop." She clapped her hands to illustrate the point. "But I can get a new hard drive."

Chee said, "Yeah, and with a computer, a lightning strike kills the power and you're out of business." He smiled at her. "The Lieutenant's brain seems more like a computer, supporting your theory, but my happy balloon brain is not convinced."

The next morning she awoke early, as always. She dressed quietly and went outside to watch the sun rise. She sang her morning song and blessed the day with white cornmeal, thankful for it. Thankful for her relatives, for Chee, for good health, for a career that meant something.

She made coffee for them both in the little pot on the dresser while Chee was in the shower. When she heard him turn off the water, she hollered in, "Did I tell you Dashee is joining us this morning? I'll go for a run later."

"You're cooking eggs in that microwave for us?"

"Wish I'd thought of that. No, we're meeting at the restaurant next door."

Chee emerged from the bathroom, rubbing his hair dry with a towel. "I noticed a softer side to Palmer last night. He thanked me."

"Really?"

"His son's accident might have shifted things inside him. I'm going to check with Officer Skeen this morning, see if there's any news on the wreck."

"I hear the Lieutenant's voice in my head." She spoke more deeply. "'There's no such thing as a coincidence, Manuelito.'"

"Do you believe that?"

"Yes, especially when it comes to crime. You know how people believe that God has a plan for the universe and that we're a tiny bit of it, but because our part is so small, we can't see how it connects?"

Chee nodded.

"Well, I think that's how coincidence works. Part of the complicated web of life."

They walked to the adjoining building that held the restaurant. Dashee sat at a table with a half-empty cup of coffee in front of him. They scooted in on the other side and quickly ordered breakfast.

Dashee said, "I hope you guys have that electricity problem figured out for the session today."

"You bet," Chee said. "I drove to Bashas' yesterday and got a box of Hopi flashlights."

"What?"

"You know, those wax things that start up with a match."

"Oh, you mean Navajo flashlights. Good thinking, bro."

Chee sipped his coffee. "Seriously, Ward texted me last night that the session is a go. We'll have power today as far as I know." He had alerted the captain to Bebe Durango's warning.

Bernie said, "Chee mentioned that grazing problem. It sounds like a mess."

Dashee put his cup down. "Mrs. Bitsoi is one stubborn lady. Reminds me of my aunt. Nothing I say gets through to her."

"That's because she doesn't speak Hopi," Chee said.

The waitress took their orders: ham and eggs for Bernie, pancakes for Chee, and more coffee for Dashee. Chee moistened a wedge of pancake in a puddle of syrup. "Hey, I heard you gave your delegates good advice yesterday: 'Be careful and don't get blown up.'"

Dashee turned to Bernie. "How do you live with this guy?"

Bernie shrugged. "I'm used to lame jokes. And he's a pretty good cook."

Dashee said, "I haven't heard you complain about Darleen. Did she go to that art school in Santa Fe?"

"She hasn't decided yet. She's taking classes in Shiprock for her diploma."

Dashee nodded. "Is she staying out of trouble?"

"As far as I know. She and a friend might be on their way here to watch the session. He wants to make a video of it."

"So what brought you here?"

Bernie said, "You mean besides Chee? The mystery of the dead man at Shiprock. And the more I learn, the more confused I get."

Dashee chuckled. "You think too much, that's your problem. Why don't you give it rest, go for a hike today while the weather is good. The old ones' bones are telling them that winter is close. I know a good trail for you, and you don't even have to drive into the park itself."

Chee said, "That's a good idea. I have a map in my unit. That might be helpful."

Bernie said, "Are you sure you won't need my help today with security or something?"

"I would love to give you the bodyguard duty, but I'm stuck with it. You can help me at the reception tonight." He handed her the keys to his unit. "The map is on the passenger seat."

She was out and back in no time. She stacked the dishes to one side and spread the map out on the table. Dashee studied it.

"I don't see it on here." He took a pen from the pocket of his uniform shirt and made a sketch on a napkin.

Chee smiled at Dashee's drawing. "This looks like the way to find buried treasure or something. What's this X?"

"X marks the spot where the trail splits. Bernie, you have to go right." He moved the paper closer to her. "Just follow this dotted line."

She looked at the napkin and tapped the X. "What if I go left here?"

"You can't unless you're a Hopi." Dashee sketched in a rainbow in the margin. "The X is a good place to start back up, too. I've seen tracks of a mountain lion on the trail a couple of times in the summer, never this late in the year. Just to be safe, make some noise as you go down that way. Sing or something. Don't surprise it."

Chee said, "You're sending my wife on a trail frequented by a mountain lion? *Náshdóítsoh?*"

"No, *tocho*. It's a Hopi lion, one of us peaceful people. He hasn't eaten anyone yet." He turned to her. "You're more likely to see snowflakes than *tocho* out here. And if you meet him, well, you can talk your way out of anything. You know, more people die from bee stings and mosquito bites."

"Or car accidents. I'm not worried about it." Bernie finished her coffee and picked up Dashee's map as she scooted her chair away from the table. "I need to call Mama and check to see what's new on the bombing case before I leave for the canyon."

Dashee said, "Your mama must be like mine. One of those ladies who know everything before it happens. Ask her what Mrs. Bitsoi is up to while you're at it."

Bernie laughed. "I left out the part where I call Cordova at the FBI, or Largo to find out about the bombing."

"I heard that FBI guy is leaving. Transferred to San Diego."

"Really?"

Dashee shrugged. "That's what I heard."

Chee nodded toward Bernie. "She had more contact with him than I did, but I thought he was a decent guy, easy to work with. How come we get this news from the Hopi express?"

Dashee said, "You're just giving me another reason to brag, you know."

Bernie said, "Actually, Cordova told me he's going to Michigan."

Chee looked at her, surprised.

"He mentioned it when we drove out to talk to the dead man's grandmother. Guess I forgot to tell you."

"So much for your computer brain theory, honey."

She called Mama from the hotel lobby. Mrs. Darkwater, Mama's neighbor, answered the phone. Ever since Mama had been sick, Mrs. Darkwater had taken Mama into her flock, checking on her at least once a day.

"Your mother is fine. She's going with me to Farmington today to get some presents for my grandson. His birthday comes next week."

Mrs. Darkwater wanted to talk about the Shiprock bomb. "Terrible. Who would do something like that?"

"That's what the investigators are trying to find out."

"Too bad that young man who got hurt out there died. No way for him to make restitution for that mess."

"We don't know yet if he was connected to the explosion or if he was just in the wrong place when it happened."

"Who stands in the parking lot when the game is on?"

Mrs. Darkwater's appraisal matched her own. No basketball fan who had driven to the Shiprock would miss the game.

After Mrs. Darkwater shared a few more opinions, she handed the phone to Mama.

Her mother sounded strong and happy. "That lady who wants to weave, well, she's doing pretty good. She makes mistakes, but she knows how to laugh at herself."

"I'm glad." She wished she had time to work with Mama. She knew how to weave, beginner-style, but Mama had more to teach her.

"Daughter, you sound sad. Are you still thinking about that bomb and the one who died?"

"Yes, but the Lieutenant is helping me figure things out. I'm in Tuba City with my husband and I'm going for a hike when we finish talking."

"Is it snowing there?" Then Mama said, "Hold on."

Bernie heard Mrs. Darkwater's voice in the background but couldn't pick out the words.

Then Mama spoke again. "We're leaving. You be careful."

Bernie went back to the hotel room, noticing that the sun was out and the morning light shone clear and sharp. She saw her laptop, still in its case, on the desk and checked her e-mail for a note from the Lieutenant, a follow-up from Cordova, or something from the office. Nothing.

It was the FBI's case, wasn't it?

She loaded her backpack with water and a jacket and made sure she had something to snack on. She had the cornmeal she brought for a prayer at the confluence of the two rivers if she managed to hike that far. She put the holster with her gun on her hip.

When she reached for her phone, she noticed that she'd missed a call from Lona. Swallowing her hesitation, she punched in the number. After five rings, a mechanical voice came on and Bernie left a message. "Sorry I didn't catch you. I will be away from the phone most of the day, but I'll try you again later."

Then she climbed into her well-used Toyota and headed south toward Cameron.

The drive worked its magic. The morning sun brought the landscape to life—iron reds, subtle grays, warm browns. She passed the country she'd seen with Palmer, the dinosaur walkway, and rolled across the bridge over the Little Colorado River, the place where, after miles of meandering, the river begins to make its rock-rimmed descent to the canyon's ancient floor. She cruised by the Cameron Trading Post oasis and took the traffic circle onto Highway 64, Desert View Drive, the route into the park.

There were two main ways to approach the Grand Canyon by vehicle. The southern route went through the village of Tusayan. With a collection of motels, restaurants, gas stations, and various tourist-focused businesses, Tusayan accommodated hundreds of thousands of visitors who came to enjoy the South Rim's attraction each year. Beyond the settlement lay forest and, after a few miles, the more popular entrance to one of the nation's most popular parks.

She preferred the eastern route through the Navajo Nation, arid and open, with miles of views unblocked by trees. As directed by Dashee's map, she stopped at the turnoff for the Little Colorado River Tribal Park. The viewpoint area sat far above the sacred confluence of the two rivers. She saw some open-air booths, similar to the ones at the dinosaur tracks. She looked at the map again before putting it back in her pack. It showed the trail but, she realized, not where it started in relation to the parking lot. She could probably poke around and find it, but better to ask.

The first vendor she talked to shrugged her off politely. The next person she asked, a woman seller of cedar-bead necklaces with a toddler-sized daughter, offered to show her the trailhead. She told a young man in the booth to watch the child.

The women walked together, past a sign that warned of snakes, scorpions, and other possible threats to hikers. The critters slept now because of the weather. They crossed flat sandstone the color of coffee with milk. As they approached the canyon's edge, Bernie remembered hiking down another trail in the canyon, and how she had imagined plunging to her death with a false step. She hoped Dashee's trail wouldn't be as treacherous.

After about ten minutes, the woman stopped and indicated with a swoop of her chin a place where the path angled off the plateau, heading downward. She looked at the sky. "You'll be fine. It gets slick down there when the rain or snow comes, but it's nice today."

"How long would it take to me get to the river?"

"Depends on how fast you go. My brother back there, he makes it to the Little C in three hours."

"He's the one with your girl?"

The woman nodded once. Bernie figured, based on age and experience, it might take her an extra thirty minutes down and more than that coming back up. Seven hours? Because of November's short days it would be dark before she reached the rim again, and she didn't want that. But she'd hike awhile to get a sense of the place. Maybe she'd make it to where Dashee had drawn his big X.

The gray and brown stone walls that frame the Little Colorado's narrow gorge lack the Grand Canyon's panorama of color. The buff-colored limestone at the start of the trail—the same stone that paved the dinosaur walkway—is evidence of a shallow sea that covered this spot some 250 million years ago.

Bernie's muscles gradually warmed as she moved down into the canyon. She breathed the fresh, cool air, listened to the wind, and appreciated the lack of highway sounds and human-made noise. If she was wrong and the attack on Palmer was tied to the mediation, then perhaps being in this land itself might help her puzzle out why young Horseman was dead.

She reached a switchback and surrendered to the meditative rhythm of the descent.

SHE HAD CLIMBED TOO far away from the parking area to hear the vehicle pull in or to realize that the driver didn't have to ask where the trail started. He went right to it and began to hike toward her.

She froze when she heard the voice calling her name.

The second time he yelled, she responded, "Who's up there?"

The voice called out a name she didn't recognize.

"I didn't catch that."

"I'm Clayton Secody. Sergeant Chee sent me. I have a message for you."

She didn't know a Clayton Secody and had never heard Chee mention him.

"What's the message?" She put her hand on her gun. She heard the rhythmic steps on the trail and the lighter clatter of small dislocated rocks. Then a young man rounded a corner. A lanky Diné with a Dallas Cowboys cap greeted her in Navajo. Why would Chee send a stranger to interrupt her hike? Why hadn't he just called her?

"We haven't met, but I'm a friend of your sister," he said.

"Darleen. Where is she?"

"She's up in her car, waiting for me. She said she couldn't hike down because her shoes were too smooth for the rocks."

Darleen had never been interested in physical activity. Bernie liked the "smooth shoes" excuse.

Clayton cleared his throat. "Sergeant Chee asked me to tell you that you went off with the keys to his unit." Bernie remembered that she had planned to ask for a background check on this guy, CS, and wished she had already done it. He seemed normal, but that's what the neighbors always said about mass murderers.

Bernie patted her pants pocket and felt Sandra's rock and a telltale lump. She remembered borrowing Chee's keys when she went for the map. "So, how did you find Chee?"

"Oh, we stopped at the meeting to see what was going on. It looked crazy. People arguing in the parking lot. Tons of signs. TV trucks. That's where Darleen saw the sergeant, and he came over and gave her the message about the keys and told us where you were hiking."

"Did it take long to find me?"

Clayton smiled. "No. I'm from the Bodaway Chapter. From around here."

Bernie said, "If I give you the keys, can you take them back to Chee?"

Clayton said, "Sure, but not until tonight. We're on our way to the Grand Canyon for that program they do about condors. I'm shooting a video of that and then the condor specialist agreed to let me tape an interview with her. I have to be there early to set up but we could drop them off later."

"He'll need his keys before tonight." In fact, he needed them before now and he's probably peeved about it, she thought. "I'll hike up with you."

As she'd expected, the climb back to the trailhead took more energy. Even though Clayton was years younger, Bernie noticed that he was breathing hard at the pace she set. They focused on the hike, not conversation, and she appreciated the cool November temperatures. They finally reached the overlook with its vendors and the parking area and saw Darleen waiting at a picnic table. "Hey, sis. I'm glad you met CS."

"He gave me the message about the keys. So you ran into Chee at the Justice Center?"

Darleen nodded. "I felt bad for him. There was a guy being totally rude."

"What did he look like?" Bernie wondered if the man was one of the protesters she'd seen on TV.

"Weird. His face was white below his eyes all the way to his neck." Darleen moved a finger along her own face to demonstrate. "But his nose and his forehead were tan."

CS said, "Make a picture of him. You're brilliant that way."

"I can try." Darleen extended her hand toward Bernie. "Let me borrow that notebook you always haul around and a pencil or something."

Darleen put the book on the tabletop and started to draw. After a few minutes, she showed them her sketch of a man with a bald head. She had shaded to illustrate his uneven tan.

CS examined the picture. "That's him all right. I didn't notice that he had an earring."

Bernie looked at the face. She'd seen the man at the meeting yesterday. She wondered if he was on the FBI's list.

Darleen said, "So what's up with the Cheeseburger? He looked totally serious."

"From what you said, the situation was tense. He's in charge of keeping the mediator safe."

"Oh, right."

CS said, "We've got to go. I don't want to miss the bird talk."

Bernie walked with her sister and CS to Darleen's car, a miracle on four tires. She noticed CS reached through the window to open the driver's door for Darleen—the only way to do it

"Do you know much about cars?" Bernie said.

He shrugged. "She's the expert on this one."

Darleen said, "I know how to put in the gas, turn on the headlights, adjust the radio, and push the brake to stop." She laughed. "I know how to check the oil, turn on the windshield wipers, fix a flat, and call somebody if we break down."

"Would that somebody be me?"

CS said, "I've got relatives out this way, but if you want, we'll call you or the sergeant if we need help."

Darleen said, "Don't worry. We'll be fine. We made it this far. Hey, the Cheeseburger said to tell you Lieutenant Leaphorn called. I almost forgot."

After they left, Bernie pulled out her phone and looked at it. She had two bars for the strength of signal; not great but worth a try.

She dialed Leaphorn's number, and he—or maybe it was Louisa—answered on the third ring. The voice broke with static.

"It's Bernie. I'm having trouble understanding you. I'll call from the road when I get—" She heard the dreaded five tones of a lost call. She put the phone on the seat next to her, along with Chee's purloined keys.

She started the Toyota, happy that the sun had warmed it. She could kick herself for walking off with Chee's keys and knew she'd get some ribbing about it, especially after her computer brain speech last night. On the positive side, she'd done some hiking and had a chance to look CS in the eye. She pulled out of the parking lot and headed northeast toward Tuba City.

After a few minutes, she heard the rumble of her phone vibrating. Sure that it was Leaphorn, she pushed the button to answer and put it on speaker without looking to see who was calling.

"Did you hear about Robert?" A distressed female voice joined her in the front seat.

"Who is this?"

"Lona."

It took her a minute to line things up. Robert was Palmer's son; Lona was Palmer's ex. Lona was Robert's mother. "I heard. I'm so sorry. How is he doing?"

"What I meant was, did you find out what happened to the car? What caused the wreck?" Lona sounded exhausted.

"The police said it was a rollover, a one-car accident."

"I think there's more to it. You know someone wants to get at Aza. What if he thought this was a way to do it. Poor Robert. I told him to stay here in Phoenix, but . . ." Her voice trailed off.

"Lona? Did I lose you?"

"I'm here. Just thinking. First my boyfriend and I split up and then poor Ricky. Robert couldn't even talk about that, it upset him so much. And now this."

Bernie said, "I admire Robert for wanting to see his dad. That took—"

Lona interrupted. "That's not the only reason he's out there. My boyfriend, I mean my ex-boyfriend, does a lot of business in the Four Corners and he offered Robert a job. Those two have a lovefest going on. By acts more like a dad than Aza ever did."

"Guy?"

"No, By. Byrum, my former boyfriend. If it hadn't been for Robert I would have kicked him out of my life sooner." Bernie heard a stifled sob. "Robert drives better than I do, better than Aza. I don't think this was an accident. Will you let me know if you hear anything?"

"Yes. And will you let me know how Robert is doing?"

"Sure. I'm at the hospital now, but they won't let me see him."

Bernie shook off the gloom left in Lona's wake and focused on driving. Cameron lay a few minutes ahead and a longer delay wouldn't add much to Chee's irritation with her. She'd stop and go into the gallery for a minute to see if they still had that rug of Mama's. If so, she'd take a picture. Mama enjoyed seeing where her rugs had gone. She said it must be like learning how the grand-children were doing; grandchildren of whom she had none.

Bernie parked and called Leaphorn again. The case was weighing on her. Too many loose ends, too many disconnects. She listened to the phone ring and wondered what the Lieutenant had come up with about Rick. She wondered why Robert was so fond of By. Probably something as simple as an adult male paying attention to him, something, according to Robert anyway, that Palmer never did.

She left a message on his home machine. Then she called his cell and could tell by how quickly it went to voice mail that he'd turned it off. She left the same message, with a touch of worry in her voice. She decided the rug would wait for another day and headed on to Tuba City.

21

Joe Leaphorn felt better than he had in months.

He had gotten up early, dressed, and headed right to his office. He reviewed notes he'd made the night before and added some new ideas. After a while he smelled the distinctive and wonderful aroma of fresh coffee, closed his computer, took his cane, and walked to the kitchen.

"You're up early," Louisa said. "Like old times."

He opened the cabinet door, took down his favorite cup, put it on the counter, and carefully poured it half full of coffee, as he'd done for years. Even if it was bitter, old, too strong, or otherwise vile, he wanted his coffee hot. And since his injury, the shaking in his hands would have created problems with a full cup.

Louisa mainly drank tea, but she always had coffee in the morning. Like many tea drinkers, she made the coffee weak, but he didn't mind. It was still coffee.

The weekly *Navajo Times* arrived that morning, and Louisa had placed the newspaper by his bowl and spoon. He wasn't crazy about oatmeal, but he knew it was better for him than the fried eggs he loved and ordered at the Navajo Inn. There it sat, the same meal that greeted him every morning except for when he went to the inn for those breakfast brainstorming sessions with the police honchos. Louisa served it up grayish white, bland but abundant. She offered a pitcher of skim milk, honey, and little bowls of walnuts and chewy raisins that made it palatable, but far from delicious.

"Can I have some of the paper?" She stirred the nuts and raisins into her bowl. "I'll let you know what's going on this weekend."

It was a recurring joke between them. She'd say something like, "Look, the Rolling Stones are playing at the Flowing Water Casino. Let's go."

And he'd say, "Who? Never heard of them," and then, "Not tonight, dear."

He handed her everything except the front section. Reading the paper challenged him. Not counting some letters to the editor and an occasional column by the reigning Miss Navajo—part of whose job was to promote the use of the Native language—the paper was written in English. He used it to exercise his brain, translating the headlines, looking at the pictures, and then, if the story seemed interesting or unusual, laboring to understand it.

The first page's big news concerned the ongoing scandal with the Environmental Protection Agency over wastewater from abandoned mines that had contaminated the Navajo Nation's precious water. He glanced at it, and then at the story about a grant for schools in Crownpoint and another about the resignation of a tribal department head after some political squabbling.

At the bottom of the page he saw a color photograph of a group of mostly white people with a few Indians, all waving protest signs. The article concerned the Grand Canyon development mediation. The people looked cold. In the background he noticed a round-faced Hopi officer whom he knew he had met. Ah yes, Cowboy Dashee.

A smaller picture showed a man in a white shirt and Pendleton jacket. He focused on reading the caption, which named the

man, Aza Palmer, and mentioned that a trip to visit the proposed
development site near the confluence of the Colorado and Little
Colorado Rivers would be part of the mediation experience.

Leaphorn stirred the honey, walnuts, and raisins into the oatmeal, added milk, and took a bite. Same as always. Unfortunately.
When Emma shared this table, they ate whatever she found in the
refrigerator for breakfast—leftover beans warmed up in the skil-
let with a tortilla, fruit her relatives had given them, toast, lunch
meat—always with coffee. On special days Emma made blue corn
mush and fried it for a special treat. She'd laugh if she burned it and
serve it anyway because they'd both grown up wasting nothing.
He ate what she offered, burned or otherwise, with gratitude for
her smile. Would he ever get over missing her?

He tried another spoonful of oatmeal. Something about the
smaller picture tickled his brain. He stared at it again.

Louisa glanced over to see what had captured his interest.
"Good article?"

"Ya."

"I thought that Grand Canyon development idea died long ago."

He tapped the story with his index finger. "No."

He wondered what memory, what connection that he couldn't
quite access, the image of Aza Palmer in the photograph triggered.

She said, "I've been reading about blood sugar and how adding
a bit more protein helps keep things regulated, like the way we put
nuts in the oatmeal. You're lucky not to have diabetes, you know.
So many Diné suffer from that. We *bilagaanas*, too."

"Ya." He straightened up in his chair. Another piece of the
Horseman puzzle slipped into place. He finished the last of the
oatmeal and reached for his cane. "Die-bees," he said. "Tanks."

"Diabetes?" She raised an eyebrow. "Did that help you figure
out what you've been worrying over?"

He nodded. Then he offered her a thumbs-up. Emma had never
cared about the details of his work, only worried that he might get
hurt. Louisa liked puzzles.

"You're working on something intriguing, I can tell by the look on your face." She smiled at him. "Good luck."

Diabetes. He thought about that as he walked back to his office. The disease plagued the Navajo Nation in ways the early Diné could never have envisioned. Indian Health Service doctors attributed the problem to poor diet, obesity, lack of exercise, and perhaps a genetic propensity. As in mainstream America, it often led to amputations, kidney failure, blindness, heart problems, and more. Leaphorn sat at his desk and closed his eyes. He took himself back to little Ricky's home, before the boy came to live with his grandmother. He smelled the hot rancid air inside the filthy trailer; the stench of unwashed clothes, soiled diapers, and unemptied garbage. He heard the whimpering baby and the woman's drunken snoring. He remembered the clammy feel of her skin when he tried to wake her.

He recalled how the little boy picked up the baby and attempted to soothe him. He could still hear Ricky saying, "Maybe there's a bottle," and see him opening the ice chest, empty except for cloudy water in which floated two oversized cans of high-octane beer. He pictured Ricky standing next to the gurney and his mother, semiconscious, swatting him away. He remembered the boy cringing and moving away to stand next to him, staring at the ground. He could still feel the boy's little hand as it reached for his.

Leaphorn recalled saying something like, "Get your other shoe and we'll go to your *shimásani*'s place." But his memory found nothing about diabetes.

He stood, stared out the window for a moment, and sat down again. He began to recall the scene at the grandmother's house. He heard the grandmother's puzzled *yá át ééh* as she stood outside near the ramada, and saw her look of surprise and concern as she studied the police car. He could still see Ricky running to her, grabbing her long skirt. She had asked about the baby. Not, he recalled, about the mother.

He took his mind's eye around the ramada, the shelter where

the family cooked and slept when the weather was warm and it reminded him of the familiar smells of his own summers away from what people call civilization. He remembered the order and stability of Mrs. Nez's place, the sound of insects and a horse in the distance, the whine of a dog. He felt the welcome cool of her shade and the smoothness of the plastic cup in which she'd given him water. When he was done, she filled it again and offered some to the little boy. He reexperienced his relief at knowing Ricky was safe.

There was something else about that day, that place. He was sure of it.

He rewound the memory to when he had driven up to the house. He saw a newish pickup with Arizona plates, and he remembered thinking that it was odd for a woman living by her wits and well-honed habits of frugality to have a truck. He remembered asking the grandmother if he could do anything for her before he left. She said, "No. That man cutting wood will be coming in soon. He has to check his sugar." Leaphorn recalled the racket of the chainsaw.

Then he remembered the second child who was there. A slightly older dark-haired boy wearing glasses and a watch with a green dial similar to Ricky's.

Leaphorn opened his eyes, aware that Louisa had spoken to him. He felt her warm hand on his shoulder.

"Did you doze off? Would you like more coffee? There's a little left."

He nodded yes to the second question.

"I'll bring it to you."

On a hunch, he e-mailed Chee and Bernie with a question. He settled in to wait, but to his surprise, Chee responded a few minutes later.

"Strange question, But yes, Palmer has diabetes."

The man working with Mrs. Nez that day little Ricky Horseman arrived in Leaphorn's police car was diabetic. The man was Palmer. But the more he learned, the less he seemed to know.

His visit to Mrs. Nez had been almost twenty years ago. It was time for a road trip.

When Louisa came back with the coffee, he showed her his plan for the rest of the day, typed in English so she would understand. He smiled when she volunteered to go with him, just as he'd hoped she would.

22

Never again, Jim Chee told himself. Next time anyone one asked him to be a bodyguard, he was saying no. Even if the person asking was the chief of police himself and even if the person who needed protection was the Navajo president. No way. No how. Hey, even if the Navajo president himself asked him, he'd say no.

He rolled his head from one side to the other to jar his brain awake. Never again. Period.

After typing out a quick response to Leaphorn's question, he had moved to the back of the room in an effort to watch both Palmer and the characters who'd come to share their views about the development. He thought of Bernie, embarrassed when Darleen told her that she'd run off with the keys to the police unit. He and Palmer caught a ride to the meeting with Dashee. His sweet wife was in for some serious ribbing when he saw her again.

Palmer sat at the table with the delegates. Chee noticed that he'd put his jacket on. The room seemed colder than when the session had started, despite the crowd of people and the abundance of hot air from the speakers. The hefty Anglo woman at the microphone was relating her frustrating experiences finding lodging at the South Rim in the summer, speaking in favor of an additional hotel. Even she wore a sweater.

The most exciting thing that had happened so far had to do with Cowboy Dashee.

Chee had been standing there for more than an hour when he heard the door open. The terrible squeak from yesterday had been fixed, but the door still made a racket. Dashee entered, spotted Chee, and motioned toward the hallway.

From the look on Dashee's face, he expected a problem.

"I saw a neighbor of the Bitsoi lady when I was driving in this morning," Dashee said. "The woman said Mrs. Bitsoi plans to take her sheep out to the highway tomorrow, down the hill toward Moenkopi, straight for US 89. The lady said Mrs. Bitsoi told her she plans to get all dressed up, too."

"It looks like she's moving her flock like you asked."

His friend narrowed his eyes. "I'm not joking about this. She'll reopen old wounds. She'll make a statement in front of the TV cameras with the sheep and the dogs milling around, and her all decked out in a velvet blouse and squash blossom necklaces. She wants to time it for when your president shows up so he will have to say something in response or look like a coldhearted character." Dashee shook his head. "Then our tribal leadership will have to respond. We'll all be embarrassed. You know she's breaking the law." Dashee's voice climbed to almost a shout. "You know all this. Don't make us the bad guys."

Chee said, "Calm down, friend. You're right and I'm on your side." How could any television newsperson resist the arrival of dozens of sheep, dogs, and a woman with fire in her eyes at the Justice Center? Mrs. Bitsoi knew that the Navajo Nation president planned to attend the meeting tomorrow. "I would talk to her about the animals, but I have to stay here to keep an eye on Palmer."

"I know. I'm just giving you a heads-up. That's one furious lady. I'm glad I couldn't understand her when she gave me what for in Navajo."

"Tell you what. I'll ask Captain Ward if one of the other Navajo cops can go out and talk to her."

Dashee smiled. "Tell him not to ask Redbone. Mrs. Bitsoi doesn't like him. Long story."

Back in the meeting room, the woman had finished speaking and the next person stood at the mic. He said his company had constructed other resorts and casinos in conjunction with various Indian communities in Arizona.

"But before I use up my five minutes, I want to complain that it's cold in here. Mr. Palmer, could you get us some heat?"

Palmer looked up from his notes and said, "I'll look into it. Thank you. Please proceed." Then he motioned Chee to the stage. "See if someone can turn up the furnace."

Chee found Silversmith, who knew whom to talk to. A young man in a maintenance uniform with the Navajo Nation seal embroidered on the pocket fiddled with the thermostat and disappeared. Another speaker went to the microphone, and then another. The meeting droned on.

Silversmith came up to him. "Bad news. Maintenance says there's something wrong with the heating system, not just in here, but throughout the whole building. It's dead."

"Dead?"

"The system manager, the guy who knows everything, is on the way. We thought it might have something to do with the power outage yesterday, but . . ."

"But what?"

"The crew thinks somebody might have messed it up on purpose. You know. Vandalism."

Sabotage was a better word, Chee thought.

"Are the two federal agents still around?"

"I'm sure they are."

"Let them know about this."

The current speaker kept to the time limit, more or less. Two more shared their opinions.

Chee had heard it before. The most irrefutable argument was that many different people held the area being considered for the resort sacred: tribes who had lived in the canyon before there was a national park, before John Wesley Powell, before the Spanish explorers. What if a developer made an offer to build a secular playground at Bethlehem, the Wailing Wall, or the Kaaba in Mecca?

The speakers continued to share opinions; the room grew colder.

Silversmith slipped him a sheet of paper, whispered *For Palmer*, and disappeared. The mediator had not scheduled a break, so Chee made his way to the stage. The man at the mic, talking about the possibility of uranium mining in the canyon and how a resort might fit with that scenario, didn't miss a beat.

Palmer met him at the edge of the platform. Chee handed him the note and saw him read it and frown. Chee said, "I've got news about the heat, too."

"Good news?"

"No. The maintenance crew can't fix it, so the system manager is on the way. I'll tell you more later."

Palmer tapped the sheet of paper. "Do you know anything about this?"

"No. But here's something else we need to talk about. An angry woman could be headed toward Tuba tomorrow with a bunch of sheep she wants to introduce to the president."

"That's what we need here. Another chute for the rodeo. Meet me in the back room in a few minutes."

Palmer walked to the podium, surveyed the crowd, then clicked on the microphone as soon as Uranium Man finished. "Ladies and gentlemen, let's take a twenty-minute recess. When we return, I hope to have more information about the heating problem."

A woman seated on the aisle grabbed Chee's arm.

"Can you tell me where the restrooms are?"

He gave her simple directions and heard her opinion on why public buildings should all have more facilities, especially for large meetings like this one. Then his phone buzzed with Bernie, the car-key thief. He'd call her back after he talked to Palmer.

Most of the delegates stayed onstage, some chatting with one another, some checking messages, all of them looking tired and cold. He went to the back room but didn't find Palmer. They had traveled this road before, so Chee stayed calm. He walked out the big exit doors and saw Palmer leaning against the wall, phone in hand. Chee heard him say, "I know. I'm sorry. I'll try . . ."

He acknowledged Chee with a glance and pressed the phone against his arm. "Can you make a call and see how Robert's doing?"

"No problem."

"And find out what's up with the heat? And get me a Coke and a candy bar. I'm fading. I know you don't want me to die on your watch."

Chee called the hospital, learned that the nursing supervisor was with a patient, and left a message with his number and Palmer's. He went inside and spotted Silversmith, who agreed to keep an eye on Palmer until Chee returned from the candy machine and had an update on the furnace crisis. But Silversmith wasn't interested in talking to the Bitsois.

"Captain Ward asked me about that already, but I know the family. They've been angry about the relocation settlement for years and let me know about it. I told the captain you could handle it better than me, and I'd babysit Palmer." Silversmith raised his eyebrows. "Why not leave it to the Hopis?"

"They say they don't have a guy who speaks enough Navajo."

Silversmith made a clicking sound with his tongue. "Navajo, Chinese, Russian? It don't matter what language you use. I know; I've talked to them. Those folks just want to raise a ruckus."

"What's new with the heat?"

"Nothing yet. The system manager and team just got here."

At the candy machine, Chee spotted the M&M's that inspired the silly TV commercials he liked. When he reached in his pocket for the candy money, he felt the envelope for Blankenship. Another errand-boy assignment, but this one self-imposed. He'd wrap it up today. He inserted some coins and pushed the button, then extracted a Coke from the next machine. By the time he returned, the delegates had settled back at their table and Palmer again stood at the podium. Chee told him about the heat guru's recent arrival, gave him the Coke, and put the candy on the podium next to the microphone.

Palmer tore open the bag, sprinkled several into his hand. "What about Robert?"

"The nurse wasn't available, but I left a message for her."

"Let me know." He slid the candy discs into his mouth.

Chee moved to his spot at the edge of the stage and noticed Silversmith heading toward him. The officer kept his voice low. "The big guy found a big problem with the furnace. You want the details, or shall I just brief Palmer?"

Chee felt his phone buzz and ignored it. "What's the bottom line?"

"No heat today. The experts who might know what makes it tick have to come from Flagstaff, and they won't make any promises that they can fix it. Even if they can, the building will take a while to warm up again."

"Go ahead and tell Palmer."

He watched the conversation. Palmer went to the microphone and asked the person in the audience who planned to speak next to wait. The mediator moved to the middle of the stage and huddled with the delegates for several minutes. Then he walked to the podium.

"Ladies and gentlemen, we will resume public commentary in a moment. The heating system won't be repaired today. I will recess the session when I determine that the room has grown too uncomfortable. Tomorrow's public input and the scheduled visit by the Navajo Nation president will be postponed."

Chee heard grumbling in the crowd, but he liked the change of

plan. Fewer opportunities for Palmer to come to harm. He looked
for Dashee, relieved that his friend could tell Mrs. Bitsoi to postpone the presidential sheep walk, but didn't see him. If the captain
agreed that Silverman could watch Palmer, Chee would meet with
Mrs. Bitsoi, maybe even tomorrow.

Audience testimony resumed: a thin, suntanned man with the
Silvery Minnow Protection Association who brought big photographs of the tiny fish. The next speaker, an advocate of expand-
ing air quality controls at the canyon to reduce haze, sounded
hazy himself.

Instead of taking a lunch break, which would have provided
Chee an opportunity to give Blankenship the envelope, the delegates ordered sandwiches to eat at the conference tables.

Chee remembered his phone buzzing earlier and reached to
check it.

It was a text from Bernie: *Doing a favor for Cowboy. He says
hi. Sorry about the keys.*

He shoved his cold hands into his pants pockets and leaned
against the wall.

23

Bernie had been raised to treat others with respect, especially her elders, but the cantankerous woman Dashee had persuaded her to talk to had worn her patience thin. It didn't seem to matter what she said; Mrs. Bitsoi remained determined to take her sheep into Tuba City during the meeting tomorrow, to make a statement about an issue that had been decided long ago. Decided in a way that Mrs. Bitsoi, her family, and many others saw as unfair, but decided nonetheless. Bernie knew that sometimes letting people talk, and listening to them, helped difuse an emotionally charged situation. But that approach hadn't worked here. At least, not yet. But Mrs. Bitsoi talked on.

They stood at the sheep pen. The story had unfolded gradually in the familiar rhythms of Navajo. Listening to Mrs. Bitsoi was the verbal equivalent of watching her mother weave a rug. Word by word, carefully moving forward. Mrs. Bitsoi started with her sheep, descendants of sheep her grandmother had raised.

Bernie considered words precious, not to be used in excess, and Mrs. Bitsoi already had said the equivalent of the giant Navajo rug on display at the museum in Window Rock. And she talked on.

Bernie understood the anger and sadness. Her hiking clothes did a good job of keeping out the November cold, but other ladies she knew would have asked her in and offered her something to drink.

Cowboy Dashee, after explaining the situation over the phone, met her outside the Justice Center, led her to the Bitsoi place, and made the introductions. He told Mrs. Bitsoi, politely, that the Navajo president would delay his visit to the meeting in Tuba City because the Justice Center had no heat. He stayed long enough to hear Bernie tell the woman, in both Navajo and English, that her livestock were trespassing on land that belonged to the Hopi, and by law her family had to remove the animals or the Hopi tribe would be forced to take action. Dashee did his best to look stern and official, nodding in agreement. Mrs. Bitsoi had said nothing.

Bernie gave Dashee credit for trying to make things easier on this lady and her family. But he was a police officer sworn to uphold the law. He'd driven away an hour ago, leaving it to Bernie to dissuade Mrs. Bitsoi from introducing her flock to the Navajo Nation president and persuade her to relocate the trespassers instead.

Mrs. Bitsoi's dog watched from a distance. Its muzzle was white with age, in contrast to the black of its winter coat. In another winter or so, Bernie thought, the dog would be too old to work the sheep. Mrs. Bitsoi hadn't mentioned any relatives who lived nearby, but Dashee had indicated that there were some. Even difficult women had people who looked after them. That was the way it had always worked in Navajoland. But now, raising sheep and cattle wasn't enough. Young people needed a paycheck, and moved to Flagstaff or Phoenix or Albuquerque. Most did their best to stay in touch, but work, school, and children complicated things. She was lucky to have a job that enabled her to stay close to Mama.

The sky had grown heavy with the promise of the season's first snowfall. A time of possibilities, she thought, including the possibility that she could persuade this intractable woman to act reasonably.

"Come inside now, girl." Mrs. Bitsoi finally led the way. She sounded tired. "We will make some tea."

Bernie found a strainer and a glass jar of tea leaves near some canned tomatoes. She saw a metal pot on the top of the stove. It wasn't as cold in Mrs. Bitsoi's hogan as it was outside, but the house was far from warm. The woman stoked the fire.

It took a while for the stove to heat up enough to boil the water, so she sat with Mrs. Bitsoi, who seemed to be done talking. Bernie enjoyed the quiet broken occasionally by the roar of a truck as it made its way up the highway.

When the water was ready, Mrs. Bitsoi made a cup of tea for herself and one for Bernie. The warm drink smelled like sage and autumn, like the tea Mama made. Bernie breathed in its nostalgic aroma with gratitude and wondered what she could say to change the sheep lady's mind.

When Mrs. Bitsoi put her cup on her lap and wrapped her strong hands around it for warmth, Bernie talked about why moving the sheep to Tuba City was a bad idea, both for the sheep and for the Bitsoi family. She explained that, while the Navajo president might be sympathetic, he lacked the power to change the law that clearly said her *dibé*, the dear Navajo sheep, were trespassers.

Mrs. Bitsoi set her cup on the table. "The *dibé* and my grand-mother's mother lived here before the law said we could not stay. Our president, he will be down there." She pointed with a nod of her head toward Tuba City. "I didn't vote for that man, but he needs to know what's going on. That's why we will walk to Tó Naneesdizí."

Bernie said, "This summer, I saw someone moving her sheep. The dogs tried to keep the flock together, keep them off the high-way, but there were too many cars and the road was narrow. Her son was in his truck and he had his flashing lights on to warn driv-ers, but someone came on the other side, driving too fast, and she couldn't stop in time to avoid hitting one of the sheep. By the time I got there, the sheep was dead." The road where she'd seen the disaster was Highway 87, the way to Hopiland from Winslow. But the road Mrs. Bitsoi planned to take her sheep along carried just as much traffic or even more.

Mrs. Bitsoi kept her gaze on her cup.

Bernie said, "I have read about other Diné in the same situation as you. Some of these also resist, but the law has not changed despite their wish that it would." The Navajo Nation had argued against the land settlement back in the 1970s and lost. When the appeals were exhausted, it was time to move on. "The Hopi policeman who has been talking to you about this. He doesn't want anything to happen to you or the sheep, but he has to do his job. You told me your job is to take care of the wooly ones out there."

Mrs. Bitsoi raised her cup to her mouth, took a swallow, then spoke. "My grandmother's mother, she raised the ancestors of my sheep. She saved a few she loved most from the bad time when so many were killed."

Bernie knew that many elderlies had experienced firsthand what history books called "livestock reduction." They remembered watching government agents herd the animals into side canyons and kill them. The meat, which could have fed many families, and the wool, which could have been spun and woven, was left to rot. The old ones probably still saw dead sheep in their nightmares.

When Mrs. Bitsoi spoke again, Bernie heard the determination in her voice. "My grandmother and my mother taught me about the sheep. Sheep are my life, my family. We will stay here. If that Hopi policeman needs to take me to jail, well, what can I do about that?"

Bernie drove back to Tuba City in the dark, feeling like a failure. She thought of another elder of strong opinions, Lieutenant Leaphorn. She'd tried to call him before she left for Mrs. Bitsoi's place and missed him again. When she got back to the hotel, she'd check her e-mail and see if he'd sent her anything about Rick Horseman's death.

She had passed Coal Mine Canyon when her phone buzzed. Chee. Finally!

"Honey, where are you?"

"Driving back from Mrs. Bitsoi's place."

"So Dashee sweet-talked you, eh?"

"Oh, he knows I have a soft spot for the *dibé*. But Mrs. Bitsoi didn't listen to anything I said."

"Are you close to the hotel?"

"A few miles out. Why?"

"We have to leave for the reception in a few minutes."

"What reception?"

"For the mediation." She heard a touch of frustration in his voice. "Did you forget?"

"Do I have to go?"

"Palmer asked me twice if you were coming and I told him yes."

Before she could object Chee said, "I might need your help. The Arizona officers won't be there tonight."

"I hate stuff like this."

"There will be food. Once the crowd starts to thin out, you can leave."

"Any news about the Shiprock investigation?"

"Yeah. The group from California—Save Wild America— looks clean in this case. The feds are offering a reward for information."

"Any more threats to Palmer?" She turned on the car's heater. The warm air felt wonderful on her frozen toes.

"No. But the heat is out in the building, and it could be sabotage. Palmer canceled tomorrow's session, but the delegates are going to take a bus out to see the potential hotel site. What happened to Robert spooked him. He must have smoked a pack of cigarettes already today. I've called the hospital so much I have them on speed dial."

"How is Robert?"

"Still in intensive care."

Bernie remembered the young man's agitation when he left

Cameron after their conversation. "Did I tell you that Robert said Rick's death was his fault?"

"Why did he say that?"

"He wouldn't talk about it." And, she thought, she hadn't pushed.

Chee said, "Oh, Leaphorn asked us if Palmer was diabetic. I told him yes, so you can ignore it."

"Odd."

"I'll ask him about that when I get a chance. I have to leave for the event in about twenty minutes. Do you want to go with me or meet there?"

"I just pulled into the parking lot. Let's go together."

Bernadette Manuelito wasn't one for fancy clothes, so she was glad she could attend the reception in jeans. She wished she'd brought her special-occasion boots, but wearing the trainers would be more comfortable. Luckily, she had her heart-shaped earrings, the ones Chee's cousin had crafted. They always made her feel special.

They met Palmer in the lobby. He wore a different white shirt, this one with silver buttons and blue edging around the collar.

"I finally heard from the hospital," Palmer said. "Robert is still unconscious."

"I hope he comes out of this OK," Chee said.

"Me, too." Bernie decided not to mention the call from Lona.

At the reception, Chee found a seat where he could observe Palmer as he chatted with the delegates and other guests. Bernie surveyed the room, already half filled with attendees.

The food looked delicious, beginning with fry bread, each plate-sized piece separated with paper towels. The hotel staff had filled the shallow aluminum bins on the steam table with other things Bernie liked: pinto beans, ground beef, and corn chips—the makings for Frito pie. She noticed little hot dogs on toothpicks, the sliced tortilla rolls, some with peanut butter and jelly inside and some with what looked like dried beef and cream cheese. She saw barbecue sauce for the hot dogs and chopped onions, red chili sauce, and grated cheese—the toppings to join the beef on the fry bread for a Navajo taco or on the corn chips for Frito pie. Then came the expected bowl of salad greens, virtually untouched. Too bad CS wasn't here.

At the end of the food parade sat plates of perfectly round cookies, oatmeal on one side and chocolate chip on the other, a platter with grapes and wedges of oranges, and bowls of red Jell-O topped with dollops of whipped cream. A bin of canned soft drinks and a large coffeepot stood at the end.

It looked like too much food for the delegates, but among the people in the room she saw clusters of faces she hadn't spotted onstage. The Navajo tradition of hospitality reigned. The staff wouldn't challenge anyone who came for food and a soda unless Palmer gave the order. When she'd gone to receptions at the university in Albuquerque, for instance, she thought it odd that people hadn't brought their children along. Now she understood that mainstream culture preferred "adult only" events. But she didn't like it. Children added joy to anything.

A man came up to her as she was contemplating the food. He was clean-shaven and wore a knit cap. There was something vaguely familiar about him.

"Hi. I didn't see you at the session. Are you representing one of the tribes?"

"No. I'm here with my husband, Sergeant Chee." She knew to discourage flirting early.

He nodded. "Thomas Blankenship."

He extended his hand. She took it and told him her name. "Chee has something for you."

"Yeah, he told me. He wanted to give me an envelope from an old Navajo woman. I thought he was joking."

Bernie summarized the details. "How do you know Rick Horseman?"

"I don't. Never heard of him. Chee can return whatever it is back to Granny." Blankenship took a sip from his water bottle. "So do you live around here, Bernie?"

"Depends on how you look at it, I guess. I'm from Shiprock. How about you?" She wasn't good at small talk, but she had learned something about it, dealing with so many white people. She learned to answer a question and then ask one.

"Oh, I'm from Page. I'm the delegate for the Association of Outdoor Recreation Professionals. Actually, 'delegate' sounds too formal. I'm just a die-hard river rat."

She knew a question was on its way.

"Have you taken a trip down the Colorado?"

"No." The idea of spending so much time on or in water made her uncomfortable.

"You have to do that. You've been to the Grand Canyon at least?"

"Yes. What do you think about the Canyonmark plan?"

He frowned. "Canyonmark wants to give the lazy jerks, too fat and out of shape to even get out of their cars at the overlooks, a cushy place to stay. The resort will destroy the environment, including the river. Guys like me, river contractors who want to live free and make a buck, will be out of business because of the mess their construction makes. Don't believe what they say about environmental protection. All that's just bull . . ."

She followed his glance, and it settled on Palmer, who was at a table with the Hopi delegate, Mr. Keevama, his wife, a little girl in a pink dress, and a smaller boy in black pants with a can of orange soda.

Blankenship said, "After something like the Shiprock bomb, people always wonder if there will be another explosion, don't they? But those sodas in the buffet over there, they're more likely to do people harm. I saw Chee come into the session with a soda and candy and give them to Palmer. No wonder Palmer's thinking is so off base."

Bernie badly wanted a Coke. "Palmer's diabetic. Maybe he was having a blood sugar issue."

Blankenship raised his eyebrows again. She noticed that his nose and forehead were as brown as a pecan shell, but his cheeks looked chalky white. Bernie realized why he seemed familiar: Darleen had sketched his face as the man who had treated Chee rudely.

Blankenship took a sip from his fancy bottle. "What do you do?"

"I'm a cop."

"You're in such good shape, I thought you might be a physical trainer or something. Do you work out a lot?"

Too personal. Time to change the subject.

"Mr. Palmer's son told me you wanted to hire him to do some work for you, spying or something. How do you know Robert?"

"Oh, I ran into him somewhere. Spying? That's a hoot. I asked him to do some research but he declined. He sure doesn't like his dad." Blankenship laughed. "He's in good company there. This whole meeting thing is a sham, a way for Palmer to add another star to his résumé. You know, he encourages the wackos—self-righteous defenders of little fish and abandoned pueblos and Indian groups who could put their whole tribe in a minivan—to think they're legitimate. But no one cares about the hardworking people who love the river and the canyon and make our livelihood there. Our clients have invested a big chunk of change and a lot of energy getting ready for the trip of a lifetime, their dream adventure on a magnificent river. And the resort would threaten that."

"It's a complicated situation." Bernie stood a little straighter. "I'm going to get something to eat."

"Be careful. Nothing healthy on that buffet except the fruit and salad."

Bernie walked toward the food. A woman wearing a turquoise-and-coral choker moved the same direction, and Bernie let her in the line first. "What a gorgeous necklace. Do you know who made it?"

The woman put her hand to her neck. "I don't know. My mother got it for me in Fruitland at the Hatch Brothers Trading Post when she and my dad made their first trip out west."

"Hi. I'm Bernie Manuelito." She saw the question in the woman's eyes. "My husband is the sergeant providing security for Mr. Palmer and I'm backup. I'm a cop, too."

"Jessica Atwell. I'm not good at parties like this."

"Me neither. Are you a delegate?"

"Oddly, yes." Atwell smiled. "I represent the Archaeology Conservancy."

"Why is that odd?"

"When I retired from Crow Canyon and moved to Santa Fe, I started volunteering with the conservancy and one thing led to another. My dad was an archaeologist who worked at Chaco Canyon in the summers, and Mom and we kids tagged along. That's where my interest in archaeology began. More than you wanted to know, right?"

"No, it's interesting." Bernie took a plate and followed Atwell down the buffet line.

Atwell took some of the tortilla rolls. "I saw there was a threat on Palmer's life. Is that why your husband is here?"

Bernie nodded. "Mr. Palmer's car blew up. The FBI is trying to figure out why."

"That might be a big job." She lowered her voice. "I heard the tribe that runs the other resort was behind the attack. Some people think he favors environmentalists because of the way a couple of his other mediations in Indian Country turned out. A lot of people aren't fond of Palmer."

A man with his gray hair in braids came to stand in line behind them.

"Jessica?"

As soon as he spoke, Bernie recognized the gravelly voice as the man who had called Palmer and driven off with him. Atwell introduced her to Denny Duke and then said, "I'm surprised you're here, Denny. Last I heard, you Paiutes didn't have a seat at the table."

"Palmer invited me. I guess he feels guilty. I heard that he's in the pocket of the developers."

Duke turned to Bernie. "You're not from around here. Are you part of the Diné delegation?"

"I'm from Shiprock. Not a delegate."

"I understand that some Indians are so riled up that they are workin' behind the scenes. You know about that, miss?"

"No."

Duke said, "Who's paying for this shindig?"

"I heard Canyonmark was," Atwell said.

"I just got hungrier." Duke patted his belly. "Nothing like letting the opposition buy you dinner." He winked at Bernie, and she remembered where she had seen him before. In the lobby of the Pit after the explosion.

Bernie glanced in Chee's direction. He motioned, *Come on over.* She filled her plate, grabbed a Coke, and headed toward his table. The seat he'd saved for her provided a clear view of Palmer and the Hopi family. She settled in. "What's up?"

"I got a call from Largo. The FBI analyzed their surveillance photos from the demonstration and the session here yesterday. One of the people they saw resembles a man arrested several times on various charges, including stalking a lawyer who represented a resort developer. They think they saw him in the photos you took at the Shiprock bomb scene, too."

She took a bite of the burrito she'd built. "That's interesting. You see that tall guy, the one in the white hat?"

"Yes."

"He's the medic I mentioned who helped me at the blast site when the rookie freaked out."

"Why is he here?"

Bernie took a sip of her Coke. "He told me he's a contractor who might be taking a job with Canyonmark. Nice man."

"Have you seen Blankenship here yet?"

"He was by the wall talking to the woman with the turquoise choker. I mentioned the envelope to him. He said he doesn't want it."

"Too bad. He's getting it anyway." Chee took the last bite of the Fritos with onions, chili, and cheese. "Did you try this? Tasty."

"As good as at Chat and Chew?" She loved Shiprock's little carryout-only place near the pawnshop.

"It might depend on how hungry—"

Chee rose from his chair in a single quick motion and left the table. Bernie followed him with her eyes.

The man in a yellow jacket had entered the reception room with a galvanized bucket in his right hand and headed directly toward Palmer and the Keevama family. Chee moved to intercept him.

Palmer stood up. "Hey there, what's—"

The man lunged toward Palmer just as Chee grabbed for him. The contents of the bucket flew out as Yellow Jacket screamed obscenities. Chee felt the shock of cold water through his clothes and a thunk of something solid as it hit his torso. Palmer's white shirt clung to his skin, but the Hopis, farther from the incident, looked mostly dry.

The bucket clanged against the tile floor and bounced, a sound track for the man's rant. "You sellout. You jerk. You don't give a rat's ass . . ." Yellow Jacket struggled against Chee's grip, trying to swing at Palmer. His voice was an angry yell. "You want to turn the water into a death trap for fish. The whole river will die unless you protect it. You and all of your phony delegates."

The Hopi children hid behind their mother. Chee had seldom heard a Hopi man shout, but Keevama raised his voice. "Stop it. Behave yourself. Show some respect."

The room fell quiet, as though the man's explosion of energy had sucked the air out of the space. All eyes were on Yellow Jacket and the Hopi. Chee noticed that Palmer remained remarkably calm. A non-Native man in a polo shirt and a woman in a snug sweater, both of whom Chee labeled as FBI, had moved closer.

Yellow Jacket turned his outrage toward Keevama. "You Indians stink as bad as the developers. You talk a good line, but

in the end you just want the money. You don't care about your
fellow creatures if they get in the way of your pla—" Yellow Jacket
looked at Chee as if noticing him for the first time. "Let go of me."

"You're under arrest." Chee kept his grip on the man's damp
arm, pulling him toward the exit. He saw something shiny on the
floor. Fish. Dozens of them, small, silvery, and still. Dead. The
impact he'd felt, he realized, came from some of these poor things
striking his chest when the crazy man tossed out the water.

"Did you kill those fish?"

"They were already dead, man. I got them at the grocery.
Got your attention, huh?" Yellow Jacket raised his voice again.
"Thousands of these will die if the project is approved. Hear that,
Palmer?"

Chee shivered at the jarring sight. He never ate fish and never
went fishing. He shared the ancient Navajo belief that fish served as
messengers between the Holy People and the five-fingered beings.
He felt Yellow Jacket try to twist away.

"First Amendment rights, brother," he yelled. "You Indians
know what it's like to be ignored, discriminated against. But now
you're working for the Man."

Chee felt his anger build and fought the impulse to squeeze the
man's arm more tightly. He noticed a person next to him, pointing
his cell phone at them, no doubt recording the whole affair. He
saw Bernie next to Palmer, professional and alert for other signs
of trouble.

He ushered Yellow Jacket to the door, the FBI agents right
behind them.

Outside, he felt the chill of night air on his wet skin. The polo
shirt man and the woman in the sweater showed him their creden-
tials, explained that they were from Phoenix, assigned to the bombing case. "We'll take it from here. This guy has been on our radar."

Yellow Jacket uttered a string of obscenities that concerned the
agents' parentage. "You know you don't have anything on me.
Federal Bureau of Ineptitude."

The man in the polo shirt said, "Let's start with assault and resisting arrest?"

Yellow Jacket swore some more as the agent reached for his handcuffs.

"We've got this, Sergeant. You might want to find some dry clothes."

"Is either of you the agent who's replacing Cordova?"

The woman said, "I know it's not me and it's not my partner here. You probably have more information than we do."

Chee jogged to his motel room. When he took off his damp jacket, he realized the envelope for Blankenship was soaked, too. He set it on the bathroom counter.

By the time Chee returned to the party, the restaurant staff had arranged yellow plastic signs around the wet places and the bucket was gone. A young Diné woman about Darleen's age worked on the mess with the same disgust Bernie's sister would have shown if she'd been asked to clean up dead fish.

Palmer, still in his damp shirt, was chatting with Atwell. He had a plate of food on the table in front of him now. Bernie sat next to the Hopi elder, Palmer within easy reach. Chee joined them.

Keevama said, "Your wife was telling me that she went out to talk to the Bitsois. Officer Dashee has been very patient with them."

Bernie said, "Mrs. Bitsoi was the only one at home. I got the idea that she's in charge and does most of the work. She spent a long time telling me about her sheep."

"I think those sheep are the only ones she doesn't argue with," Keevama said.

Chee said, "Is everyone here OK?"

Palmer said, "I'm fine."

Keevama shook his head. "What a crazy man. My wife and the children left. She felt uncomfortable after what happened. I'm asking Officer Dashee to go with the delegates to the site tomorrow. It would be good to have those federal agents, the ones who went outside with you, inspect the bus before it leaves. We don't want another explosion."

Chee nodded in agreement. He wondered if it would surprise the feds to learn that Mr. Keevama had figured out who they were.

Keevama turned to Bernie, "I heard you were there when the bomb went off in Shiprock. Do they know who was responsible for that?"

"Not that I've heard. It's still under investigation."

Keevama rose. "I need to get home. I told my kids I'd bring them some cookies and I need to talk to them about what happened, make sure they're not scared."

Bernie rose, too. "I could use a cookie and some quiet myself. I'll walk with you."

Gradually, other delegates began to drift out. Chee looked fruitlessly for more bad behavior as he watched Palmer socialize. He wished the day had ended several hours ago.

Bernie took her cookies back to the motel room. When she went into the bathroom, she noticed the damp envelope next to the sink where Chee had left it. She opened it, planning to separate the money so it could dry. As she slipped out the limp hundreds she felt something fastened to one of the bills. She saw a yellow Post-it. Someone had printed on it in big block letters: "DOWN PAYMENT."

24

Joe Leaphorn parked his truck a respectful distance from Mrs. Nez's hogan and waited. Not much had changed.

"Are you sure this is the right house?"

"Ya." He nodded in Louisa's direction.

"I'm amazed that you could find it after all those years. You drove straight here."

He hadn't actually. He'd made a couple wrong turns that looped back to the road he wanted without his having to turn around. Louisa had been sleeping and hadn't noticed.

He waited for the front door to open, but it didn't. He saw no vehicles in the driveway either.

Louisa stretched in her seat. "Either nobody's here or nobody wants to talk to you."

Then, just as he had begun to consider leaving, a truck pulled up next to them with two women inside, an old one and an even older one who was driving.

The truck's passenger cranked down her window, and Leaphorn lowered his. The warm air escaped quickly.

The woman driver leaned across the seat toward him and spoke in Navajo. "I remember you. I have been thinking about you after what happened to my grandson. Come inside and help us start the fire." She moved her lips toward Louisa. "You come, too."

Leaphorn was glad he kept some work gloves in the truck. It had been a long time, before his head injury, since he'd done much physical work. Splitting the firewood into burnable pieces got his blood moving. Louisa assisted with hauling it into the house, and they filled Mrs. Nez's bins.

Mrs. Nez's sister put the coffeepot on and then settled on the couch with what looked like a quilt under construction. When the coffee was ready, Mrs. Nez served them each a cup, already sugared. Louisa said she would sit by the fire with her book and let them talk. Leaphorn knew she'd want him to give her the details later.

Mrs. Nez opened the conversation in Navajo. "You still a policeman, or did you get too old?"

"I work now and then giving police officers advice and helping people with problems. Grandmother, do you remember how we met?"

She nodded. "You brought my grandson here to keep him safe when he was a little boy. You were kind to him."

"There was another child at his mother's place, a baby that cried a lot. When the ambulance took his mother to the hospital, they also took the baby with them. I could tell you had worries about him."

"That one is dead now, too." Mrs. Nez swallowed. "Gone a long time ago."

Just as Butterfly's notes had said.

Mrs. Nez stirred her coffee. "Why are you here?"

Leaphorn had anticipated the question. "The woman officer who talked to you about your grandson had some questions about what happened to him and she asked me to help. I knew you would be the best person to come to for the answers. I would like you to tell me about the one who died, how he grew up and what kind of a man he became. Because of my work as a policeman, I know he had some trouble."

Mrs. Nez let the request and Leaphorn's statement linger for several minutes, hanging in the air with the aroma of piñon and juniper from the fire. She sat back in her chair. She was thinking, Leaphorn knew, and missing the young man who had shared her home and her life.

"Yes, that grandson had trouble his whole life but he was a good boy. I called him Zoom because when he was little he liked to push those little toys cars around and he'd make that zooooom sound. So cute and funny." Her smile faded. "Zoom's mother would drink and find mean men. The boy would come to me. Then she would stop for a while, and Zoom would live with her. She loved him, but she loved beer better. By the time that second son came, she was using drugs, even though she lied about it, and had more boyfriends. One of those men hit the little one. When the baby died, she sank down further with more men, more drugs, more beer. Mrs. Nez looked past Leaphorn, out the window toward the mountains. "When the baby died, Zoom changed. He felt guilty. He thought he should have saved him, even though he was still a little boy himself.

"Zoom lived here with me here for a while, and that was good. His uncle, the one we called *Bizaadii* helped him, taught him how to be a Navajo. But then those people who think they know everything said that my grandson should be back with his mother."

Leaphorn knew she meant the child welfare workers.

"He met some bad boys. He starting drinking, not going to school much, stealing little things, They said he tried to drive off in someone else's car. I knew he was going around in cars he didn't buy. When he had no place to live, he asked if he could stay with me again. We had a ceremony for him. He stopped drinking and smoking *naakai binát'oh*. He wanted to become a good man."

Naakai binát'oh, Mexican cigarettes, marijuana, was common on the reservation even in Leaphorn's early days as a policeman. It was as easy to find on the rez as it was in the rest of America.

Mrs. Nez sipped her coffee. "I forgot something. When *Bizaadii* moved away after the baby died, that's when Zoom started having problems."

Mrs. Nez sipped her coffee and Leaphorn used the pause to ask a question.

"Can you tell me about *Bizaadii*?" The nickname referred to someone who liked to talk.

Mrs. Nez nodded. "Did you know I had two daughters? The younger one, she had a baby in high school and that boy, we called him Rocket, stayed with me, too. Then she married the baby's father, the one we called *Bizaadii*, and they moved away. But in Arizona it was just the three of them. No, the two of them, because her husband was at work or in school and didn't have time for her or that boy. After they divorced, my daughter found a better man, that Mr. Lee. I thought he was Navajo when she told me his name. I never met him, but he's a *bilagaana* like your lady." Mrs. Nez turned her chin toward Louisa, who was engrossed in her book. "My daughter said he liked to wear a white cowboy hat. Mr. Lee treats my grandson Rocket real good but my daughter kicked him out because she still loves that *Bizaadii*. That's all I have to say."

Leaphorn watched Mrs. Nez raise her gaze to the window and the vast spaces of Navajoland beyond. He let the silence sit, watching the vehicles in the yard catch the cool fall sunlight. Then he spoke. "Officer Manuelito noticed that your grandson's truck was here at the house, not at the gym where he got hurt. The officer thought his girlfriend might have picked him up."

Mrs. Nez squeezed her lower lip with her teeth, then released it. "It could have been."

"But it wasn't, correct?"

"The girlfriend wanted to marry Zoom, but they couldn't until he saved money, so they broke up last month. A few days before the big basketball game, Rocket came over. He was doing some work out here somewhere with Mr. Lee. He said Mr. Lee had a friend, a man with a funny name, who needed to hire someone who knew about cars. The next day my grandson went to Shiprock, and when he came back, his spirit was restless, like when he used to get into trouble. I asked what worried him. At first he didn't answer, but then he showed me money in an envelope. He said the job was putting something in a car and that he would be paid more after the job was done."

Leaphorn straightened in his chair.

"I asked what he had to put in the car and whose car it was, and my grandson said the man would tell him at the basketball game. Zoom needed money, but the secret part made him nervous. That's why he asked Rocket to pick him up to go to the game. He wanted to talk to Rocket about the job."

Mrs. Nez looked at the back of her hands. "If it was something bad, I know my grandson wouldn't do it. He left the envelope here with money to go back to the man."

"Did you ever meet that man?"

Mrs. Nez said, "No, but I saw him once, just as I got to the house and he was leaving. A tall, thin *bilagaana*. He wore a white hat."

She rose and refilled their cups. The liquid looked darker now and smelled more acidic. Leaphorn sipped the coffee, seeing the pieces of the puzzle fall into place and knowing what he had to ask next.

"Someone saw a man who looked like your grandson inside Mr. Palmer's car before it blew up. Why would that be?"

Mrs. Nez's face fell slack. She shook her head.

Leaphorn put his cup down. "Was your grandson angry with *Bizaadii*?"

"Not Zoom. Rocket was the angry one. Rocket wanted Mr. Lee to be his dad, and I know Mr. Lee treats him good. But my daughter said no because her heart still belonged to *Bizaadii*."

Leaphorn told Mrs. Nez a little about the shooting that left him walking with the cane. After answering his questions, it seemed only fair that he answer hers—even those she left unspoken. They listened to the crackle of the wood in the stove and the gentle snoring of the sister, who had fallen asleep over her quilt.

As he rose to leave, Leaphorn recalled Bernie's suspicion that Mrs. Nez had lied about Rick knowing Palmer. Mrs. Nez told Bernie that Rick never mentioned Aza Palmer, never said Palmer's name.

"You and your daughter called Aza Palmer *Bizaadii*. Did Zoom call him that, too? Or did he call him Mr. Palmer, or Aza?"

She raised an eyebrow, surprised at the question. "He called him *shidá'í*. He called him uncle, of course."

"Did Sergeant Chee take care of that envelope?"

"I don't know."

"I found it here with funny name on it, and I remembered Zoom said that he would have to go to the meeting in Tuba City to give it back. They wouldn't let me in the meeting, so I gave it to Chee. I thought I could trust him."

"I've trusted him with my life," Leaphorn said. "I'm sure he did the right thing."

As soon as he and Louisa left Mrs. Nez's house, Leaphorn started an e-mail. He flinched at the idea of Louisa driving his truck, but he wanted to focus his full attention on writing what he needed to tell Bernie, including the strange notion of two *bilagaanas* in Mrs. Nez's circle, each wearing a white cowboy hat.

25

A streamlined white coach the length of a small school bus arrived outside the Tuba City Justice Center. Chee and Dashee watched it pull into the parking lot.

Dashee looked at the sky, then back at the bus. "Half the population of Moenkopi would fit inside that thing. Where is your guy anyway?"

"Over there on the phone. Probably thinking about a cigarette before we leave."

"No need to be in a hurry." Dashee glanced overhead again. "The canyon will be foggy. No one will be able to see much."

Chee looked at the sky, brilliant blue and crystal clear.

"Foggy, huh? Like in those movies filmed in San Francisco?"

"Like the ones where the ships are getting closer and closer to each other but the captain can't see anything." Dashee swooped his hands up from his sides and clapped them together. "Then, ka-BAM! I haven't seen weather like this much. But when it comes, it's usually in November. They call it an inverse weather system. Why don't you mention it to Palmer?"

Chee said, "Why don't *you* mention it? The day looks fine to me. You're the one who lives out here."

"You're the bodyguard."

"You're the weather expert."

"What are you two arguing about?" Sergeant Redbone's voice startled Chee.

"We're talking about the weather. Dashee predicts heavy fog."

"Yeah, that fog is something. The whole canyon disappears. My wife was telling me how beautiful it looked on her drive to work this morning."

"You found someone to marry you?" Chee laughed. "Never thought I'd see the day you got so lucky."

"Believe it or not, she says she got lucky."

Dashee said, "See, I know about fog. So, is your wife a park ranger?"

"No, she has a job in the big bookstore at the visitor center. She grew up out here, went to school in Flagstaff, got a degree in library science, worked in Prescott for a while, retired with a nice pension, and then took that gig at the canyon. That's how I met her." He turned to Chee. "After you found Bernie, I figured there was hope for this old bachelor, too. Is Bernie here?"

"Not yet."

"Do you think Palmer knows about the fog?"

"No." Chee looked at Dashee.

Dashee said, "It's a blessing. Rare and beautiful."

"Palmer and the delegates might not see it that way. They might just see clouds where the canyon used to be. Somebody should mention it." Redbone looked at the bus. "Why didn't he rent a smaller van?"

"Beats me," Chee said.

Dashee said, "That's one of the buses the tour companies use to drive people up to First Mesa for the Walpi tour. I guess Palmer wanted to make sure there was plenty of room for us cops to go, too. And Mr. Keevama is bringing his wife and kids. Maybe Palmer's going to toss a bone to some of the protesters and let them ride along today to see the fog."

Redbone angled his ample weight toward Chee. "You heard any more about the problem with the heat yesterday?"

"Yeah. Looks like it was vandalism, the same as the power going off. It should be working again tomorrow."

"Wow. Any idea who did it?"

"No. Captain Largo told me the feds now think the young guy who died in the explosion might have links to the bomber after all. One of the witnesses saw him in the car before it exploded."

I'm following the bus in my unit, just to be on the safe side." Dashee chuckled. "Mr. Keevama has a meeting at two, so I'm going to drive him back here if the field trip runs long. I told his kids they could ride with me. They're excited about being in a police car."

Chee noticed Palmer motioning his way. "I gotta see what the man wants."

Palmer got right to the point. "Delegate Jessica Atwell has to attend a teleconference with her husband and her mother-in-law's doctors. The old lady is in a nursing home, and they have to make some emergency decisions about her care. She won't be done in time to catch the bus with us. You need to wait here and then give her a ride out to the site. "

"I have to stay with you. You know that, especially after the vandalism and the dead fish."

"Help me out here, Chee. I can't postpone the trip long enough for Atwell to take her call. She can't drive herself because her husband has their car."

"Why not go without her?"

"The delegates and I made a promise that everyone would have access to all the same information." Palmer shifted his black bag to his other shoulder. "Do it. You hate this bodyguard stuff anyway."

Chee said nothing.

"OK, then figure out how to solve this."

"Ask someone else to be a chauffeur."

More cars had pulled up. He saw Blankenship, with a hat pulled over his ears, and Duke, with his jacket unzipped, talking together. The information Bernie had shared from Leaphorn's interview with Mrs. Nez fueled his dislike for Blankenship. And Duke was on his bad list from last night's escapade even though Palmer had gone with him willingly.

Protesters milled about. In addition to Save Wild America, Chee saw some homemade signs that read "Let the Fish Swim." He noticed Bernie keeping an eye on things.

Palmer spoke quietly. "Have you heard anything about Robert?"

"Not yet. The nurse promised to call me if there's any change." Chee hesitated. "Any change for better or worse. Did someone brief you about the fog?"

"Fog?"

Chee explained what Dashee and Redbone had said about the weather. "Dashee said he's seen this kind of fog before, and that it fills the canyon from rim to rim. With this and Atwell's problem, you could—"

Palmer cut him off. "Cancel? No. This is the only day we have the bus. I can't control the weather, and besides, the drive out there and back will help build camaraderie. What about Bernie? Could she chauffer Atwell?"

"I don't make decisions for her. You can ask her. She's over there."

Chee noticed how Palmer stood a bit straighter as they walked toward Bernie. And he noticed that his pretty wife didn't notice.

"Hey, Bernie, I need a little favor."

"First, how's Robert?"

"No change."

"Well, that means he's not worse."

Palmer said, "Could you give Ms. Atwell a ride out to the proposed development site?" He explained the reason.

Chee said, "Dashee is driving the Hopis and the feds will be on the bus with me. It might be good to have the unit out there."

Bernie said, "Will there be lunch?"

Palmer explained that he had arranged for a food truck. "That's why Duke is here. He and his mom are cooking and serving. Come on, Manuelito. Atwell has me in a bind."

"OK. I'd like to see the site." She smiled at him. "Great jacket, by the way. I love the turquoise."

Palmer put his hands in his pockets. "These coats last forever." He gave her Atwell's phone number. "She will meet you in the hotel lobby as soon as she's done. I'm going to start loading the bus."

Bernie said, "Before you go, tell me something. How well do you know Blankenship?"

"Mostly by reputation. He's a raft contractor and speaks for the association. Before that he worked for some environmental group. Passionate guy. Why do you ask?"

"A friend of mine thinks he might be dangerous."

Palmer laughed. "You're starting to sound like your husband. See you at the canyon."

26

Back at the motel Bernie opened the door to her room and saw the neatly made bed, the fresh towels in the bathroom, and the three one-hundred-dollar bills just where she'd left them. She knew she and Chee were lucky that the hotel had such an honest cleaning staff. She put the money and the note back in the envelope and then inside the room safe. It was good that Blankenship didn't want the money, she thought, now that it might be evidence.

She called Cordova to discuss the links between Robert and Rick and Palmer and Blankenship the night of the bombing. She couldn't reach him and didn't leave a message; the interconnections were too complicated. She put the book she was reading in her backpack and went out to the police unit.

As she parked at the Hotel Hopi, she felt her phone buzz with a text message. Darleen? No, a reminder from Sandra about a staff meeting next week. Not hearing from her sister made her edgy, especially when Darleen was a long way from home with someone male. CS seemed trustworthy, but so did a good scammer.

She sat in the lobby waiting for Atwell, called Mama, and listened to the news, mostly a progress report on Mrs. Bigman. "She comes every week. I try to show her what to do, and she tries to learn. She picks me up in her car and we go to that senior center. They keep it warm there. Next time, she says she's coming early so we can have lunch. The food is for us elderlies, but that one can eat if she pays a little." The woman had begun to grasp the basics, Mama said, but Mrs. Bigman made a lot of mistakes. Mama said it with a smile in her voice.

"Daughter, are you still at Tó Naneesdizí?"

"I am."

"You sound like you have something on your mind."

"I'm waiting for a lady who is part of that big meeting about the Grand Canyon. I'm giving her a ride."

"Do you know why that young man died?"

"Not yet."

"Remember this: it wasn't your fault. Just like when your Lieutenant friend got shot. That wasn't your fault either."

Bernie helped herself to the hotel's free coffee and pulled the novel from her backpack.

A light touch on the shoulder interrupted her reading. "Hi there." Jessica Atwell wore a knee-length coat with a fur-trimmed hood and looked as though she'd been crying. "Thanks for being my driver. Sorry for the trouble. I'm ready to go. I've never ridden in a police car."

As Bernie drove, Atwell tearfully volunteered the details about her mother-in-law's illness. Bernie expressed her sympathy. "With that family situation to deal with, how did you make the time to be part of the mediation?"

"I care what happens at the canyon, and the Archaeology Conservancy board of directors had no one else with, well, how shall I say it? With the right temperament. It's good in a way. Gives me something different to focus on."

Bernie adjusted the rearview mirror. "How long do you think the mediation will take?"

"I don't know. If Blankenship has his way, we will fire Palmer and disband, leave things as they are. He joined some us for dinner after the party last night. He believes Palmer sees the canyon as a place for people to admire from their car windows or buzz over in helicopters. He thinks Canyonmark will destroy what he calls the 'wild soul of the Grand Canyon' by making it easier for people to visit who can't walk without help, who can't breathe without oxygen tanks, who aren't what he calls 'normal.' He said those old coots—that's what he called them—gave up their right to visit the canyon by not taking care of themselves, by watching movies instead of running marathons."

Atwell took a tissue from her purse and blew her nose.

"Mom is one of those old coots, I guess. She's in a wheelchair now and on oxygen. She always wanted to see the Grand Canyon, but she can barely make it from her bed to the toilet. That guy is a first-rate horse's—" She interrupted herself. "Bernie, did you see that?"

"What was it?"

"A big animal."

Bernie looked in the rearview mirror and scanned the roadside. "Probably a deer. They're common here, a problem actually."

"No, it looked like a huge coyote or a muscular oversized fox, but the tail was different. I just caught a glimpse. I'm glad it wasn't in the road." Atwell stretched her hands toward the heater vent. "What's going on with the weather? Is a storm coming? It feels cooler."

Bernie said, "I hear there's fog at the canyon. I bet it's beautiful."

She turned off the main highway at the designated spot and followed the dirt road over Navajo reservation land toward the potential construction site. After a few minutes of bouncing along, she saw the bus, a scattering of parked vehicles, and a red-and-black food truck. She noticed Duke and an ancient woman puttering outside, setting up menu signs and condiments. The delegates stood in clusters. "I think they're waiting for you, Jessica."

"I better get over there. Don't worry about taking me back to Tuba; I can jump on the bus."

Bernie grabbed her backpack and scanned the group for Chee and Palmer. She found them, as well as the FBI agents whom she'd seen at the reception, now wearing official logo jackets. She spotted Durango and a few other protesters. Fish Man must still be in jail, she thought, or he'd be here, too.

Palmer motioned toward them.

"This way, you two. We're ready to go to the site. Delegates, stay together. If you have kids, keep an eye on them. We're going to walk from here for about twenty minutes to give us a better idea of the scope of the proposal and some options. And you'll see something splendid, too—the canyon filled with fog."

Chee trotted up to her. "Thanks for being a chauffeur." He told her Palmer would lead the short hike to an overlook where the delegates could imagine the resort. "He will point out where the development might be based on plans A, B, and C. Of course, no one will see a thing unless the fog lifts."

"I'm eager to look at the fog," she said. "I hear it's like a lid of clouds, and if you hike down far enough, you'll be free of it."

"After the tour we get the lunch, more talking, and the bus back to Tuba City. You can leave after lunch if you want."

Bernie said, "Atwell filled me in on Blankenship on the drive over. He sounds like a creep."

"That's how I see it," Chee said, "but Palmer doesn't take him seriously."

"What are those cars doing here? I recognized Dashee's unit, and I figure the black sedan is FBI. But the others?"

"Some protesters followed the bus. Some vehicles were parked when we arrived. Palmer believes they are probably hikers because several trails start from here, but I'm on the alert just in case."

Bernie noticed the group beginning to assemble for the hike. "I'll hang back here with the stragglers. You get to hike with the big guy."

Chee said, "Don't lose contact with the group. It would be easy to get lost in the stuff."

PALMER ASKED THE NAVAJO delegates to lead the way; he positioned himself in the middle of the pack with Chee behind him. The trail demanded that they walk single file. Wisps of fog rose over the canyon rim, but for the first minutes of the group's hike descent, visibility was perfect.

Bernie flashed back to another hike she'd taken in this same area a few years ago with Chee and Dashee. That time, she had walked all the way to the river. She had touched the dark rock at the canyon bottom, the oldest thing on the planet. She'd tried to impress Chee with how tough she was. Today, she had nothing to prove, but Rick Horseman's death and Blankenship's possible role in it weighed on her. After negotiating several welcome sets of switchbacks that slowed the rate of descent, the trail widened to an overlook. Palmer and the Navajo delegates encouraged the group to cluster there. Below them, an ocean of white filled the immense space between the canyon's rocky shoulders like cotton batting in a giant's quilt.

She walked down the path a bit farther as the delegates assembled for Palmer's talk, far enough that she could hear only the sound of her boots against the surface of the hard-packed trail. She stopped and inhaled the cool air, enjoying a few moments of solitude. Then, out of the edge of her vision, she saw something move. Something tan and large. A mountain lion? She tried to remember what, if anything, she'd read about the relationship between *náshdóítsoh* a guardian of the mountains, and people trespassing in a lion habitat. All cats were curious, but mountain lions had a deep and wise fear of humans.

She stared at the place where she'd noticed it and then looked up and down the slopes.

Whatever it was, it was gone.

27

The field trip had served its purpose, Palmer thought.

Although the fog blocked the view of the confluence and the possible construction sites, the delegates marveled at its beauty. He heard the little boy say it looked like whipped cream on a giant cup of chocolate.

The Navajo delegate who had led the hike explained to the others how rarely this weather came to the canyon and how blessed they were to encounter it. Some nodded in agreement. The Hopi and the Hualapai delegates volunteered impromptu stories about fog and their cultural viewpoints of it, and the Havasupai woman said she'd toss in a few tales after lunch or on the bus back to Tuba City. Even Chee had calmed down a bit out here. If Robert— No, he corrected his thinking. *When* Robert recovered, they'd come here together. The boy had offered him a second chance at being a dad, and he'd accept the invitation if he could arrange time off.

When the fog stories ended, Palmer opened his black bag and gave them each a map that showed where Canyonmark planned to develop, describing the construction sites that would be further evaluated if the resort were authorized. He restressed that the goal of the mediation was to help the Navajo Nation gather insights its leaders could use in making such an important decision.

The walk back to the spot where lunch awaited, an uphill hike, took longer than Palmer had expected, and he noticed the signs of low blood sugar. The stress of the past few days had upset his routine, and he knew he should monitor his diabetes more closely.

Despite his initial misgivings, the Paiute food truck worked as an excellent demonstration of the juxtaposition of commerce and nature, offering warm food especially welcome on a chilly day. As contentious as they were, none of the delegates complained about it, not even Blankenship. He wondered if Denny Duke and his aged mama could cook and serve quickly enough, but Duke had assured him he'd get a helper or two. As the group drew closer to the truck, the familiar smell of French fries made his mouth water.

The temperature, in the low fifties, allowed for eating outside if people kept their coats on. The delegates, some family members who had tagged along, and even the protesters who had followed the bus settled down to eat. Duke called them to the window to order, table by table. Mama Duke bellowed out the numbers when the food was ready.

Palmer found a place at a folding table across from a man named Crenshaw, the National Park Service delegate. Chee the ever-present sat next to him. Crenshaw must have jumped the line because he already had lunch, a barbecued beef sandwich, fries, and an apple.

"So, what happens when the session resumes tomorrow?" Crenshaw popped a fry into his mouth.

"Well, it might not be tomorrow. We have to check on the heating issue. But whenever we resume, I'll wrap up the public comments. Then we'll see if you delegates can agree on what issues to discuss."

"I'm glad you arranged this trip." Crenshaw picked up another fry. "I think it's good for all of us to realize that our decisions aren't just theoretical. They'll have an impact that will last long after we're gone." He turned to Chee. "Isn't that right?"

"Sure thing."

Crenshaw mentioned the National Park Service's detailed approach to planning, and how long it had taken them to release their latest draft to the public because of interagency disputes about the focus. "And those arguments were among guys who basically already agreed about everything. I think these sessions could take until hell freezes over to resolve anything."

"I hope not." Palmer began to experience that sagging, lightheaded detachment that came when his body was off-kilter. "Excuse me. I need to use the facilities." He picked up his leather bag and slung it over his shoulder.

Chee started to rise, too.

"Sit, for goodness' sakes. I'll be right back. I'll yell loudly if I fall in."

As Palmer left, he heard Crenshaw launch into another topic. "The police presence here, all this security? Well . . ."

The lecture faded as he neared the outhouses. The fog was rising, drifting up to the lunch area. Perhaps by the time they left, it would have vanished. They could go back to the overlook for a quick view of the canyon's cloud-free magnificence. That would give Chee one more thing to worry about.

Even though having a bodyguard was a pain in neck, he liked Chee. The man had a sense of humor and a smart, attractive wife. Joking was one of the many things he had enjoyed about his marriage to Lona. Had he ever told her she was one of the few people who kept him from taking himself too seriously? Probably not. He could add that to his long list of regrets.

Palmer disliked outdoor toilets, but he needed a private place to check his blood sugar and inject the insulin before lunch. After years of experience, he did the test quickly. He pulled out the pouch where he kept his insulin pen. He would give himself another injection that kept him alive. Then food to offset the dose. Everything in balance. He smiled. The Navajo Way. Before he could give himself the medicine, the door burst open. "Just a minute," he said, and then he saw the man and felt the gun pressed hard against his spine.

The voice was hard, too. "No noise or I'll shoot. If you listen, you might live."

Palmer nodded. He felt dizzy and his head ached. "I'll listen."

The man, a person he'd seen helping Duke and his mother at the food truck, ignored him. He'd noticed the fellow in the audience at the mediation, too, but he couldn't conjure up the name.

Palmer tried again. "Say what you have to say. I'll listen to you. You don't need to threaten me."

Instead, the man grabbed his arm and pulled him toward the door. He picked up the insulin pen Palmer had dropped and put it in his pocket. He pushed the mediator forward, away from the outhouse, away from the delegates, toward the gaping hole of the fog-shrouded canyon.

Palmer swallowed his fear. He'd been in tough spots before, although never at gunpoint. "Talk to me. What's this about? If you've got issues with the development, tell me what I need to hear and then let's have some lunch. No need for a weapon. I won't harm you."

Palmer felt the gun push harder against his backbone. The man's voice was an ugly snarl. "You've already done your damage. You cost me the woman I love and the son I always wanted."

CHEE WAITED FIFTEEN MINUTES, then stood, leaving Crenshaw in midsentence. "Palmer should have been back by now. I need to find him."

On his way to the toilets, he saw Bernie sitting with Atwell and the Hopis.

He told her that Palmer was gone. "I'll check the outhouse. I'll yell if he's there."

She nodded. "If he's not there, I'll go to the bus and then I'll walk down the trail we took earlier."

Chee said, "I'll hike the other main trail. Let's meet here in twenty minutes."

She said, "If he's not in the john, you should tell Dashee and the agents. They can help us."

"Right. All this might embarrass Palmer enough that he'll act like a grown-up. I'm sick of this hide-and-seek stuff."

The porta potties were the old-fashioned wooden kind with a simple peg latch. The doors to all three stalls stood open, the interiors unoccupied. He found Palmer's leather bag on the floor in the one on the far end. Chee decided to come back for it—or tell Palmer where it was—after he found the man.

He turned around to see the two FBI agents. They continued the campsite search while he went back to tell Bernie, who acted on their plan. Then he found Dashee.

"Have you seen Palmer?"

Dashee looked up from his sandwich. "You let that guy get away again? Check the bus. Maybe he's in there taking a nap."

"Bernie's doing that. Cowboy, you're in charge while we're searching for him."

Dashee grew serious. "Mr. Keevama would like to talk to the delegates, share another story about why we hold this place sacred. I'll tell him to go ahead when everyone finishes lunch if you guys haven't found Palmer. And we'll ask the Hualapai woman to speak. That will keep things calm for a while here. Good luck."

THE COACH DRIVER, SITTING with a plate of food on her lap, opened the door when Bernie knocked. No, she hadn't seen Mr. Palmer since the bus had unloaded.

Bernie called Palmer's name as she hiked down the trail, moving as quickly as she could through the fog. It would be easy, she thought, to slip and fall here, especially now that the fog had come this high. Maybe Palmer had walked away from the group to have a cigarette or catch a few minutes of quiet. He should have told Chee, she thought, not just disappeared.

After about ten minutes of searching, she reached the overlook where the group had stopped. If Palmer wanted privacy, he needn't have hiked farther than this, but there was no sign of him. The trail continued through the fog, deeper into the canyon. At some point it must connect to the main trail that originated on the rim, the route Chee would check.

She felt uneasiness in the pit of her stomach.

"Palmer, are you down there?"

Only silence answered.

28

Bernie continued down the trail, past the overlook and a few more switchbacks. The route grew steeper and required concentrated focus. She searched for Palmer's tracks, calling his name, disappointed in the lack of response. She zipped her jacket against the thick cold.

Then she heard what sounded like a muffled human voice above her on the slope, invisible in the fog bank. "Palmer?"

No one called back. Hikers, she thought. Or maybe it was a single hiker talking to his dog or even himself. Or maybe even Chee or the feds calling for Palmer, the same as she had been.

She heard the voice again—no, two voices this time, both male, a rumble of conversation confused by the fog. She couldn't tell if they were hiking up toward the rim, or away from her on the long trudge toward the river. "Palmer! Is that you?"

The voices stopped. After a few moments of silence she heard rocks colliding with other rocks and then a louder, crashing sound of someone or something falling and sliding far above her.

"Palmer?" She looked up the trail and beyond it into the boulders and vegetation that clung to the slope until everything disappeared into the gray cloud. She didn't see any rocks rolling her way, but she knew the noise had come from the slope above her and to the right, probably the location of the other trail. To investigate it, she would have to forge her way up the slope. The disturbance meant something was wrong, and the odds were high that Palmer was involved.

She used her hands and arms as well as her feet and legs to climb toward where she'd heard the noise, stopping to catch her breath when she had to, wishing the fog had stayed in the canyon so she could see what lay ahead and locate the connecting trail more easily. Each time she stopped, she listened for other human sounds, called Palmer's name, and heard only silence in reply.

She paused again when her lungs called for mercy. Maybe Palmer had returned to the lunch area. Maybe Chee had found him and she should head back—it was long past the twenty minutes they'd agreed on. But the feeling in her gut and the memory of the argument and the scrambling above her told her to give the search a few more minutes. She was bound to find the other trail soon.

She came to a place where the hillside flattened. She took a sip from her water bottle and reassessed the situation, looking for a sign. On the slope above her to the right, she spotted a splash of turquoise through the chilly fog, the same color she's seen in Palmer's coat. "Palmer? Palmer, are you up there?"

She muscled her way up toward the color. When she got closer, she knew she had found his prized Pendleton. She heard a moan.

"Palmer!"

She saw him a few yards below the place where the discarded jacket lay, his white shirt nearly invisible through the fog. He sprawled on his back, wedged between the trunk of a ponderosa and a rock. His pressed jeans were streaked with dirt. Without the tree, he would have continued sliding, probably with enough momentum to break his back and fracture his skull. She squatted next to him, grabbing the tree for balance. She could see his chest lift and sink. He was breathing, but barely. She touched him as she said his name again.

His eyelids fluttered open.

"It's Bernie. I'll help you. Don't try to move."

He looked at her with a hint of recognition, then closed his eyes again. She noticed his paleness, and that sweat beaded on his forehead. His lips trembled. She didn't see any obvious bleeding, a good sign in an otherwise difficult situation.

"Try to relax now. We'll get you out of this."

He opened his eyes and found her face. "Whaa happen?"

"I think you fell."

She removed her jacket and gently placed it over him. Palmer's shoulder pushed against the tree in an awkward, painful-looking position. She took his cold hands in hers. "Don't worry. We'll get through this." Her backpack had first aid supplies. She knew Chee would be looking for them. She felt the tension in her neck and shoulders relax a bit.

A rustling above her caught her attention. She glanced toward it, attempting to see through the thick fog. "Hello! Is someone there? Chee? We could use some help."

The rustling came closer. "Bernie? Is that you?"

It wasn't Chee's voice. "Who's there?"

"Byrum Lee. You're way off the trail. Are you lost?"

"I'm fine. It's Palmer."

The rustling stopped. "Palmer? What's going on?"

"Looks like he had a bad fall."

"Hang tight. I'll be right down."

"No, it's too steep. Find some help. Get Chee. We'll have a challenge getting Palmer out of here."

Lee kept coming. "I'm an old medic, remember?"

She heard rocks jostling loose, skidding footsteps.

"Is he conscious?"

"Barely."

"Did he tell you what happened?"

"No. I just found him. It looks like he fell."

Palmer squeezed her hand, and she saw terror in his eyes. He shook his head no.

The clattering overhead grew closer. She heard a change in Lee's tone. "I can see Palmer's coat now. Climb back to the trail and start to hike out. We'll probably need a copter to evac him. Go get that process started. I'll stay with him."

"Palmer's frightened. I don't want to leave him alone. What are you doing here, anyway?"

"I was helping Denny Duke and his mom at the food truck. And I figured it would be good for someone with some emergency experience to be on the trip, just in case something went wrong. I noticed Palmer walking out toward the rim, looking down at the fog. He was stumbling. When I didn't see him come back for lunch, I got worried, so I went searching for him."

Looking for Palmer but not calling his name? "Did you tell Chee?"

"I didn't have a chance. You should go for help. Every minute you wait increases the chance of his dying."

She heard Lee traversing the slope as he spoke, knocking rocks loose to cascade toward her and Palmer. She heard him swearing. Then came a different noise, a dry, shuffling sound like a person riding the soles of his boots down a scree field.

She spoke softly to Palmer. "Are you afraid of Lee?"

He nodded, but she knew confusion sometimes accompanied diabetic shock. Still, it was odd that Lee could arrive again to help an injured man. Odd that a medic and building contractor would volunteer to work at a food truck. She recalled the Lieutenant's warning about coincidences.

Lee appeared above them. He took the last few steps toward the place Palmer was wedged and turned to Bernie.

"Let me in there so I can assess the damage."

She noticed that he had a backpack, larger than hers. Was it filled with emergency supplies? She moved away slightly, and Lee crouched next to Palmer, resting his hips against the tree. "Hey there, can you tell me where you hurt?" He reached for Palmer's wrist.

Palmer flinched. "Stop." His voice was a trembling whisper.

"Easy man. I'm just checking your pulse." Lee turned to Bernie. "You've got to go up the rim and find some help. His heart is racing. His skin is cold. We can't do anything for him here."

"Do you have a space blanket or something else in your pack that will help him stay warm? Maybe candy that could bring up his blood sugar?"

"Stop with the questions. Go for help."

Palmer said, "No."

The fog had grown thicker. It reminded Bernie of the heavy smoke in a sweat lodge, but instead of being hot, she felt uncomfortably cool without her jacket. As she slipped on her backpack, she watched Lee adjust his position, and she saw him put his hand on Palmer's left arm, just below the questionable shoulder. He leaned down.

Palmer's howl of pain made her wince. He struggled weakly to free himself from Lee and moaned.

"You're hurting him. Stop it."

Lee's voice had a sharper edge now. "He's delirious with pain. I think his back is broken. I've got something in here to help him, something to take care of that." Lee reached in his pocket and pulled out what looked like an oversized marker.

"What is that?"

Palmer's eyes opened wide. "Insulin. Bastard."

"It's something for pain." She heard the tension in Lee's voice. She knew he was lying. Lying and dangerous.

Palmer's voice rose. "No."

Bernie put her hand on her gun. "Show me what you've got there. I can reassure him. Tension always makes pain worse."

"What? Say again?"

She knew he had heard her. Then she saw the flicker of a smile.

"I'll show you. Stand up so you can see better." Lee moved toward her as she rose, clutching the device in his hand. He lurched and pushed against her, hard.

The unexpected contact launched her off balance before she could draw her weapon. She felt the bone-jarring impact of rocky ground. The energy of the fall and angle of the slope forced her body quickly downhill, sliding headfirst, gaining momentum. Using her legs and heels, arms and fingers, she struggled to slow her descent and to change her position to avoid the worst of what lay before her. She moved too fast for the terror of the situation to catch up with her. The speed of the fall outdistanced the pain.

Finally, her side slammed into the stump of a dead ponderosa and she stopped.

Stunned, she took a minute to gather her wits, let her heart rate slow to what could pass for normal. She lay still, afraid to move or even breathe, reconstructing what had just happened. The push was no accident. Lee had probably shoved Palmer, too, and planned to make sure Palmer was dead before she'd interrupted him. What was happening to Palmer now? She forced her breath to quiet so she could listen more closely to possible sounds on the slope above her. At first, she heard only the rush of her own blood in her ears. She stayed motionless, and then noticed the stones clattering. She put her hand on her gun in case Lee had begun the descent to check on her.

Then the noise began to fade. He must be climbing up, away from her.

As she surveyed the bodily damage the fall had caused, she recognized that bone-chilling cold seeped from the ground into her skin, into her blood, and now seemed to circulate into her heart. Her palms stung from the abrasions made by the rocks as she'd struggled to break her fall; her hands were bloody, and several nails had snapped off to the quick. Her back and her hips ached. But fingers and toes, arms and legs responded when she gingerly tested them. Motion hurt, but it was possible. She inhaled deeply, thankful that her ribs didn't scream with the pain. She winced as she moved her neck, but the effort didn't make the throbbing in her skull any worse. She could see and hear.

Not only was she alive, she realized she was furious.

Lee had tricked her, made a fool of her from their first encounter at Shiprock. The details would sort themselves out, but her rising anger provided a surge of energy. She forced the pain aside and pressed her sore hands against the frigid earth to push herself to sitting. She decided to wait a moment for the light-headedness to pass before trying to stand. Another fall meant disaster, but she couldn't linger long. She knew Lee would kill Palmer if, in fact, the man wasn't already dead.

Then she heard something or someone approaching from behind. Lee? No, he would have made more noise. She turned her head and watched the mountain lion gliding toward her. The big cat walked cautiously, pausing after each step. She could see its ribs as it came closer. She readjusted herself to watch the animal as it circled to stand in front of her. She felt primal, brain-stopping terror, the hardwired response of prey to a predator. But, simultaneously, the cat's grace and beauty stirred her sense of wonder.

Náshdóítsoh stared at her with its bright carnivore eyes and growled as it paced. She looked back and held its gaze. Slowly, she moved her hand to her gun and felt its reassuring presence. She didn't want to shoot, but she couldn't let the lion kill her without some attempt at self-defense

Then, from that place in her pounding heart that knew *hozho*, she began to sing the song her grandmother had taught Mama. The song of courage and protection Mama had sung to her and to Darleen. A song about the beauty that surrounded them; a song honoring the lion itself.

Náshdóítsoh stopped walking. It lowered its muscular body to the ground and raised fur-lined ears. *Náshdóítsoh*, the guardian assigned by the Holy People to protect Turquoise Girl. *Náshdóítsoh*, the one who helped The People by sometimes leaving behind for them a portion of the deer and elk it killed. She could feel the cat watching her. Its rope-like tail twitched.

She studied the broad nose and golden eyes rimmed with deep black, and then her eyes settled on its strong paws as she sang. She noticed the way stiff white whiskers stood straight out from its snout and the triangular shape of its head. Her voice grew stronger, her hand resting more lightly on the gun. The song's rhythm and repetitions, its poetry and simplicity, became her prayer. She appreciated the mountain lion, not only as an animal to be reckoned with but also as one of the mysterious First People in existence before her tribe of five-fingered beings came to walk the earth.

When she had finished the words she remembered, she added new verses to praise the animal's long legs, its thick winter fur, and the taut muscles beneath the sand-colored coat.

Then, as silently as it had arrived, *náshdóítsoh* rose and turned away, bounding down the slope with fluid grace, disappearing into the fog.

She ended the song and closed her eyes.

After she stopped shaking, she stood and removed her backpack, encased in dirt from the fall and the downhill slide. She pushed the crust off with her bloody hand, unzipped the front pocket, found her red emergency whistle. She slipped the whistle into her pants pocket. She felt something small and smooth, the talisman Sandra had given her. *Náshdóítsoh.* Bernie adjusted her pack and began the painful climb up the slope, fueled with adrenaline and a sense of both power and peace. She put the whistle in her mouth and blew as she hiked, when she could spare the breath. Chee must be searching for her and for Palmer. If the noise alerted Lee to the fact that she had survived, let him come. She wouldn't hesitate to defend herself. And she'd protect Palmer, too, if he was still alive. The lion had taught her well.

She used her sore fingers for balance and leverage, inching her way up, hoping she was on course. The fog made the task harder and left her disoriented. Without the struggle against gravity, it would have been tough to know up from down.

She reached a section of the slope where she expected to see Palmer, or at least encounter something familiar. But nothing looked familiar. Rocks, bare patches of earth, scrub oak, the long brown needles fallen from the ponderosas, the darkness of their trunks and rich vanilla smell of the bark enhanced by the fog's damp presence. She called, "Palmer?"

She heard a moan. She yelled again, heard nothing encouraging. Was she hoping for too much, wishing too hard? She spotted a footprint and then another and realized they were her own from before the fall. She came to a place where the slope flattened slightly. As she waited for her heartbeat to slow, she noticed something turquoise ahead of her on the ground.

Palmer looked worse than when she'd left him, but she found a pulse as she pressed her sore fingers against his neck. She blew her whistle. Again, and again.

As he looked for the mediator he'd been assigned to keep safe, Chee's anxiety grew. Palmer wouldn't walk off and leave his precious black bag in an outhouse. Whatever had happened, happened because Sergeant Jim Chee was still the screwup Lieutenant Leaphorn, his mentor, knew him to be.

Then there was the Bernie problem. They had agreed to regroup in twenty minutes, and the deadline had long since passed. His curious wife could have found an interesting plant, gotten mesmerized by the view, and lost track of time. She knew how to handle herself outdoors, but the thickening fog made finding the trail confusing for anyone. No reason to worry, he told himself, but he worried.

He called again and again for Palmer. Maybe the FBI team would find him first. Maybe they already had. Maybe Bernie had found him and they were eating lunch right now. He eased his way along the narrow, winding dirt path that led deeper into the fog bank and ultimately to the heart of the canyon. The fog had muffled the natural sounds of the birds and the wind. With no proof the mediator had come this way, he'd turn back in a few moments. He saw rocks, dirt, bits of vegetation that disappeared into the grayness. Then, out of the corner of his eye, he spotted movement: a tan, muscular, long-tailed shape heading away from him. He whispered its name, *náshdóítsoh*. He watched it, a creature on earth before the birth of the Hero Twins, disappear as quietly as the fog.

Then he noticed a place along the side of the trail where the soil had been freshly disturbed. He squatted and found a print made by a waffle-soled hiking boot, a smallish indentation. Bernie's? Then he heard a whistle, too sharp to be a bird cry. "Bernie!"

Chee climbed toward the sound. The whistle came again, and he yelled, "I'm coming. Keep blowing."

He found her squatting next to Palmer. She'd wrapped her jacket around him and held her hands against his face and neck.

"What happened to him?"

"I'm not sure. I'm glad you're here. We have to get him out of this place."

He bent close to Palmer. "It's Chee."

Palmer didn't respond.

Chee touched his face. "The nurse in ICU called. She said to tell you that Rocket opened his eyes. He wants to see you."

Palmer's face shifted to a trace of a smile.

He looked at Bernie, noticing the dirt on her clothes, the blood on her hands. "What happened to you?"

She shivered and he saw the glistening in her eyes. "I sang to *náshdóítsoh*. And Lee tried to kill me."

29

Chee said, "Where is Lee now?"

"I don't know. I heard him scramble up the hill."

Chee noticed how she winced as she moved closer to Palmer. "You might have cracked something in that fall."

"I'm OK, lucky I didn't split my head on one of those rocks."

Chee said, "I'm hiking up to call for a copter and let the feds know about Lee."

"Oh, no, you don't. Guarding Palmer was your job, remember? You're stronger than I am, and getting him out of here is going to be tough." Bernie hobbled toward him, and he saw her grimace. "You stay here. I'll go for help."

He shook his head. "Protecting Palmer is my job, just like you said. I don't like his condition. I'm not injured. I can get help for him faster. You know that, don't you?"

She looked at him for several long seconds and he knew from the jut of her chin that she wanted to argue. Finally, she said, "If you see Lee on the trail, be careful."

He unzipped his jacket and draped it over her shoulders. "I promise."

She shrugged off the coat. "You keep it."

"No. What if you or Palmer go into shock?"

She nodded. "Don't hike up this way. Climb down between those two rocks and you'll hit the main trail. It's longer but quicker."

She watched him make his way down the hill until he vanished in the fog.

Palmer's skin was gray and his breathing shallow. She put Chee's jacket over him and then hobbled to retrieve the beautiful turquoise Pendleton.

The voice startled her.

"You're too smart for your own good." Lee sounded tired. Tired and desperate. "If you and Chee had been slower, I could have finished Palmer off with his insulin pen. Not a terrible way to die, and it would have made life simpler for all of us. But now, well, we have a problem."

Bernie couldn't see where the voice came from. She drew her gun.

"No, you have a problem. Chee knows you tried to kill us, and he's on his way to the feds. I've got a weapon pointed at you. It's over. Come out and make things easier on yourself."

"I didn't want to kill you, just slow you down so I could take care of that stinkin' weasel." Lee's voice seemed to come from a large rise of rocks. "Palmer has some kinda hold on Lona. She can't see that he's all talk. And nobody should ignore his own kid like that."

Bernie said, "You helped me with that injured man. Let me help you."

"Honey, you're in the way of the mission now, so your death has to look like an accident."

She heard a rock collide with something and turned toward the sound.

"Up here." Lee towered above her, in the opposite direction from where he'd tossed the first rock. The huge stone he hurled now brushed her shoulder as she dodged away. Bernie almost lost her balance with the impact.

The exertion cost Lee his footing. She saw him stagger on a narrow sandstone outcrop. Then he tumbled off the ledge and rolled down the slope, propelled by momentum, making no effort to break his descent. She watched him fall into the deep gray gloom.

She listened for a moan, a stirring against the rocks. The man was tough, fired by jealousy and revenge. If he was still alive, he'd muster every ounce of energy to kill her and Palmer. He had nothing to lose.

She limped to where she'd seen him disappear and looked down into the gray haze, but she saw only stillness. At first she heard nothing. Then a rumbling growl rose from below her. Even though the fog tried to mute it, she recognized the song of the lion. She made her way to the Pendleton jacket and back to Palmer. She shook off the dirt, and as she prepared to cover him, she found something in the pocket. She pulled it out—a bag of M&M's, Chee's favorite. She gave one to Palmer, then popped some into her own mouth—a sorry substitute for lunch. She fed him another and, when she was sure he could handle it, a sip of water from her backpack.

The increased warmth and the sugar gradually made Palmer more alert.

"Chee?" His voice was a hoarse whisper.

"It's me, Bernie. Chee went for help."

Palmer reached for her hand. His squeeze hurt her damaged fingers, but she didn't pull away.

"What happened?"

"Byrum Lee tried to kill you."

He wrinkled his brow. "Why?"

"Jealousy. Don't worry about that now. Rest."

She had trail mix in her backpack and shared it all with him as they watched the light begin to fade and waited for rescue. She felt cold, sore, hungry, and glad to be alive. After forever, the noisy, distinctive, and welcome sound of a helicopter filled the sky.

She tugged the turquoise jacket off Palmer and waved it, hoping the pilot could see the flash of color through the trees. The helicopter moved closer, finally hovering overhead. Tricky work, she thought. Their rescuing angel looked like a bottom-heavy dragonfly. She saw something red leave its belly, swaying in the breeze. No, two somethings—a person and a big pack.

The EMT, a man in his forties, introduced himself as Scott. He looked at her battered hands, but she directed his attention to Palmer.

"He's diabetic and he had a bad fall," she said. "His shoulder could be a problem."

"What about you?"

She shrugged off the question. "There's another man down the slope. From the way he fell, I think he's unconscious or worse. I called out to him, but he didn't answer."

"Show me."

She moved gingerly to the spot where Lee had disappeared. Scott yelled his name loudly, with no answer.

"I'll have search and rescue deal with him. We've got to get Palmer some help, and you don't look too good either, Officer."

She helped Scott place the rescue harness around Palmer and watched the mediator swing on the cable as he ascended to the belly of the helicopter and the waiting arms of another medic.

"Come on," Scott said. "You're next. You get a lift outta here."

"No thanks. I can hike out."

"No arguing."

Bernie looked at the harness and the swaying line that spanned the breathtaking distance between the ground and the hovering dragonfly with more trepidation than she'd felt at the sight of the lion.

Scott extended the harness toward her. "We've got an injured man up there, remember? Get going."

She slipped it on and squeezed the fetish in her pocket as Scott secured her harness to the cable.

30

Chee found Bernie in the ER waiting room at the hospital in Flagstaff.

She gave him the update on Palmer. "Besides the fractured shoulder, he has broken ribs. He's in surgery."

"How about you?"

"They said I have a bruised back, cuts, scrapes, the usual. They gave me something for my headache and muscle pain and predicted a few days of soreness. Worst of all, I'm starving. The cafeteria is one floor below us!"

"I brought you some clean clothes and those earrings that you like."

She looked in the bag and smiled at him. "Almost as good as a sandwich. Thanks. I'll change and let's eat."

Chee didn't like hospitals. He couldn't free himself of the idea that people died there. He thought about suggesting that they go somewhere other than the cafeteria, but he wanted to be close when Palmer got out of surgery.

She dressed quickly. They ordered a Coke for her, coffee for him, hamburgers for both, and took their trays to a vacant table.

Chee said, "How was your ride to Flagstaff?"

"Fine, once I got inside the helicopter. I wondered if I would get sick. I kept remembering how airsick the Lieutenant always gets. The fog lifted, and I got to see the canyon from a condor's perspective."

"Cool." Chee felt his phone vibrate. "It's Cordova." He took the call.

Bernie sipped her Coke and thought about ordering a second hamburger.

"She's banged up, but she says she's fine. Here."

He handed his phone to Bernie.

Cordova said, "I wanted to let you know we just arrested Blankenship."

"For being a jerk?"

Cordova chuckled. "We had him on the radar from a protest in California. They matched him to the surveillance video but it took a while because he shaved his head and he'd had a beard and long hair in California. He was behind the vandalism at the Justice Center, the problems with the power and the heat."

"Did Blankenship say anything about the bomb at Shiprock?"

"No. He denies involvement in that. I heard you took care of Lee pretty good."

"I just stepped out of his way and let gravity do the job. Did search and rescue find him?"

"What was left. A big predator had a meal out of him." Cordova cleared his throat. "Take care of yourself, Manuelito. If you and Chee get to Michigan, look me up."

She gave Chee his phone and put her drink down. "I'm stunned about Lee. How can a guy who seemed so nice and helpful—"

Chee said, "I forgot to tell you. Leaphorn sent an e-mail about his conversation with Mrs. Nez. She saw the guy who hired her grandson to mess with the car. You know, the envelope said that down payment should be returned to Blankenship, but she described the man as a tall, thin *bilagaana* with a white cowboy hat. That's Lee."

He stopped talking as an attractive Navajo woman walked up to their table. She looked at Bernie.

"Are you Bernie Manuelito?"

"That's me."

"I'm Lona Zahne."

"Lona! Your smile has hardly changed since high school. This is my husband, Jim Chee."

Chee stood. "Join us." He waved toward an empty chair.

"Thanks, but I'm here with a message for you, Bernie. Rocket— I mean Robert—wants to talk to you."

"How's he doing?"

"Much better, thanks. He's young and strong, and that will help him recover. He said you asked him a question and he didn't tell you the truth. Finish your food and come up when you can." She gave Bernie the room number.

After Lona left, Bernie said, "You told Palmer that Robert wanted to see him. Was that true?"

Chee smiled. "Of course. Robert might not have actually said it, but he does. Why else would he have been such a pain in Tuba City?"

On their way to the stairs, they encountered Denny Duke. The old Paiute broke into a grin. "Hey there. I have something for you to give Mr. Palmer." He showed them Palmer's black bag. "I found it in the outhouse."

Chee said, "Yeah, I remember seeing it there."

Bernie said, "What happened to the delegates after Palmer disappeared? Did everyone behave?"

Duke said, "Ma'am, you'd be surprised. They listened to the Indian stories, and then Mr. Keevama asked everyone to climb back on the bus. He said Chee and you were looking for Mr. Palmer and that the FBI was helping."

Like all good storytellers, Duke paused. "Guess what happened then?"

Bernie said, "I don't know. What?"

"Mr. Keevama told the delegates they should cancel the mediation until future notice. The Navajo representatives agreed, and then they acted like it was really their idea. The rest of them went along with it, even the Canyonmark dudes." Duke laughed. "The Grand Canyon has been there a long time. It will still be there when the next plan to change it comes along."

He said to Bernie, "You know, I met you at that big game in Shiprock when you helped keep everything calm. You did real good."

"I thought I remembered you."

"My neighbor's grandson is a Chieftain. He's on the team, but mostly on the bench."

Duke gave Palmer's bag to Chee. And he was gone.

ROBERT'S FACE WAS SWOLLEN, and an ugly bruise stretched between his right eye and his chin. His left arm was in a sling. Lona sat in a chair next to him. Chee took his familiar place against the wall.

Bernie walked over to Robert. "Hi. Your mother said you wanted to talk to me. Is it all right with you if she and Chee stay here, too?"

"Sure." Robert looked down at his damaged arm, then raised his gaze past her to the wall with the whiteboard for patient and staff comments. "Mom told me about what happened in the canyon, about Lee hurting you and my dad. I can't believe it."

Bernie said, "He fooled me, too."

"We were at that restaurant with Dad and you asked me about the explosion, right?"

"I remember."

"Well, I know why Rick was there, I just didn't want to talk about it with my dad around."

"Do you want to tell me now?"

He nodded. "Rick knew a lot about cars, so when Lee asked me for somebody who could help his friend, some dude named Blankenship, I gave him Rick's name."

Young people like Robert didn't mind saying the names of the dead. Bernie waited.

"When we were driving to the big game, Rick told me that Blankenship had given him a bunch of money to put something in a fancy BMW. He figured it was a tracking device."

"Rick said the guy who owned the car owed Blankenship money. He wanted Rick to steal the car later, when it wouldn't be so obvious. Rick felt funny about that; he was trying to go straight but he needed cash because he wanted to get married."

Robert pushed against the pillows to sit a bit straighter. "We got to the game way early and Rick put in the tracker. We watched Aza play, and Rick noticed his number—twenty-three. He got a funny look on his face. He told me that was the number on the special license plate on the car he'd messed with—a Beemer from Arizona—and that he needed to undo what he'd done. He said he'd be right back and he went out through the side door.

"That tracking device was really a bomb. Rick went out to remove it. Blankenship must have seen him, figured out what he was up to, and set it off."

Bernie said, "One of the people I talked to about that night mentioned a young man outside the gym, standing there looking suspicious, wearing a blue sweatshirt with a hood. Was that you?"

"I went out to find Rick." Robert's voice grew softer. "I think he knew that thing might go off if he messed with it. He was just sitting in the car and he waved at me to go back inside. Rick died because I got him involved in that. He liked Aza and never would have harmed him. My dad loved him, loved him better than he loved me."

Lona put her hand on Robert's shoulder. "Aza did love Rick, and he loves you, too. He wanted custody when we got divorced, but I wouldn't hear of it. I was so furious I wouldn't let him talk to you when he called. I threw the letters and presents he sent you in the trash."

Chee walked into the hall to take a call.

Bernie turned to Lona. "Lee was jealous of Aza, that's why he wanted to kill him. And he used Robert to help."

Robert said, "Rick told me Blankenship was the guy who hired him. But I did give his name to Lee."

"Lee hated Blankenship, too, because an environmental group Blankenship had worked for cheated Lee's sister. Lee arranged the explosion and used Blankenship's name in case things went bad. That's why Lee showed up after the explosion."

"So Rick is dead because of Lee. I liked Mr. Lee."

Bernie said, "Lee wasn't all bad. He helped at the bomb scene." Lee must have wanted to make sure Rick didn't talk to anyone about his role in the explosion, but she didn't say that.

Chee returned from the hall. "The nurse said Aza came through surgery just fine. He'll be in recovery awhile, and then they can move him to a regular floor."

Robert looked at the empty bed in his room.

"I'd like it if he could be here with me."

Lona said, "Me, too."

Bernie stood. "One last question. What happened with your accident, Robert? Everyone says you're a good driver."

He looked at the faces in the room. "Rick was dead because of me. I thought I deserved to die, too. I drove too fast and went off the road on purpose. I wanted it to look like an accident so I scraped the fender against a fence first. I didn't want anyone to feel guilty. But Dad always made me wear my seat belt. I got in the habit, and that's what saved me." His voice broke with emotion. "Dad gave me another chance."

Chee handed Palmer's bag to Lona. "He treasures this. He takes it everywhere. I think he'll be glad to have it back."

Lona touched the leather. "I thought he'd forgotten all about it, the same way he forgot all about me."

"You were wrong on both counts." Chee smiled at her. "Good luck."

Chee drove himself and Bernie back to the Tuba City motel, north on US 89 and then northeast on US 160. Bernie, who seldom fell asleep on the road, snoozed with her head against the headrest, waking only when he turned off the engine at the motel.

She smiled. "Thanks for driving."

"Gave me time to think about the last few days. It makes sense except for one thing. Mrs. Nez. Did she lie to you and Cordova about her grandson knowing Palmer?"

Bernie shook her head, noticing the ghost of a headache. "Sort of but not exactly. I asked her if he ever mentioned Palmer's name and she said no. Cordova and I didn't ask the right question. Of course he wouldn't use Aza's name. She told Leaphorn the boy called him *shidá'í*. What else would he call his uncle?"

"Are you going to tell Cordova he goofed?"

"No. That's his going-away present."

When they entered the motel lobby, they found Darleen and CS waiting.

"Hey there," Darleen said. "We're heading home, but we were wondering if, well . . ."

Bernie guessed her sister needed money.

CS picked up the story. "We saw this lady with a flock of sheep out by the highway today. The animals were all over the road, and so Darleen thought we should help."

Darleen said, "She wanted to take them to Tuba City to meet our president, but I told her the whole mediation was canceled. She didn't know what to do, but CS had a good idea."

He took up the story. "I said we could do a video with the sheep and what she wanted to say, and then send it to the president. She liked the idea."

"So, sister, could I borrow your red earrings for the video? CS wants me to talk with the sheep lady, you know, ask her questions. Something colorful would look good in the shot. She invited us to camp there so we can get started right at dawn."

Chee looked at CS. "Do you need money for gas?"

"No, sir. Her car gets great mileage. The gas gauge doesn't ever seem to move."

Bernie knew the gauge was broken, stuck on full.

Darleen said, "It's my car, so I'm buying gas. Don't worry, Cheeseburger. We're cool."

Bernie took off the earrings, the ones she loved best, the ones Chee had given her after she'd seen Leaphorn get shot. She pressed them into Darleen's hand.

She and Chee watched Darleen drive away in her old car, CS shooting video out the window, capturing Tuba City and Moenkopi after dark.

Chee put his arm around her. "Did you ever do a background check on that guy?"

"No. I got kind of busy."

A FEW DAYS LATER, they were headed to Window Rock to visit the Lieutenant. Chee drove so Bernie could pay full attention to her call to Mama. They talked a long time. From Chee's perspective, the conversation consisted of his wife occasionally offering, "I understand."

Then she said something that surprised him.

"No, Mama, I want to keep my loom. I'd like to start weaving again. Maybe I can join you and Mrs. Bigman at the senior center for some lessons."

He couldn't hear Mama's response, but it took a long time. When he glanced over at Bernie, he noticed her smile and the tears in her eyes.

They had dinner with Lieutenant Leaphorn and Louisa. As always, Louisa fixed something she deemed healthy: grilled chicken breasts cooked juiceless, chewy brown rice, and vegetables Bernie had never seen before. Chee had volunteered to provide dessert and brought along brownies. Bernie and the Lieutenant each ate two.

While Louisa did dishes and made coffee, they moved into the

Lieutenant's office. He wanted to show them something and was happy to speak Navajo.

Bernie said, "You know the FBI guy, Cordova, who Chee and I worked with?"

The Lieutenant nodded.

"He sent us a picture of his field office in Detroit." She showed him the photo of the building on her phone.

"And listen to what he wrote." She read, "'I just learned that a woman from California, fresh out of school, is being assigned to work out your way. Good luck with that, you guys.'" Bernie put the phone down.

Chee said, "I hope she likes the desert. Farmington and Gallup aren't exactly LA."

Bernie noticed a basket on the table with colorful cards, the kind with balloons, dancing elephants, and space ships. Leaphorn saw her gaze and pulled one out.

"Remember the dead one from the bomb?"

"I'll never forget him."

"His grandmother saved all these cards and she thought I should have them."

Chee opened one and read aloud: "'To Ricky, May you walk in beauty and grow up to always do the right thing.' It's signed, 'From Emma and Joe.'"

"The grandmother cried when she showed me that card," Leaphorn said. "But I told her not to be sad. On the last day of his life, her grandson had walked in beauty. He had saved the life of a good man who loved him."

ACKNOWLEDGMENTS

As always, there are many more people to thank for help in bringing a novel from idea to reality than I can mention here. They did their best; and all mistakes are my own.

My editor at HarperCollins, Carolyn Marino, provided enthusiastic encouragement and specific suggestions for *Song of the Lion*. Her wisdom helped me solve problems for Bernadette Manuelito I didn't even realize I had created! Marino's fabulous assistant, Laura Brown, handles bucketsful of wiggling details with graceful efficiency and much patience.

I'm blessed that David and Gail Greenberg have taken me under their wings. This time, David helped me begin to understand the complicated details of the law enforcement response to a deadly explosion at a large public event. Generous Gail put her educated eyes on the text, making sure the words said what I meant, and eradicating a plague of unnecessary commas. She also brews a fine, fine cup of coffee.

A big thank-you to Pearl Goldtooth, the hardworking Tuba City Public Library manager who made time to introduce me to the mysterious beauty of Coalmine Canyon and share the joys of life in To'Nanees'Dizi. She and the staff help make Tuba City,

Arizona, a place where stories thrive. I'm grateful that librarians throughout New Mexico, Colorado, and Arizona have welcomed me to book festivals, fund-raisers, solstice celebrations, and cowboy breakfasts. Where would writers or readers be without the wonderful gift of public libraries and the men and women who staff them?

Despite being ignored, neglected, and grumped at, my husband, photographer Don Strel, and our son, Brandon, cooked, shopped, did the dishes, walked the dog, and more while the siren of writing seduced me. Thanks to Katie Hawkes for asking "How's it going," a question that kept me working when I didn't want to!

Besides handling details of contracts, Elizabeth Trupin-Pulli helped improve the manuscript with tactful criticism. If all agents had her talent, more authors would be smiling. My business partner and friend Jean Schaumberg stayed at my side and listened to me whine about Joe Leaphorn. Big thanks to Randy Johns and his family, Leigh Irvin, and my friends at the Farmington (N.M.) Library. Thanks to Lucy Moore for all her insights into the world of mediation and for her help in reviewing the manuscript.

I thrive with the ongoing support of the literary community in my home state of New Mexico and my hometown of Santa Fe, including our treasured indie bookstore. A shout-out to my buddies, the Literary Lunch Ladies, a little posse of writers and readers who keep each other shooting straight.

The publication of my nonfiction book *Tony Hillerman's Landscape* led to a series of educational tours to Navajoland under the auspices of Road Scholar. Although I served as a Study Guide, I learned more than I could have dreamed from the wonderful Navajo, Zuni, Acoma, and non-Indian experts who shared their knowledge with our group. Our trip to Tuba City, Cameron, and the Grand Canyon helped create this book.

Speaking of the Grand Canyon, thanks to Steven Smith and Stacia Lewandowski for sharing their story of a hike in the fog at the Grand Canyon and for showing me the beautiful pictures. You never know where a conversation will lead you.

Finally, a Grand Canyon–size thank-you to all the fans of Tony Hillerman's work who took a chance on my first novel, *Spider Woman's Daughter*, stuck with me for *Rock with Wings*, and asked for more. Without your support and encouragement, *Song of the Lion* and the two books that came before would not exist, and the stories of Jim Chee and Joe Leaphorn would be over. Thank you for embracing Bernadette Manuelito in her new role as crime solver. I am in your debt.

None of my novels would be possible without the inspired work of my dad, author Tony Hillerman (1925–2008). He introduced readers to Joe Leaphorn and the fascinating world of mysteries set on the Navajo reservation beginning way back in 1970 with *The Blessing Way*. Thanks, Dad. I miss your smile.

TO SEE DAD'S MANUSCRIPTS and learn more about his work, please visit the Tony Hillerman Collection at Zimmerman Library at the University of New Mexico, or go to ehillerman.unm.edu

ABOUT THE AUTHOR

Anne Hillerman is the author of two previous novels, *Spider Woman's Daughter* and *Rock with Wings*, both *New York Times* bestsellers. Her stories continue the popular Joe Leaphorn/Jim Chee Navajo mystery series created by her father, Tony Hillerman. Anne's novels have been honored with the Spur Award from Western Writers of America and the New Mexico–Arizona Book Award for best mystery and best book of the year.

Before writing fiction, Anne wrote several nonfiction books, including *Tony Hillerman's Landscape: On the Road with Chee and Leaphorn*, created with photographer Don Strel. She began her career as a journalist. A New Mexican since the age of three, she writes and lives in Santa Fe.

BOOKS BY ANNE HILLERMAN

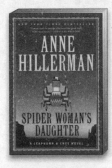

Spider Woman's Daughter
A Leaphorn, Chee & Manuelito Novel
Available in Paperback, eBook, Mass Market, Large Print, and Digital Audio

"Chip off the literary block—there are a lot of things Tony taught his daughter, Anne, and one of them was how to tell a good story. *Spider Woman's Daughter* is a proud addition to the legacy, capturing the beauty and breath of the Southwest as only a Hillerman can."
—Craig Johnson, author of the Walt Longmire Mysteries

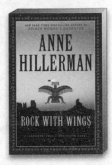

Rock with Wings
A Leaphorn, Chee & Manuelito Novel
Available in Paperback, eBook, Mass Market, Large Print, and Digital Audio

"Hillerman uses the southwestern setting as effectively as her late father did while skillfully combining Native American lore with present-day social issues." —*Publishers Weekly*

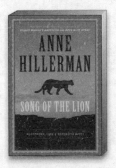

Song of the Lion
A Leaphorn, Chee & Manuelito Novel
Available in Paperback, eBook, Mass Market, Large Print, and Digital Audio

"Hillerman seamlessly blends tribal lore and custom into a well-directed plot, continuing in the spirit of her late father, Tony, by keeping his characters (like Chee) in the mix, but still establishing Manuelito as the main player in what has become a fine legacy series." —*Booklist*

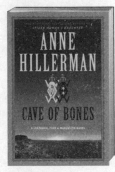

Cave of Bones
A Leaphorn, Chee & Manuelito Novel
Available April 2018 in Hardcover, eBook, Large Print, and Digital Audio

New York Times bestselling author Anne Hillerman brings together modern mystery, Navajo traditions, and the evocative landscape of the desert Southwest in this intriguing entry in the Leaphorn, Chee, and Manuelito series.

THE LEAPHORN & CHEE SERIES
BY TONY HILLERMAN

THE BLESSING WAY
Available in Paperback, Mass Market, and eBook

DANCE HALL OF THE DEAD
Available in Paperback, Mass Market, and eBook

LISTENING WOMAN
Available in Mass Market and eBook

PEOPLE OF DARKNESS
Available in Mass Market and eBook

THE DARK WIND
Available in Mass Market and eBook

THE GHOSTWAY
Available in Mass Market and eBook

SKINWALKERS
Available in Mass Market and eBook

A THIEF OF TIME
Available in Mass Market and eBook

TALKING GOD
Available in Mass Market, eBook, and Digital Audio

COYOTE WAITS
Available in Mass Market and eBook

SACRED CLOWNS
Available in Paperback, Mass Market, eBook, and Digital Audio

THE FALLEN MAN
Available in Mass Market, eBook, and Digital Audio

THE FIRST EAGLE
Available in Mass Market and eBook

HUNTING BADGER
Available in Mass Market, eBook, and Audiobook CD

THE WAILING WIND
Available in Mass Market, eBook, and Audiobook CD

SINISTER PIG
Available in Mass Market

SKELETON MAN
Available in Mass Market and eBook

THE SHAPE SHIFTER
Available in Mass Market, eBook, Audiobook CD, and Large Print